THE LOST OF NEW YORK

The Lost of New York

a novel

JOHN RIGNEY, JR.

Myrmidude Press

First Printing, 2022

print: 978-1-0879-1868-6
ebook: 978-1-0879-2038-2

Introduction

John "Butch" M. Rigney, Jr. wanted to be a writer.

Stories about his young life, growing up with his sister Maureen and brother Kevin, remain amusing, despite his two sometimes abusive and alcoholic parents who helped him become what his sister called "a throw-away kid. Nobody ever gave him a chance, helped him out."

As a youth, Butch went in and out of a series of reform schools for stealing, and jumping in a river from the Teufelberg Bridge, named after the Dutch Devil's Mountain. His brother was also a petty thief, robbing a neighborhood diner. In the early 1960s, Butch also served in the Air Force, possibly as a bargain for another jail sentence. He was stationed in Anchorage, and got out with an honorable discharge

A letter was sent to his mother –Mrs. John M. Rigney– mistakenly presumed to be his wife, of a package of papers that were left at McGuire Air Force Base in New Jersey. The early writings of Rigney are dated 1963. These "papers" may have been his early drafts of short stories (not in this edition), perhaps the letter and scant scribbled notes. A few of the short stories are signed D.Cno. with J.M. Rigney as the mailing name.

Back in New York, Butch took writing classes, hand-wrote pages of multi-syllabic words as practice. He continued writing what became the unfinished *Bugs in a Jar*, the content of which is this edition. Some of those chapters are dated 1967, so it can be assumed that this work was his final. Another less complete work includes chapters for *The Damned Deceived*. An impressive novella-length short story, "Flat-Leavers" will be in the second edition.

How Butch managed to stay alive and work, his social interactions with fellow parolees, and the desperate needy romances of the women in his life, are captured in muted colors, and –between the self-taught grammatical limitations– often poignant lyricism.

By the mid-1960s, his sister Maureen, then married, took Butch to a meeting of Alcoholics Anonymous, where a well-known speaker dared anyone who wanted to have a drink that he would give them two dollars. Butch responded to the offer a bit too enthusiastically, and was asked to leave.

His sister managed to attend the High School of Performing Arts, and soon escaped the poverty and desperation of Rigney's world, with a marriage and move to Ohio, where she and my father raised our family.

While nearly every other family member visited us, and we them in the following decades, Butch remained a mystery. Rigney wanted to be a published writer. He had even sent one work to a literary agency, but it was returned by American Authors Inc. of Madison

Avenue. Did he continue writing, give up, or did the reality of his life overtake any ambition? Or was it simply his addictions to alcohol, heroin and other drugs that took over?

The entire box of original pages was allegedly found with Butch at his Bailey Place home when he died, of an overdose, with two ladies of the evening at his bedside, on December 6, 1967.

The manuscript and letters were shipped to my parent's house after they attended his funeral. The box of his writing remained in our attic for decades, in a yellow plastic box. My curiosity, and penchant for annual cleaning and sorting of our home's treasure trove of memorabilia and toys in our attic, led me to the box full of hand-typed stained onion-skin pages, along with letters, a few rent receipts for 3422 Bailey Place, The Bronx, 63, New York.

I couldn't see which chapter went with which story, or if any of it made any sense, but it fascinated me before I was even a published writer. A few years ago, I shipped them to San Francisco. In 2009, they were sorted, scanned, converted to text, and edited mostly for punctuation and grammar, not much else. The sad tone of desperation pervades the characters of Rigney's stories, each intertwined with a needy sorrow.

John "Butch" Rigney wanted to be a writer, but died thinking he never could be. The sad thing is, he already was.

– Jim Provenzano, March 2022

Chapter 1

One and Two

Once upon a time, an old man's restaurant, located in this neighborhood near a corner, had a sign above the plate glass, with the words in brushed paint:

The Old Man's Restaurant, est. 1937

It was an old sign. The words in red edged with black were faded, the background of the sign a dingy white. It had been there as long as the old man had, for a long time. The front of the restaurant was painted yellow, its flakes exposing another brighter yellow. Beneath the window was the word CIGARETTES in gold leaf. The door was twelve feet high and thin. In the summer, to hold it ajar was an old heavy iron. Within was a long counter topped by marble. There were booths in the rear and a jukebox that played without coins, twin telephone booths next to it.

The floor in the back between the booths was smooth, sometimes waxed. On the rear wall above the telephone booths was a picture of Franklin Delano

Roosevelt waving a cigarette holder. The glass covering was dusty, greasy and spotted. To the left was a door painted a glossy maroon red. Behind it was a dark room stocked with soda cases and paraphernalia long discarded and forgotten. There was a bathroom back there and an old bed that was comfortable.

Between the booths were wooden tables painted mahogany, but made of pine. A mirror ran along one wall, tinted blue. The walls were orange, just painted.

The old man, Frank Benello, was a stocky, hairy, cranky old man. His hair was short, coarse and brown, his eyebrows bushy, his forehead perpetually creased as if he were forever troubled. His eyes were deep brown, an expression of utter doubt playing in them, unless amused contempt came in as relief. He walked slowly with a limp and slight stoop. He disliked the world, confessing periodically how sorry he was to be born to it, wishing he had permission to leave. But he made the best coffee in the world.

A group of young men and women lived here with him at that time, now. The old man condemned them all, at least outwardly he condemned them. In him, he feared these people. He feared them their youth, their impetuous curiosity, their impulsive actions.

He feared the madness that impelled them thoughtlessly to waste the youth they had, the daring they shoved in laughing at established rules believing themselves not a part. The malicious humor they employed toward almost anything they did not understand and the cruelty that enforced them to act. Their lack of fear frightened him and their exuberance turned him pale. He did not understand them and warily guarded their

approach, admiring them, hoping they would never awake from their temporal, sanguine irresponsibilities.

When he opened that morning, Bob Coffin was sitting in the back in the first booth playing solitaire. Of them all, Bob was his favorite, the one he believed most likely to succeed. He was a tall good-looking young man who had been six-two since he had been thirteen.

When he smiled, he showed beautiful teeth, and because of those teeth he smiled often. His brown hair was thick and short, light now because of the summer sun, his skin darker. His eyes seemed always to be amused, though often his feelings were not. He was a quiet, sometimes taciturn young man to whom the old man could tell his troubles and sometimes question.

After the old man had placed the heavy iron against the door, he asked, "Ey, you bring inna papers?"

"Yup. Make some coffee, uh?"

"Yeah, yeah. Fer Christ sakes, gimme a minute. Whadda you think, you own this here place?"

"Uh uh."

"Friggin phone's ringin' all las night. Whas a matter wit you? You stop givin' out this here number ah?"

"Mm."

The old man banged things around while making coffee behind the counter in the large stainless steel urn. "You eat chet?"

"I ate chet. Marie was opened early."

"Yeah, whadda you think, you're funny? What time you got here?"

"About six."

"Why so early? Didn't get inna bed yet, huh!"

"Couldn't sleep. Come on, stop mumblin'. I'll play you some poker."

"Aw, nahh. You tell 'at Johnny to stop cuttin' up on my tables."

"We own this one."

"I don' mean 'at one. I'm talkin' about the uddah ones. Goddamned kid an' 'is knifes. What's a matter wit him? He crazy?"

"I don't know. Who called last night?"

"Some girl, ahh, what's a name, wait a minute, ah, Marge. Yeah, somebody like that. Ah, can't remember. Ask Alice. She answered a couple times."

"She would."

"You guys gotta be more careful."

"Bout what, Frank?"

"Ahhh."

He went on making coffee. Bob grinned, counting cards. He played for an hour, listening to the old man grumble while drinking his coffee.

Near eight, Alice came in, singing high because she had an unshakable belief that she could. Most times she wore her blonde hair long, curled only at the ends, which barely touched her shoulders.

She was very aware of her own body, boldly, with a youthful exuberance displaying it, wearing tight-fitting clothes, finding a satisfying female enjoyment at male reactions. She was not pretty but certainly attractive and, in a careful selective way, promiscuous.

Now she wore her blonde hair tied behind her head in a ponytail, a bright summery blue blouse, and very short white shorts. She greeted the old man with a happy, "Good morning, Frank!" She laughed. "Honest, love. It really is."

Stopping across the counter from Frank as he began pouring her a cup of coffee, "Is that fresh?"

"Yeah, yeah. Ain't it always?"

"Well then give it to me."

He handed her the cup. "Aw, gwan inna back wit him." His thumb pointed.

She turned, her voice rising, "Oh, hey, Bobby. What are you doin' up so early?"

"Nothin'. Come on back here."

"Right there, love. Frank, I wish you would buy cream."

"Aw, git the hell outta here."

With her cup and saucer, she walked back, sitting in the booth across from him.

"My, isn't it a lovely day?" she said, stretching her arms overhead, arching her back.

Bob raised his eyes from the cards, watching her, smiling, asking, "Whad are you doin'?"

Grinning, "Why, love. Nothing."

"Um, I'm not Tippy. I'll take you back there." His head nodded toward the maroon door.

She laughed. "I wanted to wake you up. Besides, I'd probably go. Lemme finish my coffee."

He pushed the cards to her and yawned. "Here, play with them."

She ignored the cards, stirring her coffee, her eyes on her hand as she spoke. "I got in late last night. Don't ask me why I got up so early for. I couldn't sleep." Stopping as if thinking of something, then suddenly, "Hey. Does Sully really go to a doctor for his head?"

"Yeah, but it's the guts in his head, not the kind you're always talkin' about."

"Not a psychiatrist?"

"Nope, just a doctor."

"What's the matter with him? Because of those headaches he always says he has?"

"Mm. You're disappointed."

"Do you believe he has them as much as he says he does?"

"Why not?"

"I don't know. He seems like an awful easy-going guy to forever have a headache."

"An' you don't believe him, just a way for him to get attention or somethin', right?"

"Yup." She smiled as his eyes went up and his head turned away from her. "All right, love. I believe, but it could be, that's all."

"Let it go, Alice."

"I have . Ask me why I didn't sleep late."

"Why didn't you sleep late?"

She chuckled a moment, then, "Because I was thinking."

"Good."

"It's not."

He gathered the cards together, asking disinterestedly, "How come not?"

Flatly, "I'm tired of Tippy. I think he's a queer."

His mouth dropped a little. His eyes came over to hers, then he laughed. She watched him, smiling, playing with a card she picked up. He slowed, breathing deep, shaking his head, "Oh Christ. You an' those books a yours."

"The books have nothing to do with it, love." Her voice had been heavy, her head bowed, eyes turned down on herself. His laughter went deeper.

She went on. "I was with him in a car last night and all he did was feel me, cautiously."

Shrugging, after calming himself, Bob said, "He always said he wanted a virgin wife, right?"

"That's only an excuse for his immaturity."

"You better take it easy. I'm gonna think you're one a them broads 'at can't get enough, a whatever the hell they call 'em. Read about 'em in one a your books."

"I did. He's a lovely looking man, but he's a boy."

"He's shy. He got one a them 'plexes you're always tellin' people they got. Whadda you call it. You upset his libido."

"That's why I think he's queer? Besides, you don't even know what libido means."

"Mm, don't knock 'im, honey. He's a nice-lookin' guy. You got nobody to replace him yet."

"Yet. I will."

"Yeah. Freddy got shot at last night."

"Not again. Oh, for God's sake. He's insane."

"I guess."

"When he was on his way home again?"

"Mm."

"They're going to kill him one of these days."

"Freddy don't think so. I think he gets kicks outta it."

"I do, and I think his father is as insane as he is."

"Uh uh; cheap, not crazy. Where'd you go last night?"

"After we left here, we drove around all night and he told me how beautiful I was, that's all. I think he should see a doctor."

Grinning, he winked. "I do, too, if he ignored those big bubbs a yours."

"You're right. A girl called last night. She wanted to know when you'd be back. I told her to call this morning about ten. She sounds cute; sexy over the phone, anyway."

"That was Marge?"

"Yup, that was her name. Hey, Bobby. Does Jimmy use junk?"

"Ask him. You know, Alice, you are nosey one. Ask the ole man to bring us more coffee."

"No, I'll get it. Let him pat my ass and he'll be in a good mood all day."

"You think a awful lot a that ass."

"Mm, hm. So do you, love."

She took the empty cups and walked up front. He rubbed his face with both hands, stretched, then sighed back against the plastic cushions. Picking up the cards, he began flipping them upward, forming a pile. When she came back, she said, "Oh, by the way, you're taking me to the lounge tonight." She placed the cup before him.

"You're outta your mind."

Her expression and voice sweet, both of her hands taking one of his, "Please, love. I promised I'd meet someone there."

"Uh uh. Place gives me a headache. Costs too much, too."

"I'll pay. Come on." She laughed when she saw his expression, a high laugh with humor. "It's not that expensive."

"All the way down to midtown? Oh, I don't think so. No, I don't know."

"Aw, come on, Nance. It's really a swell place. They have a combo an' a dance floor. Come on, huh?"

There was hesitation on the line, slowly, doubtfully.

"I'm not sure. Will you let me think about it? Call me later this afternoon. I'll tell you then. All right, Louie?"

"Yeah sure, okay. But no kiddin', it's a great place."

Later that afternoon, Bob was standing in front of

the old man's, staring without seeing the other side of the street. The sun was hot. He was wondering where to go, what to do with himself.

"Hey, man."

"Whadda you say, Jimbo? Where you been?"

"You know. Lookin' aroun'."

"Um, you been lookin' around a lot, huh?"

"No sweat, ace. Where you goin'?"

"Don' know. Feel like swimmin'?"

"No. I seen Blanche last night. She was askin' about you."

"You tell her I love 'er?"

"Yeah, sure. Wadda pig she's now."

"Yeah I know. Stuff knocks hell outta broads faster. They start junkin', seems like they give up all their secrets."

"Yeah. She's bangin' for niggers now."

His eyes came away from the other side of the street to Jimmy's, asking as if inquiring about something that had nothing to do with the conversation.

"Oh, whad you expect?"

"Yeah, yeah. I know. You goin' to the lounge tonight?"

Bob shrugged. "I don' know, I might. I feel lucky."

"Let's go get Frankie's care, take a ride."

"Mm, good idea. Let's."

"Hello, Nancy?"

"Oh. Hi, Louie. How are you?"

"Uh, okay, Nancy. Did you think about it? I been there before. We'll have a ball."

"Well, yes I did. I really don't know. I'd like to, but I don't think it's such a nice section. I don't know what my parents would say."

"Aw, come on, Nance. It ain't that bad. There won't be any trouble, an' I'll get you home before twelve if you want."

"Yes, I would have to be home early. I have to go out tomorrow."

"Yeah, sure. Don't worry about that. What time you want me to pick you up?"

"Is eight all right?"

"Sure. What colors you gonna wear? I wanna get some flowers."

Oh, thank you, but please don't bring any flowers. I'm sorry, I don't like them."

"Huh? Okay then, I'll meet you at eight, uh?"

"Yes, fine. Thank you for calling."

"Yeah, sure. So long, Nance."

"Goodbye."

Tippy walked into the kitchen in his drawers. He was a tall boy, his skin very pale, hair almost white and thin, it never seemed combed. His sister Marcy sat at the table in a half-slip and brassiere, sipping tea, dunking a roll. He grabbed an empty white bag from the table, "Whad you do, eat alla rolls?"

Marcy, who appeared to be a smaller female imitation of him, though her hair was always combed and looked it, her skin as pale, eyes, set wide apart, were light blue.She said, not nicely, because Marcy never spoke nicely, she couldn't help that, "Yeah, for breakfast. I'm havin' my lunch now. You sleep all day; tough."

He balled up the bag and threw it at her, bouncing it off the top of her head. "You little bitch. I'll punch you inna mouth. Don't talk to me like that."

She put the cup down, placing her hands on either side, palms flat.

"Don't you talk to me like that, an' watch who you're throwin' things at, you slob."

He leaned over and smacked her cheek. Her hand caught his arm as he was withdrawing it. She dug her nails in. He yelled, "Whadda you? You little bitch!" He started around the table with his fist cocked, ready to flatten her against the walls.

She stood, voice loud, "Get outta here, you rotten bastard." Her fists tight, ready to fight, when their mother came into the room.

"Cut it out! What the hell's a matter? Tippy, git outta there." To Marcy, "Happy you shut your filthy mouth before I let him smack you?"

She whirled to her mother. "I didn't do anything. That bastard started it. He smacked me."

"Yeah, you little whore. Next time, I'll knock your teeth down your throat."

"Like hell you will, creep."

Alice and Bob were walking along the street. It

was late afternoon and the street was crowded with screams of children and old ladies sitting on tenement stoops gossiping about the past, projecting themselves into the future, forgetting the present.

Alice was trying to con him, holding one of his hands in hers, walking close, speaking softly. "Come on, Bobby. As a favor. I'd do it for you."

"Hell, there ain't nothin' there but noise. Ask Frank!"

"Oh sure. He'd try to get in me five minutes before we left. Like why not tell me to ask Jim?"

"Ask Jim."

"Yeah, and be ducking punches as soon as we stepped in the
door."

"So go with Tippy."

"Hey, like, you are helpful one. I said I wanted to meet somebody, somebody else. Will you, please, love?"

"Mm, yeah."

She laughed, bumping her body against his.

The lounge was now a downstairs dance hall. It used to be a poolroom, and still smelled of poolroom smells, of cold drafts, smoky ones, soft chalk, balls that were shiny and hard, and numbered sticks. Of men around tables and in corners, of hard shots, sharks and marks. Of whispered hushes long faded, of deep urinal odors forever there. Of saliva ground deep under, the pounding dulling feet of womenless men. Of dreams dreamed in glory past, walls, and of the tired, run over, all gone with nothing left of the triers but a weak dance hall set in a fast perishing dream running by.

In place of the lights that were bright only over the cold green felt they covered, garish colored lights played on idiot-colored walls. It was wide and ugly, the heat, the smoke, loud combo, the bar and mostly the crowds made it the place to go, so everybody went.

The fans set in corners whirred for nothing, not disturbing the smoke that formed and lay in the air, hovering over everyone.

Mugs stood near a whirring-for-nothing fan, his fat moon face shining with perspiration, his heavy body wet and gritty.He grinned when he saw them.

Bob yelled. "Whadda ya say, ace? Bouncin' tonight?"

Nodding. "Yeah, hot. Lookin good, Alice."

She said, but it was lost in the noisy roar, "Thank you, love."

Bob yelled loud as the combo soared. "What about a table?"

"I dunno. Frankie's awright? He got one. He's with Sonya. Gotta table fer eight, awright? How's things?"

"I'm same. You were down Jerry's last week, uh?"

"Yeah, yeah, wanned somebody he could trus. Sheee, made a million. That yoyo knows howda runna bar like I know howda pray. Shoulda been there. Folla my wake. I'll cut a path."

Mugs was a heavy short bull-necked fighter. When

he started off, they followed the path he cut between the frantically dancing couples, who were trying to keep time with the imprisoning rhythm of the combo that blared in there heads. There were over a hundred couples dancing close together searching for room. On the dance floor proper, the added heat from the packed bodies was near unbearable. Over toward the rear where the windows were, it cooled appreciably. They were the only windows that slanted open. There, the smoke and some heat swooped up in a rush, escaping into the night air.

The table Frankie had reserved was over near a post slightly away from the others that were crowded together. Some sat four, others eight, ten, twelve, twenty four. There were bottles and pitchers of warming beer on the tables with waxed cardboard containers that held fast melting ice cubes or just water and glasses were piled in small pyramids.

They were as far from the combo as they could get, yet it was overwhelming, even there. The talk, loud laughter added to it, felt as if they were being assaulted in waves of colorful noise, light, heavy, dark, piercing.

Bob sat in a chair, loosening his tie, asking Alice as she sat down, "I must be bugs one, eh?" Then, asking Mugs, "Where's Frankie?"

Mugs thumbed over his shoulder, indicating the dance floor, then beckoning him close, yelling in his ear, "Wanna see the best lookin' head I ever seen in my life'?"

He nodded.

Mugs pointed, Alice busily making a drink from Frankie's bottle, followed his eyes and Mugs, pointing a finger and grinned.

But as he turned, Bob saw another girl.

Nancy was a beautiful, remarkably tall girl with hair that was deep black. Her eyes darker, they were sometimes purple. They were large and at times she did not at all care for them, because she felt they revealed too much of what was within her, and she could be shamed. Her short hair curled inward, framing her face, a face composed of carefully detailed, finely molded features that had to take much time and care to develop, or an extreme accident, fragile sustenance dwelling within. She was then an outrageous definition of pulchritude, one lovely young lady.

He breathed softly, asking Mugs, but not expecting an answer, "Who the hell is she?"

"Don't know, ace, but the jamboney with her is lost; first time here, I guess. Name's Nancy."

His eyes still on the girl, "How do you know?"

Smirking. "Come on, I'm a bouncer, man. That's house policy."

"Mm."

"You gonna try an make 'er, you better hurry up. Frankie ain't seen her yet. Whadda bout Alice? You with her?"

His eyes came away from Nancy a moment to Mugs, sarcastically, "She likes you. You're a bouncer."

Mugs dropped his eyes, looking around, saying softly, "Yeah, yeah. I'll dance with her later."

Bob's eyes were back on the girl. He asked, "What's she so scared for? What's she afraid of?"

"Don't know. Bad guys, I guess. She looked like that when she first came in. When I told her I was a bouncer, man, the broad looked relieved, like she's somethin', somethin' like that I'd marry."

Bob turned to him smiling, "Would you?"

Mug's laughed, a small hoarse sound with embarrassment. "Yeah. How's Alice feelin' tonight?"

"Fine. Warm. Careful nobody tells Patrice on you."

"Ah, yeah. Be back later. Gimme a clue you find any troubles, now." Mugs made his way through the crowd to stand by his fan, a lonely husky inhibited little man with his company of fists.

Alice grinned, pointing to the girl, "She's beautiful, Bobby."

He could not hear her, so he nodded. She held the bottle, indicating a glass. He nodded again. She pushed the bottle, glass and soda over to him.

He turned, watching the girl seated at a table for twelve bend her head as if listening to the young man she was with. She smiled, her eyes turning up, over to him.

Not often, within the compass of human intercourse on a social level, there develops between two strangers, a man and a woman, a communication not yet defined explicitly or with a satisfying degree of clarity, other than poetical, a degree of human emotion not yet exploited; an understanding by two individuals, an attraction wherein each knows that they have been solely put upon this earth for just that reason, for this time. That was the attraction then, when she turned to him and that was how it was at that time. Then her eyes fled. They rested in his a moment and fled.

She stood after that, the young man with her leading her to the dance floor.

He felt Alice tugging his sleeve, turned, a little annoyed, then saw the drink in her hand and she said, "I made it for you, love. Say thank you."

He nodded thanks, his eyes going back to the dance floor until Jimmy came over, smiling. He was tall and thin with small eyes and a big nose. He was high on junk then.

He bent, kissing Alice's cheek, turning to Bob, whispering in a low scream, "Man, whadda night. Things are movin', uh. You feel it?"

He nodded, pushing Jimmy out of his way with his arm. But he had lost her and damned Jimmy quietly.

Frankie came off the floor with Sonya, laughing, pushing her ahead of him, waving to Alice, going over to Bob, yelling in his ear, "Hey man. You made the broad, uh?"

"Who?"

His eyes were still on the dance floor.

"Come on. Who do ya think? Marge."

"Uh, no. She was busy."

Frankie straightened, looking down at him, grinning, saying something that was lost in the crowd's roar. Jimmy spoke in Frankie's ear. Frankie nodded, taking Jimmy's head down to his lips, saying something that made Jimmy's head come up, his expression disbelieving. Frankie nodded, smiling wide.

Bob watched the girl and the young man come off the floor, then saw Sonya smile at him shyly, so he winked, mouthing with his lips, *"Hello, babe."*

Sonya was a meek olive-complexioned girl who thought she was in love with Frankie. She was very shy, timorous. Her voice sounded as if she were whispering at all times. She kept her head close to her shoulders, but she would without hesitation do anything Frankie asked or that she thought he might want her to.

Frankie, with wavy hair that was curly, black, combed over, and almost feminine good looks and a well-proportioned body that he spent hours tanning, combined with a personality that made young ladies cry, and a queer promise to kill himself over, enjoyed it all. Jimmy said something in his ear that made him laugh then shrug his shoulders, sitting beside Sonya. He held out his hands, shaking his head. Jimmy still did not believe him. Frankie pointed to the bottle. Sonya began mixing drinks.

Bob caught the girl's eye at the other table again and tried holding them, but they left. He was not sure of the moment, but knew the next that they were gone, turned away as if frightened. Alice, who had been watching, found herself pitying the girl.

Mugs came over then, roaring in her ear to dance with him. She roared back. "You're outta your skull! I'll sweat."

Mugs smiled an indefinite grin and nodded. Bob leaned over to her saying, "I'll be back later. Dance with the guy."

"No. You go to hell. I want to be fresh. You dance with him."

Kissing her neck, he chuckled.

"Jimmy'll tell Tippy on you."

"So, let him. He doesn't own me."

"Really."

He moved for the table the girl was sitting at with the young man, an odd feeling playing in him. He bent for her ear. When he spoke her name, it was as if he were repeating it to himself.

"Teach me how to dance, Nancy?"

Her head snapped around, her eyes wide. He could not believe eyes could be made to be that wide. She hesitated, as if unsure, then smiled with a soft throaty laugh.

The young man sitting next to her frowned. His brows came together and he was angry. She wanted to dance with him. She had felt his eyes on her from the moment he and the blonde girl he was with had sat down. Twice she had glanced back, meeting his eyes for a moment, then flushed, turning away quickly, feeling too much and too silly. A glance could not do all of those things, she was sure, only in fairy tales or novels.

She was going to say yes, when Louie, the young man she was with, answered for her and she was afraid Bob might believe him.

"Look. We're alone. We're not dancing."

His eyes did not leave hers. They seemed to be laughing. She was thrilled because of the excitement that seemed to come from him.

"I know. That's why I asked."

Her smile grew as she started to stand.

"Yes, yes. Now I would like to." The last was meant for Louie, to excuse her for asking him to take her off the floor a little while ago; she had been tired.

Alice's eyes narrowed. She turned to Jimmy who was mixing drinks, standing next to her. Pulling his head down to her lips by the tip of his tie, she said, "I knew there had to be something wrong with her. She's too tall, isn't she?"

Jimmy turned his head, his eyes following her pointing finger, and said low in appreciation, "Like, wow. Holy shit, that's some piece. Who's she? How'd he meet her?"

He turned back to Alice, who shrugged, "He met her tonight. She's about to meet him."

Jimmy moved his lips to her ear, whispering, "The chump with er ain't goin' for it. He might have some troubles."

"Mind your business and everything will be all right, yes?"

"Shee, no sweat. Who'd you come wit?"

"Him."

"Yeah. I'll take you home later."

"Thanks. Don't."

She was smiling now, waving.

"Ey, that's Dicky," said Jimmy. "He gots the hots for ya?"

"Yes."

Nancy turned her face up at him, her hands on his forearms, his around her waist. She felt warm, warmer than the heat from the dance floor, and she was thirsty. Her voice was soft, with an anxious rapidity. "The music is faster. You're not supposed to hold me."

She wished she had spoken louder. She wasn't sure he had heard her. Then he nodded, saying, "I know. I can't dance."

"You can't dance, really?"

"Uh uh. I wanted to talk to you. Just move slow; no one will know."

"I thought you were fooling. It's really very warm. Do you mind if we sit down?"

"Yup. Stay here."

"Why? I mean, we could talk there. It's cooler."

"I don't wanna listen to the guy that's with you make a fool outta himself tryin' to impress you."

She chuckled softly, "Oh, he won't. They're all like that, I mean first dates, aren't they?"

"Not really. Where do you live?"

"New Jersey. I've never been here before."

"I know. Like it?"

"Yes. Well, it's nice."

Grinning, "Liar."

Quickly, "I'm not! Don't say that. Don't call me that."

"All right. I'm sorry. Why are you afraid?"

"I'm not. You talk silly. Are you laughing at me?"

"Do you wanna go upstairs? We can talk up there; it's cooler."

She stopped moving, blushing faintly, looking up at him, then away. "When? Now? Just you? Alone? Oh, no. I couldn't do anything like that."

"Don't you want to?"

It wasn't a question. To her, it seemed as if he had stated a fact. It made her angry. "Stop that. I don't like it as if you knew what I was thinking. You are laughing at me, are you, inside, I mean?"

"Uh uh. We're just goin' upstairs, Nancy. It's not that far, nothing will happen to you."

"Yes, I know, but ... How did you know my name?"

"It's hot. The band's loud. Come on."

"No. I don't know you. You don't ... How did you know my name? I am afraid, but not of you."

"Just upstairs. We can talk there. I can hardly hear you now."

"No. Don't make me go with you. He brought me. What will he think of me?"

He held her arms close to her shoulders, whispering, "Come with me, Nancy. I want to know you."

Nervously, apprehensively, "What will I say? No, I couldn't. No, please. I will give you my number. You can call me. I couldn't do anything like that. Tomorrow. Will you call me then?"

"No, now. Why are you so afraid for? It's only upstairs."

"I'm not. Yes, I am, but not like that. I've never been here. What's your name? I like you, but not like that. It's not ... Can you wait? Will you call me tomorrow?"

"I'll call you tomorrow, but come upstairs now. There's nothin' to be afraid of. It's only a street."

Shaking her pretty head negatively, her dark locks of hair bouncing, "Yes, but just upstairs. We'll come back?"

He kissed her lips lightly, walking beside her for the exit.

Frankie sat in his chair watching Bob and Nancy carefully. Alice, sitting with Dicky, who was standing beside her, saw him and turned, watched the couple leave, then chuckled. Frankie's eyes came over to hers. He frowned a moment, then grinned, winking. Jimmy's eyes were on Louie, who was searching the floor for Nancy.

They stood at the top of the steel stairs leading up from the dance hall, both breathing in deep sighs of warm night air that was cooler. It was a soft summer night with clouds overhead high and remote, with some stars that were scattered because of the clouds.

She stood close to him, her hand on his arm. "I left

my purse downstairs." She smiled, adding, "The music is almost as loud here!"

He pointed to the cars parked along the curb. She went with him. "Do you come here a lot? What will that girl say, the one you were with?"

"Nothin'. She's a friend goes with a buddy of mine."

"Oh."

Grinning, "An's trying to make another."

She did not understand so she ignored the remark. "It seems so late, the dark."

"Yeah, the lamp post ain't workin'." He pointed to the dead lamppost down from them about twenty feet. He was leaning against a parked car. She was standing in front of him, his hands cupping her elbows, bringing her closer.

Smiling, her head moving slowly from side to side, "You won't, you wouldn't do anything, will you?"

Freddy was up on the small stage with the bright red in the background and the four-piece combo that wore white dinner jackets with ties and dungarees without cuffs and sneakers that were orange. Freddy was singing the only slow song of the night, and the bodies on the dance floor were hushed close together, not moving other than a slight swaying. Freddy sang slow, whispering into the mike.

Freddy was small and thin, his features, his body seemed intense. When he spoke, he spoke with such rapidity it was for the most part not understandable. Everything he did was done with a rapidity, except now.

He sung slow and soft, until a break when the trumpet came in and deafened him, snapping his eyes that were almost closed, while jerking his body. He turned and growled something to the trumpeter, then went on singing, not as slow.

Kip came in alone, squeezing her way through the crowded dance floor as Freddy was singing. She was sorry she had come because she hadn't realized how hot it was until she had paid her way in. She was a pretty kid with neat cute features and an awful lot of honey curls all over her head. She had a neat figure; thin, everything small.

When she got to the table Mugs had told her where they all were. She was disappointed because then the only one there was Jimmy, who had his chin on his chest as if studyinghis hands that were lying on the table before him.

She frowned, sitting across from him, turning to listen to Freddy sing, just as the trumpet snapped Freddy's eyes opened and she giggled, more when she heard the low giggle run throughout the dance hall.

Freddy turned and said something to the trumpeter that she thought must have been something fierce, because the trumpeter, although unperturbed, looked at him a moment, then at the ceiling, and would not look at him again.

Jimmy's head came up, his eyes unfocused, slowly clearing, saw her, and said sleepily, "Kipper, love. Wanna dance with me?"

Without turning to him, "Leave me alone, Jimmy. Don't start tonight. I wanna listen to Freddy."

Chuckling, "Aw, come on, baby. You know I love ya, doncha?"

She didn't answer, watching Freddy sing faster as the trumpet player played with his head up in the air. Freddy was moving the microphone from hand to hand and she wondered if he was going to hit him with it, until Mugs moved over and pulled the trumpet player's dungareed leg, saying something, shaking his finger as if warning him. The trumpet player's mouth hung, eyes round, hands in front of him, shaking his head in a masquerade of innocence. Mugs finger shook again and he turned away.

Freddy finished the song, turned to the player, thumb pointing over his shoulder toward the exit, head bobbing a few times, then he stepped down as people clapped and the trumpet player grinned and Jimmy said happily, "Aw, now lookit this. Me an' Fruits gots troubles."

Kip turned to him sneering, "You an' that fool always have."

Crushed, winking, "Aw, baby. You don' love me no more, uh?"

She dismissed him, turning her head off to the side as the combo began blasting and the crowd began contorting rhythmically.

Freddy sat down at the table, muttering quickly to himself, playing with an empty glass that was there on the table in front of him.

Jimmy asked loudly, "Whasamatter, Fruits? Gonna go up on 'im or what?"

He growled an "Aww" at Jimmy and turned to Kip, his hand going to her arm. "Hey, how are you? Where you been?" His words were falling into each other as they caught one another. Kip pulled her arm away and said, "No."

Mugs walked up the steel stairs, breathing deep, trying to free his lungs of the heat and smoke and his head of the noise that still echoed in there. At the top, he leaned against the railing, glancing at his watch, wishing the night was over, and thinking that if Patrice came around tonight, he would tell her to go home because this was a trouble night. He felt it even before Freddy had the trouble up on the stage. The feeling was all over the place, in all the corners. He thought about what a dumb bastard he was, working for the cheap bastard he was working for and was a little angry at himself.

Bob came over then. Mugs smiled, looking past him to the girl standing by Frankie's car. Bob returned the smile, asking, "Ace, Nancy left her purse on the table. Will you pick it up for me? I'll get it later?"

"Yeah, sure. How's she?"

Bob's head shook, his smile fading. "You wouldn't believe it. See you later. Thanks."

"Yeah. Okay. Take care."

Frankie and Sonya were dancing when he saw Alice

and Dicky walk out the door and said, "Oh, now. What's this?" while grinning, chuckling, pulling Sonya over to the last column.

She asked, "What, Frankie? Who do you see?"

"Shhee, look." He pointed at them.

"That's just Alice. She's with Dicky."

"Yeah, yeah. I know, dummy. She told Tippy not to meet her tonight." He laughed. "My boy Tippy finds out, he's gonna cry."

"No, Dicky's probably just takin' her home."

His eyes snapped down at her in disbelief, then back up, as Alice and Dicky went out, saying, "You know you're not stupid. You're more."

Grinning, "Wait'll Tippy finds out. Owie, is he gonna cry."

"Don't tell him. You'll get her in trouble."

"Her in trouble? Hey, I ain't tellin' him. She will. She's tired of little boy blue. Whadda head that chick is. She's strong stuff." Looking at Sonya, his smile gone, "Why don't you be like her, uh? I mean, you got nothin' mousey."

Sonya's features tightened, her tone different.

"Do you wanna dance some more?"

"No. Come on. Make me a drink."

His hands were around her waist, clasped behind her, her hands resting on his forearms, her dark eyes watching him carefully.

"Do you want to go for a ride? Let's go someplace where we can be alone."

She seemed to sigh, her body going limp without sagging, "But you said jus–" Then she gave up. "Yes, all right."

After they were seated and the car was going, she said, "I want to talk to you. I don't know why. I feel funny, a little afraid."

"Of me?"

Smiling, "No, not you."

He took her hand, kissed it, turning it over, licking her palm. She let out a surprised gasp, alarmed, pulling away, then sorry she had she moved closer.

"I never ... It felt funny."

"You wanna go down by the river? It's cooler there, nice at night."

"Yes, I would like that. I feel different, not afraid so much; well, funnier than that. Do you feel it?"

He grinned.

"In your belly, here." She supressed her surprise when his hand touched her, moving it away quickly.

"Yes, yes, there, but in my head, mostly, and I'm shaking. Do you feel like that? Don't touch me there, please."

"Mm, all right. I'm sorry."

"No. I didn't mean you to be sorry."

"I feel like that, Nancy; stronger."

He was smiling and he had a hard time beating down an urge to take her in his arms.

Patrice and Mugs stood up on the street near the lamppost that wasn't working. Patrice was a husky kid, a little older than Mugs, not good-looking, with long brown hair and a big grin, with a large bust and heavy arms and shadows under her eyes. She was warm, nice to be near. She never whispered.

"So why don't you want me to come down, finally make out with one a them young broads, huh?" He laughed quickly.

"Yeah, yeah. Hey, you shoulda seen the one that was there tonight. Whadda good lookin' kid. Whew."

"Oh, so what happened to her, fatty?"

He glanced down at himself self-consciously. "Yeah, naw, Bob, he took her. Prob'ly take her home later."

"Who? Bob Coffin?"

His grin died, expression somber. "Yeah. I don't know. There's gonna be troubles here tonight."

Eyebrows up, mockingly, "Why? Because you have that feeling?"

Defensively, "Yeah. I tole you about it. When I get it, it happens."

"I know, every time. That's why I think you start it."

"I don't! What the hell I wanna fight a buncha kids for? Drunk, too."

"You will. Is it crowded?"

"Yeah, hell yeah. About six ta every foot an hotter 'an hell."

"I know. You're sweatin'."

He took out his handkerchief quickly, wiping his face. "Yeah, hot. I ain't gonna work here no more. Hell wit it. Getta job inna bar for weekends."

"Sure, go ahead. But they'll expect you to bounce there, too."

"Not bad there, but just a neighborhood bar."

"What about Tom's?"

"Uh, uh. He jus' wants me to work days there."

"Well, it would be better, twenty dollars a day."

Indignation, but it was mild. "Yeah, yeah, sure. Then when'm I gonna see ya, huh?"

She chuckled loud, hugging him, saying in his neck as she kissed him there, "Okay, Romeo. Me an' you every Saturday an' Sunday an' late Friday nights."

"Yeah, only till we get money. Then it's different." He slapped her rump, moving away, her arms still around him, merrily saying, "Then you quit and I'm the only one workin', right?"

Laughing low, "Yeah, yeah."

Alice was staring at Dicky, her expression one close to anger, in seconds would be. She said, almost snarling, "Whadda you mean, the Columbia?"

Holding his hands up in front of him in mock defense, trying not to laugh, "No? Hell, no. It's the place downtown, not the hotel."

"You better be sure, because you're all alone if it is, love."

He waved at a cab that zipped by, ignoring him. "Be nice, slim. I wouldn't take you to that joint."

Nodding, saying flatly, "I know."

Her expression threw him and he choked from laughter as he was going to whistle for another cab.

Kip asked Frankie and Sonya as they sat down, "Where's Alice and Bob and everybody?"

Frankie smiled slow. "Makin' love, love. You should try it."

Jimmy said, "Uh uh. She don't like it. She cries."

Kip glared at him as Freddy asked Frankie, "Hey man, you hear me sing?" quickly, too quickly for Frankie to understand him, so he frowned.

Jimmy grinned. "Yeah, you sounded jus' like a faggot."

"Yeah, sure I did. Come on, Kip. Let's me an' you dance."

Since she was glaring at Jimmy, and Freddy had said everything while still turned to Jimmy, she did not realize he was speaking to her until he stood, taking her hand. She went with him, because she was sure if she did not, she would bat Jimmy over the head with a bottle.

He stopped her at a small clearing circled by forcythia bushes, hidden from the highway beyond, almost opposite a brightly lit factory across the somber flat river. Slipping off his jacket he said, "Let's sit here."

She smiled as she watched him spread the jacket out on the grass.

"What time is it?"

She sat next to him, his arms around her. He nodded across the river to the moving electric sign:

PALISADES AMUSEMENT PARK
NEW RIDES SIX NEW ATTRACTIONS
WORLDS LARGEST OUTDOOR
SALT WATER POOL
FREE PARKING
COME TO THE PALISADES

She sat closer to him. He asked, "I've never been in love. Have you?"

"No, but we can't be. We just met. It's not like that."

"Yes, it is. Now it is."

He cradled her in his arms, kissing her. It was long, the effect startling them both. She groaned. "Oh, oh see, I'm dizzy. Why do you make me feel like this for? I feel weak an' scared." She collapsed against him, her lips warm, moist, heavy. "I've never felt this way, Bobby. Don't hurt me, please."

"I can't, Nancy. As soon as I saw you, it had to be like this.Don't be scared. I won't hurt you."

She moved with him as he stretched out on the grass. Everything they were made of then was stimulated. Nancy was discovering things she never thought she wanted, all the nice things gone, still there, with different values placed upon each. So they kissed again.

Jimmy sat next to Kip. Frankie was in a hushed conversation with Sonya, speaking intently, the girl listening as intently. Freddy sat watching Kip try to ignore Jimmy, who was holding her hand, playing with her fingers, telling her a story about little piggies. Her teeth were clenched. She was staring at the window that was opened but she couldn't see out of.

Freddy was thinking about how good-looking he thought Kip was, and if Jimmy would leave her alone, maybe she wouldn't be so nasty and he could make points with her.

Mugs was over by his fan, watching two men argue with a girl sitting between them, her eyes excited. He was promising himself that he was going to kick her in the ankle when he went over to sock them both silly, when they started swinging.

Jimmy whispered in Kip's ear with his arm around her, after Frankie made her a drink and Sonya had mixed him one. Then suddenly Kip whirled, and drink, glass and ice cubes missed Jimmy because he moved away. He darted around the table, laughing, pointing his finger at her, saying, "She gots the littlest bubbies in the world."

Freddy told her to take it easy and walked her out on the dance floor. Frankie was laughing like hell, with Sonya not saying anything, her eyes blank.

Alice was no longer wondering why she was slightly infatuated with Dicky. She had decided that he was manly. A male aura of authority was about him, as if he could master anything, anyone, except her, of course.

He was husky, almost fat, with chunky features. He laughed loud from a stomach that was blubbery. They were sitting in a booth in the Columbia Cocktail

Lounge, which was a bar with a dark back room that had a piano player and a female singer and fast service.

Tonight, Kippy was loser one. She knew that. So did Dicky.

Kip said to Freddy, when he tried to stop her so they could dance, "No, I'm goin' home. That god-damned son of a–"

Her eyes fell on him as if just discovering him. "And you. You're just like him."

"Am not!"

He snapped that at her because he felt unjustly accused.

She grinned. "Okay. So you're a little less. I'm goin' home. I'll see you."

"Hey, no. Lemme walk you, huh?"

He pleaded that slowly enough for Kip to understand.

"Okay. Sure. Come on."

Kip was sure Freddy was an idiot, but a real one, afflicted. The streets they walked on were lonely and empty, just some of the hallways where lovers held each other close as if tomorrow was already gone, held life.

At the stoop of her apartment building, she watched clinically as he put his arms around her and said, slow, "Hey, you know I been waitin' to get close to you. You know, without that creep Jazz aroun'. I go for you."

Her eyebrows raised just a little bit she said dully, "You're close."

So he wrapped her in one passionate embrace that shocked hell out of her because he was so quick with so much energy and haste. When she finally squirmed free she was gasping, not from any passion, just lack of air.

"Why, you, you stupid son of a bitch."

She swung, missing him by half seconds as he danced away, grinning, saying, "I'll get you, skinny. Bet you see my way soon."

She started for him. Since their weights were just about evenly divided, Freddy figured he should allow valor to prevail, so he scooted away towards the old man's.

Kip fumed, watching him run, clenching and un-clenching her hands, watching him run. Then she thought about what had just taken place, and she started giggling, and was still giggling a half hour later.

When Freddy got to the old man's, Sully was in a booth in the back. Sully was tall, heavy, almost two hundred and eighty pounds, with crinkly dark hair and soft womanish eyes where headaches lurked behind.

An easygoing, affable young man with hardly an idea or thought of his own, generous by nature without malice, to him the people of the world mattered in this sometimes changing order; his mother –she was always first– his brothers and sisters, but they could and sometimes did hold last place firmly. Then there was Bob, Alice, Frankie, Jimmy, at times Freddy was included, and of course God was in there, too.

He was slow to anger and quick to laugh if the joke were painstakingly explained to him. But should any fool happen to run over anything told to him by one of the esteemed, which he held as sacred knowledge, he would hug them to death, squeeze the bejesus out of them.

The headaches that Alice would dearly love to have proven imaginative —so that her friends might think her intuitive, well read and smart, for the most part they did so anyway— were real. They were caused by a growth that would stop growing, when a doctor, paid for by the city in a zestful moment of metropolitan misguided bureaucratic charity, would attempt to cut it out of Sully's skull.

Sully from then on would for all purposes live no longer, though his body would not die, rather fester in a vegetated state in an institution for the mentally ill, where he would only be remembered.

Freddy stood breathing heavily, his suit jacket hanging over his folded arms that were across his chest. He was watching Sully stare down at the checkerboard on the table in front of him. "I'll play ya."

"Wait'll this here game's over."

Softly, "What game?"

"This here one." Sully pointed to the board.

Freddy's brows contracted, his voice rising a decibel. "You buggy? Ain't no game, just you."

"Yeah, it is."

"How long it's gonna take?"

"Not long. I got 'im."

Very loud, "Who ya got?!?"

"Me."

"Yer nuts, yuh fat bastid."

Complacently, "Shud up."

Freddy sat in the booth on the opposite side, watching Sully carefully. A few moments later, Sully smiled. "Okay, let's play."

"Who won?"

"Me."

Scornfully, "Aw, you didn't even move a friggin' checker."

A large friendly smile. "But I won."

Freddy's eyes went from the board to Sully's head, from Sully's head back to the board. Sully spoke slowly in a deep low boom with meaning, "Better not, ya little bitch. I'll squeeze yer mouth in fer yuh."

Freddy's head popped straight up, asking incredulously. "You'll what? My what? How ya gonna squeeze my mouth? You're crazy."

Sully warned with a dignified solemnity, "Wanna play? Shud up."

"I'm playin."

"Go 'head, move."

"Did."

"Did not."

"Did so."

Sully glowered. "Ya playin? Move."

"There, moved again."

"Whereja move?"

Coyly, "Not tellin ya."

Warmly, "Ya didn't touch a checker."

"Did."

"Did not, jus' your pinky did, but you didn't move it."

"Oh yeah, I moved twice."

Sully's large heavy hand came up and sat on Freddy's squirrel head. "You playin."

"Sure, yeah. There I just moved again."

Sully raised his hand about a foot off Freddy's head, made a fist, and slammed it down. The green of Freddy's eyes disappeared, making room for the whites as he slipped under the table.

Sully growled down at the checkerboard. "Crazy little dope, yuh."

The old man stood at the end of his counter, his body jiggling up and down, wild jets of air coming from his nostrils, tears from his eyes, as he tried to laugh quietly.

Alice and Dicky, on the ground floor of her apartment building, were kissing deeply, their hands playing at one another. He kept pressing himself against her. She felt it jut from his pants, insistently.

When they broke, Alice thought it was about time, because this would be too easy. She held him away, saying, "Whoah, like, that's enough. No more."

But he remained close to her. "Why not tonight? It's gonna be sooner or later."

"Mm-hmm. It's going to be later. Whadda you think I am? Hell no, fella. Call me in the morning."

Grinning, "How bout late afternoon?"

"All right, but it's not that late."

After one, an' I likes to sleep."

"Yeah, I bet. Come up my house tomorrow night. My mother an' father are going out."

"Good idea. When? What time?"

"After nine. Now lemme go."

He did, but watching her walk up the stairs he regretted it. Chuckling, he walked out on the stoop, anticipating another time.

Alice was singing to herself as if she had won at bingo.

Nancy whispered, "I never have. I've never. I'm sorry. Stop. We can't. I'm sorry. Bobby, I want to. I want you to, but I can't, not now, not tonight."

She lay on her back, his arms under her, his hands framing her face, his body over hers. He kissed her lightly and she cried, "Oh, Bobby, no. I wan ... We can't. Please, not now. I'm menstruating. Bobby, I'm sorry."

"Don't be sorry. We have time. I never wanna let you go. Let me hold you. I can't let you go now."

She closed her eyes, his lips touching hers carefully. They were that way a long time. Then he sat up, pillowing her head in his lap, her arms going around his waist. He gazed down at her, watching her breasts rise and fall under her dress, then turned, looking across the river, wishing he could thank someone, something, for her.

Mugs walked up the steel stairs, the last one out because he was paid to stay to watch the sweepers sweep up. It was after three and he heard his feet clank on the black steel steps.

Mug's didn't like his feet because they were fat and stubby, the toes. They were too short. They should have been longer; too short and wide. Mug's enjoyed swimming, but didn't go often because of those feet, mostly the toes. He thoughta lot about swimming in the summer, about swimming and wearing sneakers.

Up at the top of the stairs with his hand on the railing, he gazed around slowly. The street was dark, the lamppost was out, and all the lights in the stores were out, except the dim night lights glowing faintly and a clock with a light inside it. There was a faint rain, not a rain, as if it were warm steam that was light and being sprayed lazily.

Patrice was waiting for him up at the apartment they shared weekends. He wanted to marry Patrice. He was relaxed with her.

He knew it wasn't love. Love had nothing to do with it. In bed, she was comfortable, but that was all. He had had better sex when he paid a stranger for it, but she was easy to get along with. She understood some of the things that bothered him, like his toes. Hers were something like his, so it was all right. But they had to wait until she could divorce the bum she was married to.

It cost a lot of money, but not so much the money, that didn't bother him. It was the time, the waiting. Something could go wrong. Maybe she wouldn't divorce the son of a bitch after all. She said she would, wanted to, but women were funny.

He brought the small wallet-like purse that was in his hand up close, and looked at it a moment as if expecting it to move. Bringing it closer to his nose, he sniffed it. It smelled, some kind of perfume that was sweet and an old smell that he could not place. He thought about what it contained, then dismissed it quickly; just women's stuff. It opened in his palm.

When he loosened his fingers, it fell in half, the way a book would. The satin lining gleaned a little from the tiny beads of rainy spray that fell on it without noise. Then he heard someone approaching and started. The wallet-like purse slapped closed in his hand.

A guy and a girl walked by, holding onto each other. He watched them walk and continue and he felt embarrassed, as if he had done something wrong and had been caught doing something dirty. He shoved the purse in his jacket pocket, walking fast for the apartment.

He was going to tell Patrice that this was the first tine he had been wrong about that feeling.

Very early that morning before the sun came up, Freddy stole softly to the corner of the street he lived on. He stuck his head around the corner quickly, studying both sides of the street carefully with the utmost scrutiny, deliberating every shadow. After five minutes of intense concentration, he sneaked slowly from shadow to shadow.

At the front of his apartment house, rather than enter the hall where enemies could and very well might be lurking, he crept down the cellar steps and climbed the fire escape to the fourth floor, locking the unlocked window after he climbed inside. Then he relaxed, undressed, and went to bed.

"Hello."

"Oh, hello," Nancy blurted. "Hi, I missed the bus. That's why I'm late. I was afraid you wouldn't be here."

Bob's eyes were dancing with humor. "Can I kiss you?"

She turned her head, peering around at the crowded busy corner, her eyes flashing quickly from side to side. "Here? Now? No, wait."

He laughed, hugging her close to him. There was no one coming down the stairs from the subway station now. She stepped back, smiling shyly, looking up at him, then held him, tightly wrapping her arms around him.

"I'm glad I met you. Oh, you're nice, you are."

He kissed her lips. She near jumped away.

"You stop that! Not here on the street. You shouldn't."

Enjoying her indignation, he said, "I'm goin' to make love to you tonight."

Aghast, "You are not! No. Why do you say things like that for? I never have. Don't say things like that, please."

"I won't, but I am."

"Huh."

"Where'd you feel like goin'?"

"I don't know. Wherever you like."

With a charming hesitancy, her eyes averted, until the last, "That place, where we were ..."

"All right, I'm goin' to tell you how beautiful you are. Don't tell me not to."

He brought her waist close to him as they began walking, her head bobbing.

"You can."

He growled down the chuckle silently. "Have you decided you're in love with me?"

"Don't be silly," she said. "We still hardly know each other. Oh, you; we just met."

"But I was in love with you the minute I saw you."

"You. You were not. What did you mean by making love? You don't mean all the way? I won't let you. I can't, even if I wanted to."

"Can an' will."

Her mouth dropped, her eyes opening very large, making him again wonder how large eyes could be made and remain beautiful.

"I will not. Are you crazy or something? Bob, I just won't let you."

It was the same spot they had stopped at before, with the river below, about twenty feet the highway behind, beyond the forcythia bushes and rocks sloping down from the water's edge into the river.

She smiled, sitting next to him. "I like it here. We were here before, last night. This is the place, isn't it?"

"Yes. Give me your hand."

Her hand went between both of his as she stretched out closing her eyes. He gazed down at the black flat water, then turned, bending. He met her lips as they came up at him. After they kissed, she kept her head turned away, her eyes closed.

"I knew that's what we would do, what you said before. I never have, but I want you to. I thought about it all day. Can we now, when I'm still like that?"

Chapter 2

A Three-Legged Mouse

"I wonder how old he is?"

She smiled at the thrill in her stomach, the same as she always felt when she thought of him, turning from brushing her hair in the vanity mirror.

"He can't be much older than I am. He just acts that way, as if he knows so much more."

She laughed, hugging the brush to her.

"Oh, if he's just like he is, I'd love him. He doesn't seem young, I wonder how old he is? I'll ask. He'll tell me."

She turned back to the mirror, then patted her short coal-black hair.

"It's behaving that's good. It's rainy but it's still behaving."

A scowl overcame her pretty features as she heard the gruff voice of her father call from the living room just off her bedroom.

"Damn, he's drunk already and it's not even seven

o'clock. Sometimes I wish he would drink so much he'd drown in it."

"No, no; you stop that."

Taking a light bright jacket from a closet, she went quickly into the connecting bedroom, then out into the kitchen and through the side door. She walked down the street toward the bus stop to start her trip to New York.

Walking down that long street under the shadows of trees she was passing, she appeared innocent, wrapped in an unconscious beauty and lonely youth. Somehow she was temporal, as if at any time she could easily be embraced in an aura of gossamer desire that would only resolve to a longing of remembrance, long gone, hardly remembered when recalled.

It was a wet drizzly evening when he met her at the subway station. He had been standing by the newspaper vendor's shack, listening to Stan, the old man who entertained him by repeating old jokes in either an Irish brogue or Jewish accent, combining the two at times. Stan had told him a long time before that his parents had been Irish and Jewish –mother Irish, father Jewish– another time reversing the order and nationalities. Bob did not believe a word the old man said but he enjoyed him; he never failed to amuse him.

As Nancy walked by, he reached for and held her forearm.

"Hey, where you goin,' good lookin'? Thought you were sposed to meet me?"

She turned, surprised over the disappointment she

felt when she had not seen him, smiling nervously. "Oh, you! I didn't see you. I didn't know where you were."

The sincere proffering in her expression made him lose a second. Then he grinned, "Waitin' for you. How was the ride down? Crowded?"

"No, it was nice; not crowded."

They began to walk away from the bright lights of the drug store that was on the corner and the newspaper vendor, who smiled after them.

A pleased satisfied feeling was within both of them now. He asked lightly, "I thought about you all day. I told you I was in love with you, didn't I?"

His arm was inside her jacket across her back, tips of his fingers touching the side of her breast. She pressed down on them so he would not move away, glancing up shyly to see if he had noticed, she saw his lips curl upward.

"Yes. Why are you laughing? Don't."

"Mm." But his hand moved, covering her. She was not sure she wanted that.

They walked under the El as a train roared overhead with wet jinking rumbling sounds. It was darker walking here with him. She let her head rest on his shoulder, lifting her face to the warm sprinkling rain that muffled almost all sounds.

The buildings they were walking beside, to her, seemed to gleam in the warm safe darkness. His lips touched the top of her head he whispered her name.

"Nancy?"

"Yes?"

"Right now like we are, if something happened I'd think of us like this. I'd think of you more than anyone I ever met."

"Yes, I feel that way. But why do you say something will happen, what?"

He stopped walking, placing both hands at her waist, the smile on his lips faint.

"Nothin'. I was talkin'."

His voice had been low and soft and she wondered if it had been the truth, if he had just told her the truth? They walked on again his arm under her jacket her head resting on his shoulder.

"How old are you?"

She walked at the end of the block and they had turned the corner.

"How old are you?"

He was smiling when he asked. She knew it, not seeing his lips, but hearing it in his voice.

"I'm seventeen."

"Mm, nineteen. Would you marry me?"

She hesitated, then giggled.

"I've only known you for a week. "

"I'd marry you if you'd marry me."

She held his arm tighter.

"Oh, you. My parents wouldn't let me."

"First turn-down I ever got."

They walked along the pavement, wet shining oars forming a pathway between the apartment buildings with their low stoops and seven-foot-high iron fences, garbage cans in front everything in wet shining black of lighter and darker hues. Street lamps glowed their whitish circles that were sometimes pale yellow upon asphalt paved streets that now appeared as wide black blotters, soft and damp, easily torn.

The lights from apartments of the buildings shown dully in a wild cross word puzzle. Diffused whites and oranges darkened by shades, Venetian blinds, curtains and drapes to others with blind myopic eyes that were black and sometimes dumb. She felt she was within a dazzling moment, a scene set just for them that night.

"It's pretty, this street."

He looked around while walking. "Guess so. Never thought of it as bein' pretty."

A car went by. The humming tires, as she listened, looked for, gave off a muted far away glow, wistful, romantic.

"Where are we going, Bobby?"

"I don't know. I'm broke. You wanna go to the old man's for coffee?"

She frowned slightly, looking down at the black loafers she wore. "No. You said there's always so many people there. Can't we go someplace else?"

"We can walk around in the rain all night." He grinned when she looked up at him.

"Do you wanna go to my room?"

Shrugging, "Yes, I guess so."

His arm slackened around her as if it were going to fall away. She held it, her hand going inside her jacket to hold his.

"What's wrong? What's the matter?"

"Nothin'." He gazed ahead at the empty street. "Look, kid. I told you when I called I was broke. I didn't want you to come over. You shouldn't have if you wanted to go someplace."

Fear played in the background of her eyes as her head twisted from side to side and she pleaded.

"Don't be angry. I want to go to your room. I'm sorry, please don't be mad."

He regarded his hand going to the back of her head, his fingers in her hair, shaking his head with a defeated smile. Her unawareness captivated him, leaving him helpless.

"Nancy, I don't... Why do you always sound like you're gonna cry for?"

"I don't ... I'm not. I don't know why, I don't."

He took her hand that was at her side.

"Come on. We'll sit up there and talk. I won't try to con you to come to bed with me, if that's what's the matter."

She allowed him to take her hand but did not move as he started away, a pout of anger on her face, her lower lip puckered, brows together, then suddenly, "I said I'd go. Why are you speaking to me that way for?"

He turned back to her and wanted to laugh, then take her in his arms and kiss her, but he bent his head, speaking low.

"Forgive me. I'll never talk like that again, not to you."

When he looked up at her, there was too much promise in his eyes, too much laughter in his voice.

Walking along with him, displeased with his reaction as well as her hair that had started to fall across her forehead, she no longer cared much for the rain. They walked toward his building.

"You know you were the first. You were the only one, Bobby."

Her hand dropped from his and she stood, tears welling inside. He watched her, seeing her groping, as if in a self-effacing way she were trying to regain something, then realizing it was a useless search. Her head shook and he knew she was wishing she could hide, that she wanted some place to run to.

He held her tight, not allowing her to speak anymore.

"Not now. Later. Come on, we'll talk about it."

They walked the wooden stairs inside the building. It was narrow and dark. She held his hand, feeling afraid as her eyes tried to make out the doors on each landing. She whispered, "Which one do you live in? I can hardly see."

He answered in a normal speaking voice, but to her it seemed loud.

"Next floor." Then he chuckled, that was normal too, but to her loud.

"I think the damned doors all look the same." Again she whispered, "Will the landlord say anything?"

His voice had humor in it when he answered. "Uh uh. I paid the rent."

But it went by her; she was tense.

In a softer tone, his hand tightening on hers, "Don't worry. Pete's the super here."

"Oh, you know him?"

"Pete?" He opened the door on the forth landing. "Everybody in the neighborhood knows him."

After clicking on the light, he hugged her, kissing, at first she was surprised, drawing back slightly, then she moved to him. After he let her go, she looked around.

The room was large for a furnished single, with a double bed, a dull black bureau that Pete had shown him with a childlike glee, a secret compartment behind the top drawer that he never used.

The only window in the room was large, and opened to an alley and a brick wall less than five feet away. The walls were light blue. Worn grey linoleum covered the floor. On the bureau was a hot plate. She smiled, seeing him watching her.

"It's nice."

Grinning; "Liar."

She stopped a second, then smiled wider. "You. No, honest."

He slipped off his jacket, opening the door in the far wall, motioning to her. She took hers off, shaking it before handing it to him.

"I don't want the rain to get in your closet."

"Thanks. Are you afraid of me?"

"No." She smiled. "Why did you ask me that?"

"I don't know. Every time I look at you, you look as if you wanna run an hide someplace. When we talk about anything serious, your eyes fill up and you look like you wanna cry. Tell me, good lookin', what can I do to please you?"

He pointed, smiling as her eyes widened, becoming darker. "See? That's what I mean. What are you afraid of, Nancy? Do you think I'm gonna hurt you?"

"No. No, Bob."

Her head shook, her dark hair almost falling in her eyes. He smiled deeper when he saw it. Not wanting her to see and think he was laughing at her, he let it die.

"It's not you. I'm afraid that I might not be the way you want me and you'll go away from me. I mean ..."

Shaking his head slowly, "No Nancy, uh, uh. That's not the way it is. Listen to me. You're easy to love. You can't help that. Hey, I'm the one beggin' you. All I can give you is me. Hell, you can have that."

Her eyes fell away from him. "I would be happy with that."

Going over to her, holding her shoulders his smile dying, "Aw, Nancy. What's a matter? Are you scared of everything? Nothin' will happen to you."

"I know; really, I'm not afraid. I can't help that. I can stay tonight, maybe the whole weekend."

He sat beside her, not happy. "What about your mother and father? Won't they worry or anything?"

"No. I told them I was going to stay at Alice's. She

said I could, that she would tell them I was there if they called." Her hand moved. "They won't call. Don't worry."

"Why won't they call?"

Turning away, "I don't want to talk about that. I told you what they're like. They just wouldn't think of it." She smiled. "You touched my shoulders again. When we were down by the river, that's what you said you were going to call me. That's silly."

"Yeah. I'm sorry for you, Nancy. I wish I could do something."

"Don't talk like that." She took his hand between hers. "Let's not talk about anything like that. Just you and I, all right?"

Nancy lay in bed. She could hear the water from the shower that was in the bathroom next to his room, through the wall. She wondered what he looked like under it, wished she could go and see, wished she had forgotten something or just had the nerve the way he had awhile ago when she had been bathing, just walk in. She felt it was wonderful, she felt it to be pleasant and beautiful to both of them. She counted in her mind to three. 'Three,' she thought, chuckling to herself, feeling a lovely wantonness as she did.

'We've slept together three whole nights, last Saturday and Sunday and last night.'

She thought, they had all day today, perhaps tomorrow? She would call her mother, tell her she was going to stay at Alice's again. Maybe she would let her. Maybe her father was drunk, her mother, too. She scowled. "Maybe."

She laughed happily as he walked in the door, just a towel around his waist, dropping it before the door closed. She sat up.

"You're terrible. Someone might have seen you."

He shrugged, taking the underwear from the top of the bureau that he had neglected to take in with him. "The hell with them; it's raining out."

"What has that got to do with your neighbors seeing you naked, running through the hall?

Grinning after slipping on a T-shirt, "Wasn't thinkin' a the neighbors." He walked over, sitting on the bed with her, "I wasn't runnin'. I was thinkin' of an excuse to keep you up here with me all day."

Smiling, taking her in his arms, she laughed shortly, burying her face in his neck.

"You didn't even have to think of one, I want to. Besides, that's not one."

She moved so he could lie next to her, letting him kiss her breast, pulling away, laughing when she felt his teeth, then moving closer, kissing, his hands going over her body; she too moving, trying to bring him to her.

Quietly, "Wait, Nancy. We have time."

"I know. But can't we just hold one another? Can't you be inside and just hold me?"

With a soft groan containing laughter, he brought her to him.

Later in the afternoon, they both sat naked, whispering. She stretched, yawning, then laughed as his hands moved over her.

"But you promised you'd wait."

"Mm."

She watched his finger trail lazily between her breasts, then stop.

"Can men really become weak?"

He winked, smiling. "Umm, that's what they tell me. Never happened. Wanna try?"

She moved. "No, don't. I don't want you that way."

"You're silly, Nancy."

"No, Bobby, it's not that. But, well, what we have, I've never been in love, but it can't be like this. It's wonderful, but I'm afraid, as if it's going to–" She stopped, looking at him with her wide eyes holding his, then finishing, "It's as if something is going to happen to us. No, to you. Is it?"

He gazed into those wide beautiful eyes, wanting passionately to dispel her fears, more because he knew them to be true and nothing could be done, it had been already.

Taking her in his arms, cradling her, he smiled softly, because he knew he lied well then. "Everybody feels like that when they're in love. I'm a little afraid, too. But nothin' will happen. Believe me. I won't let it."

He turned from her, looking at the door as he heard the knocking, about to ask who it was and tell them to go the hell away when the door opened and Alice walked in, her hand going immediately to her mouth as she laughed.

"Whoops! Pardon me, I came just at the right time."

He laughed, tossing Nancy the sheet as she broke away from him sitting up.

Startled, Alice started backing out the door, hand over her eyes, fingers spread wide, still laughing. "I promise I'll make out I didn't see anything."

He waved to her. "Come on in. Next time, wait'll you're asked."

Nancy sat up, holding the sheet to her stomach, her eyes wide, agitated and uneasy.

Alice bowed. "Sure, like giant steps, ask permission, then ask again to make sure, huh? Did I embarrass you guys?"

"No, you didn't." He spoke lazily, stretching across the bed.

Alice smiled, turning to Nancy. "I'm sorry if I embarrassed you. Stop looking so horrified! I won't snitch. You really are a brunette, huh?"

Shocked; "Oh, stop that."

Alice went on enjoying herself. Bob was watching Nancy.

"From now on, keep your damned door locked. That's what they're for, ya know."

"Shut up, Alice. Hand me my drawers."

She bent, scooping them from a chair, throwing them at him, mocking a serious tone.

"You should keep them on, love; really."

He slipped into them, walking to where his pants hung. Alice would not be ignored.

"Everybody down the old man's was wondering about you, so I came up."

"Who's down there?"

"Everybody. Jimmy's in one of his mysterious moods, as if he has great secrets. He has a lot of money, so I guess he has. Where were you last night?"

She laughed as he continued to try to ignore her.

"Oh ho."

Squeezing Nancy's foot, "You've got him wrapped, hon. Really. I'm sorry about catching you two like that."

He growled, "You're a liar. It made you happy as hell."

Nancy looked at them both after slipping into his robe. Courteously to Alice, "Honestly, we weren't doing anything. Bobby was just holding me."

Alice deadpanned, "I know. I saw."

Nancy blushed, a warming pinkness under her eyes.

He sat on the bed, his arm around her. "Don't let her embarrass you."

"I'm not, I don't. We didn't do any– I'm all right."

She took his arm from around her shoulders, holding it in her lap, throwing her head back to stop hair from falling in her eyes.

Alice sat on the bed, still happy, grinning. "Frankie wanted to know if that was the first time you met Hanoi Bobby, down 'at the lounge."

"Umm."

"Did anyone call your house, Alice?"

"Nope, I'm going to start charging you rent if this keeps up."

"Oh no!"

Alice started laughing, her eyes going from Nancy to Bob, then back to Nancy again. Alice doubted whether any woman could be that innocent or naive.

"Hey, I'm kidding. I don't care. Do you take everything seriously?"

"Yeah, she does."

"I, oh, I do not."

But she was smiling now, the pinkness still under her eyes.

"Well, I was kidding, anyway. And if anyone calls, I'll tell them you went to the store or something and come up and get you." Looking at him, saying heavily, "Knocking first on the locked door, of course."

He moved Nancy's legs aside, pushing his head onto her lap. "Mm, when you leave, lock it, okay?"

"Bob, don't, please. Move. You tickle. Let me shower."

After she showered, she came in the room, smiling.

"Guess what, Bobby?"

He was brushing his hair in the mirror on top of the bureau. Alice was sitting on the bed. They had both been talking aimlessly since Nancy had left. He flipped the brush to the bureau top, turning to her. "You win. I give."

Her mouth opened as she began to speak, then she stopped. "Oh, you. Don't tease me. You have mice."

"Mm, where?"

She spoke, radiant and lovely as if the well-known fact were a secret, important and interesting.

"In the bathroom. One was looking at me while I dressed."

Alice grinned.

"That dirty slob."

Nancy smiled, but not fully.

He asked, "Aren't you afraid of them?"

"No. I used to have two for pets."

He took the robe she was holding.

"No kiddin'. White mice?"

"No, just regular, when I was small I bought a trap that caught them live."

His eyes stayed on hers because she was fascinating.

"I don't remember why; I think to train them or something."

Alice was becoming sick. Nancy turned to the window, looking out as she asked, "Did you?"

She turned from the window, glanced at Alice for a moment then back to the window.

"What, oh train them? No, not much. They used to eat from my hand. I wanted two, so one wouldn't be so lonely, and they could have babies, but I guess they were two of the same kind."

Alice asked quietly, not feeling very nauseous, "What kind?"

"Just mice, I didn't know how to tell."

"I think you're nuts. You should be afraid of them. I am, I hate the midget rats. They make me sick."

"Bobby, let's go have something to eat. My belly's grumbling."

When they came to the corner on Broadway, Alice turned.

"I'm going to the old man's. Maybe I'll see you two later. So long, Nancy."

She waved, they waved and walked on.

"Where are we going?"

His hand indicated straight ahead. "Marie's. She has food, an' I have credit."

"I have money."

"Mm, you can call home from there."

"Do you think she likes me?"

"Who, Marie?" She glanced over to him smiling with him.

"No, you knew I meant Alice."

"She only knows you for a week. Give her time. She'll like you. She can't help it. Do you like her?"

"Yes. But, well, she's so brash about everything, as if she's not afraid of anything."

"Sure."

"What did you keep those mice in?"

"An old fish tank I had with a screen over it, I had some wood shavings in so they would be comfortable."

He chuckled. "Comfortable?"

Her eyes fell away as if embarrassed.

"Yes."

"You don't have them anymore?"

"No. That was a long time ago. Why are you so interested?"

"It's funny. I thought you would be afraid of mice. What happened to them?"

"I don't know. They died."

He turned, looking at her curiously, almost stopping her.

"Are you telling me the truth?"

"Yes. Well, I guess they're dead. My father was drunk one night and stumbled over the tank, they left. I don't know how long mice are allowed to live for."

His arm around her waist brought her closer.

"That's funny, pet mice. What are they like?"

"Nice. They were affectionate. They used to eat right out of my hand and let me rub their backs. Sometimes when I stayed very still for a long time they would sleep in my palm." She held her hand out.

"Makin' sure they're not there, Shoulders?" He took her hand, kissing her palm.

"No. Don't be silly. You called me that again."

"Mm."

Two days later, he sat in the old man's. She had called him there early that morning, explaining why she would not be over. Her mother was not feeling well and wanted her home. She felt she should stay. He hoped her mother died, that morning anyone that spoke to him wondered if he hoped they joined him, in a way he did.

About eleven, he began to shake it, listening quietly while Jimmy expanded for the third time how he burgled a store out in Long Island City.

"So, like, I hit the roof an' a man's right behind me behin' me screamin', tellin me to stay where I was or he's gonna shoot holes all over me, but like hell, that drain pipe was made fer climbin'."

Then Bob stopped him.

"Where can I get a fish tank?"

Jimmy gazed at him, not sure, then closer to see if he really were serious, his small eyes studying. After making up his mind, he ventured, "You mean a fish tank?"

"Yeah."

"Those things they put them guppies or whatever the hell? A goldfish tank?"

"Yup."

"In a pet shop, where the hell else? Whadda you gonna do with it?"

"Do me a favor, ace. Get me one."

"Hey, Bob. Come on. You kiddin'?"

"No. How much you think it'll cost?"

"How in hell do I know how much a friggin' guppy tank'll cost? You serious?"

He stood. "Mm, yeah. Will you go over to Blumstein's an' get me one?"

"Yeah, sure. I guess so."

"Do you have any bread?"

"Fer Chrissakes. I jus' tole ya I had over a hun' twennie bucks."

"Lend me some, enough to pay for the tank."

"Sure. You mean a little glass bowl like?"

"No, you know, the kind that has steel rims an' glass sides."

"Oh yeah, you wan' it today?

"I'd get it myself, but I wanna catch a mouse."

Completely puzzled, unsure, he looked at him.

"Hey man, what's a story?"

"No story. I think they come in gallon sizes. Get one about this big." He held his hands about a foot apart.

"While you're there, get some wood shavins or something. Tell 'em for a mouse."

Jimmy stood beside him, a tall pale kid and thin.

"Aw, hell. A mouse. They'll put me inna bug house."

"Yeah. I'm goin' around to see Pete. When you get it, bring it up to my room."

"What are you gonna do with a mouse?"

"Give it to Nancy."

"Gonna shake er up, huh?"

"Yeah, hope so."

He walked down the cellar steps of the building he roomed at, knocking on the door under the stairs. Pete answered on his second knock, wearing an old sweatshirt and dirty army pants, his red pop eyes swollen, hair messed and unkempt as usual. When he saw Bob, he smiled his toothless grin.

"Hi, sport. What's up?"

"Need a favor. Will you help me?"

"Sure kid. Let's hear it."

"I need a mouse."

A slow grin. "Where, under your eye?"

"I'm not kiddin'. There must be a thousand down here. Can you get me one?"

Pete stared at him awhile, then his smile came back.

"You gots that forty-foot stare inna twenty-foot room. Stay outta there awhile."

Bob smiled shaking his head. "Pete, there's a jug a wine in it for you."

Dubiously, "Fer what, a shittin' mouse?"

"Just a mouse."

Pete was very serious now.

"How in hell many you want?"

"One. Can you get him by tomorrow?"

He asked, not quite believing. "A mouse, no special kind, just a mouse?"

"Mm, guy. Get good lookin', broad beautiful."

"Ahhh, I figured you was shittin' around."

"Hey fella, I'm not." He flopped his hand. "Come on, Bob. You ain't the kinda guy to give me no hard time. What's goin' on?"

"I'm tellin' you the truth I'm getting' a tank to put upstairs. I'm gonna keep him as a pet. My girl likes them. I'm not puttin' you on. I'll give you the buck now if you want." He put his hand in his pocket, taking out a dollar bill.

Pete looked from the money to him. "Okay, Bobby. But I ain't gonna like you much if you're puttin' me on."

"I'm not. Get me one tomorrow morning the latest."

"Yeah, sure. I'll bring one up inna hour."

Taking the money from him, Pete closed the door and groaned. "Son of a bitch."

It was after two in the afternoon when Jimmy came up with a five-gallon stainless steel rimmed fish tank, a pound box of feed and a box of cedar shavings.

"Guy said this the stuff's what they eat. Got a pound a cheese, too. How come you didn't want white mice? They had plenty a them over there."

"Thanks. She doesn't want white mice; regular, whatever the hell color they are."

Jimmy sat on the bed, watching him unpack the tank, still not at all sure he had not gone for a ride, still going for that matter.

"You mean she likes the damned things, not afraid a them?"

"Umm, that's right."

He glanced at him. "She's broad one, Jim."

Nodding, saying sourly. "Yeah sure, great."

He watched Bob awhile, then, "I thought she was awright in the head. Don't tell me she's another bug like Alice."

Bob spread the shavings in the tank he had placed on the windowsill.

"She had them for pets when she was a kid."

"What, wild mice?"

"Mm."

"Man, I'm glad it wasn't fleas or cockaroaches."

Bob turned. "You don't know what she's like. Her

eyes, they ... I can't tell you what she's like, how I feel. Let it go, Jazz."

Jimmy stood, speaking quickly, as if embarrassed. "Yeah, sure."

Pointing to another package on the bed. "That's a reflector. The guy said you might need it. Got a light in it, an' a gratin' so the friggin' thing don't hop all over you."

"Yeah, thanks."

"Don't thank me, like I think I'm bugs. There's a dish for food an' water. Figured I'd do it up brown. Goin' bugs mights well go in style, huh?"

"Think that's enough shavins? She said she put in enough to make 'em comfortable."

Jimmy laughed without mirth, falling back on the bed.

"Comf-tubble? Holy shit! Who gives a shit if the bastard's comf-tubble or not?"

"Yeah, I thought it was funny, too. You don't under-stand. You don't know her." He moved the tank a little. "She's just like that, ace."

They both looked over as the door opened and Pete walked in.

"You still wan' this bitchin' thing?"

He held out his hand. Wide, scared and square, peeking out above his thumb was the small head of a very upset mouse.

"Yeah. Put it in the tank. Thanks."

Pete turned to Jimmy. "You sure this guy's okay?"

"Hell no. He's bugs. So's his ol' lady."

Pete brought the mouse up close to his face, peering at it closely. "It's only got three legs. 'at okay?"

Bob fell back against the wall, laughing helplessly. "Yeah. Hell, yes. Oh, man. It's better."

Pete smiled, still not sure he was the butt of some joke. He moved the grating from the top of the tank, letting the mouse sniff his way out of his hand, moving at first just a few steps, then scurrying to a corner, sniffing along the sides, completely around the tank.

"You sure your girl likes these things here?"

"Yeah." Bob was still thinking of the three legs and Nancy's compassionate reaction.

Jimmy motioned with his hand to his head, touching his temple. Pete guffawed.

"Yeah, yeah. You ain't shittin'."

When they had gone, he watched the mouse, a small smile on his lips, a chuckle deep inside. It sat in a corner. Its hind leg's right paw had completely healed over as if it had never been there. It seemed to be watching him with as much amusement.

That night he bought a bottle of spray used to delouse birds, bathing the animal in the sink amidst much small chirpings. He sprayed it and the tank, filled the water and meal cups, placed some cheese next to them and laughed when it sat back on its haunches, rubbing its face with its one good paw, then deeper when it started digging down under the cedar chips for a warm place to sleep with privacy. He thought about how small it was and how silly anyone would think him if they saw him bathing a three-footed mouse.

O'Mally and his partner Keith sat in the black Ford that was parked near a corner. Jimmy came around that corner a while later. The man sitting between the two policemen nodded his head.

Bob and Jimmy were picked up early that morning.

The sun shone warm when Nancy left her house the next morning. As she walked for the bus, she felt a happy tingling sensation. She wanted to hurry. The bus would take her over the bridge from New Jersey to New York where she would meet Freddy.

Chapter 3

Shades

That summer, there were a lot of mornings that made him glad to be alive. The sun was bright, clear and warm, shadows were dark black, excitement, adventure and a promised ending fought and tumbled one another in the rolling air; things were crisp and sharp.

In roaring loud colors, around every corner was something new, something alive that could be close but going too fast, easy to recall. There were a hundred promises for a tomorrow, and more than all these, there was a Nancy.

He had his foot on the fire hydrant, his elbow resting on his knee, his chin cupped in his hand. He watched her cross the street and marveled at how beautiful she was, wearing a white dress with large blue polka dots that clung neatly to her body. Several strands of white beads around her neck and wrist, she wore sunglasses and carried a large white purse. The sun caressed, enveloped and lay upon her and the breeze teased at her hair.

He kissed her before saying hello. She looked at him with a happy puzzled expression, holding his hands.

"Oh, that was nice. Hello."

His hands on her waist, his eyes holding hers; "My, you look in the mirror this mornin', Shoulders?"

"I ... Yes, of course. Why? Is something the matter with me?"

"No, no. Hell, no. If you looked, I don't have to tell you how beautiful you are."

She smiled fondly.

"Yes, you can. You can tell me."

Her hand touched her thigh.

"Do you like my dress? It's new."

"Yeah, it looks great, kid." His voice dropped lower. "Dammit, Nancy. Don't you know how beautiful you are?"

He took her in his arms, kissing her fully.

"Stop that, Bobby. No, not here, not on the street like that. You shouldn't kiss me on the street."

"I know."

He took her hand. She walked beside him. At the corner, he stopped and tried to ignore the black Ford that came down the middle of the street. It slowed for a light, the driver glanced at him, frowned slightly, then turned to the man next to him, who nodded his head, indicating the other side of the street.

Bob's eyes went there. He saw Tony Bard walking along with Mary, who was pregnant because she was going to have a baby because she married Tony because they felt they should marry because she was pregnant. And they both had in mind a desire for a family of their own, a way to raise that family and a belief they could.

He watched them enter a hall of a building and something in him wished to Christ it was all over. Then he heard Nancy saying, happily as she leaned toward him, "Well, come on. I want to change. What's the matter, Bobby? Come on."

He waited until the light changed and the Ford putted up Broadway.

When they got to the room, she tried to believe he was in the same mood he had met her in. He sat on the bed, watching as she took off her sunglasses, shaking her head, patting her hair.

Some of the life had gone out of the words when he asked, "Did you buy that dress yesterday?"

"Yes, my mother, well, she likes to see me dressed pretty. That's what she says."

She sat next to him primly, her eyes purposely avoiding his.

He asked after a moment, "What's the matter with you?"

She started to say, apologetically, "Nothing, I don't know I ..." then turned to him saying with some fury, "No, it's you. What happened to you?"

He grinned. It was almost all gone just because she tried to look indignant and didn't make it, even with her finger-pointing.

"Yeah, forget it. Go change. We'll drive up to the lake."

"Oh, have you the car?"

"Mm. I missed you yesterday, Shoulders."

She went into his arms with a soft growl.

"Bobby, I never thought it was going to be over. I love you so much."

He held her, kissing her eyes along her cheeks, her neck. She tried to move onto the bed.

"Your dress; you're gonna wrinkle it. Take it off first."

She moved away, standing with her back to him.

"Help me. Unzip me, please."

He unhooked the strand of beads, unzipping her dress. She smiled, turning her head, slipping her shoulders out to show him.

"I'm wearing a chemise and pink panties with ruffles. Is that what you want? You like them, don't you?"

His laugh was almost a cry as he took her in his arms.

"Wait, wait. Let me hang my dress. I have a flowered bra too, Bobby. You like them. Remember, you said so?"

"Nancy, Shoulders, don't you know how much ... You don't know what you're doin' to me."

He buried his lips between her breasts. She held his head, laughing softly. She tasted sweet, like her scent.

Freddy and Sully walked up the street together. Freddy; five-feet, one hundred and one pounds. Sully; six-eight, two hundred and seventy pounds. They were headed for the old man's. Then they slowed and stopped as the black Ford headed for them.

Sully's big sad womanish eyes pouted at them. Freddy's green eyes went up to the sky. The two cops that got out were middle-aged kindly-looking gents whose eyes were hard, capped, evasive at times, as if they were not sure whether it had all gone by and they had been run over.

They patted them down, then shoved Freddy against the side of the building. It did not hurt much, but he knew better than allow that impression, so his face scrunched up in a deep long patented expression of pain. Sully stood stoically as they conked him all over his big head, his eyes gazing down at the pavement. Couldn't hurt good old Sully.

They were patted down once again and given the instructions of the day, which were as usual.

"Get the fuck outta here."

They did not stay to argue. They could have, rights and all that, they had them just like a fat pig has an ass. That's where Freddy secretly thought they kept them. He was never sure where their "Get the fuck outta here" was, the block, the neighborhood or the whole goddamned world?

She pulled the white lace chemise over her head, again shaking it and patting her hair. Her brassiere was blue with orange flowers, passion flowers. She saw him watching her and giggled softly.

"I think my mother knows. She didn't say, just looked at me funny when I bought these." Her hand touched the pink ruffled panties. "But they're so pretty, I feel so nice having them on."

She walked over, standing in front of him. His hands went around her, holding her buttocks. She looked down, her eyes half closed.

"I like that. I like you holding me there. Is that silly?"

"No, nothin' we do is silly, Nancy."

He moved her closer, kissing her between her legs through her panties. She purred low, lifting his head higher, pressing it into her stomach. He brought her down to the bed. She rolled, her eyes closed, asking softly.

"Would you rub me like that first time? It felt so nice."

His hand made slow circular motions, rubbing smoothly on her behind, his lips close to her ear.

"Go slow, Shoulders."

"Yes, all right. Tell me when you want to, Bobby. I want to right now, but you tell me when you do."

He pressed his lips on her, mumbling.

"We have all day. When do you want to go home?"

She groaned.

"Never, I never want to. I want to stay here all the time."

She moved her hips as he slipped her panties down, folding them, placing them on the chair. He kissed her behind and walked to the door, locking it, hanging his shirt on the knob, taking care with the crease in his pants when he hung them, watching her lying on her stomach making soft humming sounds.

She turned on her side as he lay beside her.

"Ow. If you just touch me, I'm going to come, I'm so excited."

He took her in his arms.

"Go slow, Shoulders. Take your time, baby."

She sighed, pushing closer, holding him.

"Oh, see, oh Bobby it's right now. Stop me, I want to wait."

He moved over her as she moved her legs, helping him.

"Wait, wait, don't move inside me. If you move, I'll be finished. Wait, let me wait for you."

Her head fell back as he moved his hand on her thigh, helping her body. He undid the strap of her brassiere from behind. She grabbed it, flinging it from her, ripping a strap as she did, trying to move with him, trying to hold him close at the same time.

He whispered, "Go easy, Nancy you're goin' too fast; wait!" Then sucked in his breath as she moved her body.

"Ohh, Christ, Nancy."

She held him almost as tight as he was holding her.

"I feel you, Bobby. I feel you right now. Oh, how wonderful. Can you feel me? I've done it, owww, Bobby I love you."

He met her lips as she moved under him. She turned away, speaking rapidly.

"Leave your hand there if you like, press harder. Oh, how wonderful. Can you feel me, you feel so good, hold me."

Blood stood on the corner with Sandy, who was a skinny homely broad, but she went to college. She read Kafka, Wolfe, Sartre, Genet and Leroi Jones and she thought *Moby-Dick* was great. So did Blood. He saw the picture and when he was about ten he read it; classic comics. Sandy told him to forget it, he never read it, so he forgot it because he wanted to screw Sandy, mostly just because she went to college.

He wanted to screw Kip, too. But she told him to forget it; she wasn't interested. He knew why; so did Kip. Neither mentioned it, but they both knew why. Blood tried never to think about it. He knew he would have to later. But right then, he did not have to, so he did not.

He stood on the corner with homely skinny Sandy and she told him about some concert, a classical concert of some kind. He hummed and nodded his head. He didn't know what the hell she was talking about, but Sandy got her kicks that way.

"Have you ever heard Prokofiev?"

"Uh, who? Uh, no, not much."

She trilled. "He's so witty, oh, really a wonderful composer."

"Yeah, huh?"

"He's dead now though. If I were only older, a few more years, anyway."

"Oh yeah, he another one a them Communist studs?"

"Well, he does come from Russia."

She laughed, a well-modulated laugh, high and hoarse. She had long sandy-colored hair. That was why her name was Sandy.

Blood was beginning to dislike Sandy even if she went to college and had all them liberal ideals that she said she had, she still couldn't be that good a screw. Besides, she was a goddamned idiot.

"I gotta go, I'll see ya."

"Why no, I was go–"

He walked away, saying, "Frig her."

He brought her head to his chest, she sighed heavily with a feline graceful contentment. Her eyes were closed a small smile at her lips.

He whispered. "You enjoy yourself, lady?"

"Oh, you know how much. Hmm, I don't ever want to move. How do you feel?"

"Hungry."

Her lips came together as she looked up at him, she said with a careful dignity that made laughter the only recourse, "You better stop that. Don't tease me, please, not now about this."

Laughing quietly, holding her tight; "Alright. I'm happy, Shoulders; tired but happy."

She was happy too. She kissed his chest, moving her legs, straddling him, her fingers tracing along his face, her arm around his neck, his hand flowing up and down her back lazily.

Tony and Mary were up on the roof landing, she watching him with interest and some fright. She was thinking about what a wonderful person Tony was and how much she loved him, but why did he have to use that stuff for?

He slipped the belt from his arm, wiping away a small streak of blood, then rolled down his sleeve. Mary was now absorbed in what it was going to do to him, how it was going to react upon him. He rubbed his face with both hands and grinned a dull slow grin that was sleepy and peaceful and in a way she envied it. "You want some, kid?"

He motioned at the soot-blackened bottle cap with the hairpin around for a handle, the little ball of almost dry cotton in it. The pretty pregnant girl shook her head. Her long thick straight black hair whirled with the shaking.

"No, I never wanna try that, not never."

Bob sat up, stretching his arms wide, then rubbed his head.

"Oh, Nancy, Nancy. How in hell I ever live without you?"

She was happy, she purred. Then he thought of that dumb mouse and wondered if the damned thing was still alive. Going over to the window, he moved the shade and the little mouse sat munching on a piece of cedar chip, his head coming up as the shade moved. It glared at him with miniature marble eyes. Bob laughed.

"Hey good lookin'. Come here."

She still felt a tender lazy sleepy feeling, wanting him beside her.

"Aww no, come back to bed, Bobby, please?"

He lay beside her nestling in his arms close, and they fell asleep.

Blood was sitting with Kip in the back of the old man's. They were talking, she laughing, when he whispered something to her. Then he said suddenly, his voice changing as if in expectation. There was hope, almost a demand, but it was faint.

"Come on downtown with me tonight. We'll go there."

Her eyes fell on him for a quick moment. Then she turned away and the laughter was all gone. "Stop, Blood. You know better than that."

"Why? I'm tellin' you, nothin' will happen. They're my friends."

Her eyes came back to him and her hand touched his cheek, the expression in her eyes was something like pity. She stood. "So am I, but we can't. It would never work. It's not only because of that but... Oh, let's forget it."

But he held her hand as she was going to turn away his voice low, heavy, fierce.

"Come on, Kip. You got me all screwed up inside. Lemme jus' talk to you. Nothin' will happen."

"No, I can't. I have to think of other people, not just you. Besides, you won't believe me, but you don't move me. You don't do anything for me that way."

She pulled away and he tried for a second to forget all about it and not know what it was about, but it didn't work for more than a second.

Kip sat with Rosey and Alice as Sully clumped in the door and boomed "Hello!" to the girls with Freddy behind him. When he saw Blood, he walked back to the booth and sat, grinning.

"Hiya Bloody, I was lookin for you."

Blood grumbled something in greeting, playing with the sugar bowl. Freddy sat next to Kip across from Rosey and Alice.

Sully asked, "Whatcha doin'? What's a matter? You look like you hurt, doya?"

Blood looked back at him a moment with blank eyes, then started giggling, breaking into laughter.

Sully smiled.

"Go over to the window, Shoulders. Lift up the shade."

She was sitting up in bed, his head in her lap.

"Oh, no. Why?"

"How's I want you to?"

"Oh, Bobby."

Her brows were together as she walked over, lifting the shade. Then her eyes flew wide and she spoke with an excited glee in her voice. "Oh, Bob, it really is! Look at him!"

Her head kept turning from the tank to him, then back again. The mouse ignored them both. He was still busy chewing a piece of cedar, holding it down with his one good paw.

"Oh, he's darling. Where did you get him from?"

"Downstairs. Pete caught him. He only has three legs. I thought that'd make you want him more."

She had been watching the mouse. When he finished speaking, she glanced at him, a happy sound in her throat. "Yes, yes, he's pretty, so pretty. Oh, Bobby. Can we fix his leg?"

"It's not there. We can't."

"But what happened to it?" Her eyes were on the mouse, who still ignored her.

"I don't know, babe."

Taking the grill from the top, she put her hand inside. Three Foot did not at all like that. He crouched low, commando-style, watching warily, and tried to scoot away when her hand came around him, holding him loosely.

Bob watched as she hardly dared move, holding her breath. The naked loveliness of her body, tense now from the effort, made him want her again.

She opened her hand and let the mouse scamper out, again going for him, letting him go. He whispered, sure he was interfering.

"Whadda you doin,' Shoulders?"

"I want to show him we're his friends, that we won't hurt him."

He laughed softly. The mouse let her run her finger down his back, as if he enjoyed it turning his head watching her, she smiled.

"See? Soon he'll know us."

"Not us, he's yours."

"Oh." She waved her hand at him. "You like him or you wouldn't have gotten him for me."

"Uh uh, I got him for you, 'cause I love you."

"Bobby, aw, don't talk like that now. Wait til later."

He sat up, surprised as tears flooded to her lashes.

"Nancy, now what the hell are you cryin' for? Can't I tell you I love you?"

She walked over and stood contritely beside the bed, head down. He almost expected her finger to go to her mouth.

"I'm sorry I ..." She threw her arms around him. "No I'm not, I'm never going home. I'm never going to leave here, Bobby."

Charley, who was Rosey's boyfriend, walked by the candy store that was in the middle of a block. It was painted an old brown color ten years ago. It had a large plate glass window and a dusty display of goodies put there ten years ago and a door that was twelve feet high. Charley walked by without noticing it. He was going to the old man's to meet Rosey, who was then asking Frankie to meet her later that night after she left Charley. But Frankie wouldn't, because Rosey didn't have enough. And the broad he was going to meet after dumping Sonja with an excuse, did.

Chapter 4

Tyro

The little girl walked down the crowded summer sun shiny street. Gina was seven, but she looked four because she was about the same size a four-year-old should be, but she was really seven. She was seven and she was pretty, because all kids are pretty until most of them grow up. But all kids are pretty at seven if you don't hate kids.

W. C. Fields was reputed to hate kids. If true, perhaps he was right. This kid was seven and she was pretty and she was walking down this street that she lived on, looking for someone to play with, anyone, really. Because after an hour she still had not found any of her friends and she wanted someone to play with, because she did not like playing alone, and no one was home in her house, except her mother and that man, and she did not like that man.

Besides, her mother did not like her around so much when that man was around, because that man did not like kids. But this kid did not like that man, anyway. So she walked down the street, feeling lonely, even if it was crowded, and then she spied one giant. He was about six hundred feet tall and weighed almost a thousand pounds and had big soft eyes and spoke low and liked her. His name was Sully. He stood with his arms crossed in front of him, gazing across the street.

She walked up and stood beside him. She stood very quietly and stared up adoringly at the big clumsy jerk. Sully chewed his gum slowly with his back teeth and watched the hallway across the street. He just stood, watching the hall across the street, and did not notice the little girl who looked four but was really seven. She edged closer, almost but not quite touching him. Tippy walked over and stood next to Sully on the other side.

"He called again. Whas takin' 'em so long? He better get outta there. They'll nab him."

"No, they won't."

Jimmy came out of the painted red store where he had just made a telephone call. He stood next to Tippy.

"The operator made me call the cops again."

Tippy nodded.

"He tole you they would. He better get the hell outta there."

Jimmy growled, "He chased me out. How come he didn't come? Aw, that crazy bastid."

Tippy said, "That broad's still down there."

Jimmy, angrily, "Yeah, she ain't goin'. Weepin' all over the place for somebody to help 'im."

Sully boomed low, "I don't blame her. 'at's her hus-band, yeah?"

Jimmy, said, "Aw he'll rap her aroun' jus' like any-body else."

Tippy shook his head. "Naw, just scare her. She's knocked up about nineteen months. Gonna have the kid right now."

She did.

The little girl touched Sully way down low, about where his thigh began. He turned, bent his head, and gazed at her. She was terribly frightened for a moment as the big soft benevolent womanish eyes took her in and the slow wide smile started.

"Hello, Gina. How are ya?"

Her head bobbed up and down about fifteen times. She wanted to laugh, she wanted to cry, she wanted to kiss him, the little idiot. Tippy looked beyond Sully to see who he was talking to, then turned back to his vigil of the hall across the street. Jimmy did not bother to look just then. Sully continued to beam down upon her and asked, "Where yer friends? They must be lookin' for you, yeah?"

Her head twisted from side to side about twenty-two times.

"You wanna sit up here?"

Her head bobbed up and down so fast that it met itself, going down as it started back up and she almost broke it. He picked the little girl up and sat her on his shoulder. She hugged his head with one arm while the other held his hair loosely, because she was not afraid way up there, because Sully would not drop her. If he did, she would be dead, but he wouldn't.

She looked across the street to the hallway they were looking at, but she did not know why. She really did not much care why, because she was happy to be sitting where she was sitting and she was in love with almost everyone in the world then.

"How long he been in there? Jim, you got your watch?"

Jimmy glanced at his watch. "Been in there twenty minutes since I called the first time."

"Aw, I'm gonna go over an' get 'im out."

Sully boomed again low. "Better not, maybe. You know what he's like, uh?"

Jimmy glanced at Sully as if he were to blame for it all, then winked at Gina, though he was not sure he saw her. A half second later he would not know if she were alive.

Gina weighed about sixteen pounds, Sully close to two-seventy. She worried that maybe she would make his fat massive shoulder tired. She bent her head and both her eyes looked into one of his. He laughed softly, his big belly bouncing up and down. She kissed him on the middle of his forehead and felt reassured. She sat up on his shoulder and watched the hall again, but soon lost interest in an empty sun-filled hall that turned into black shadows. It was nice here now, this block. So many people lived here, hundreds and hundreds.

There was a stickball game going on way up the

corner of the block where the batter was, and way down the other end, a block and a half away, the last outfielder waited, hoping he would catch this one, his palms still burnt from the last one he caught, well almost. It had popped back out of his hands and went scooting down Broadway.

And there were kids drinking sodas in front of the painted red store. Two were reading a *Super Boy* comic, one huddled close to the other as if all the information, all the answers, all the reasons for all the misery in the whole, world would be found right there before them. They weren't reading just for entertainment. It was as if it were for something more, something hell heard nothing about.

"How long now, Jim?" Tippy asked.

"Thirty. Man, oh, man, I – whoops! Oh, shit. Now lookit what's comin', will ya? Aw, Christ. That friggin' Good Samaritan bastid is busted again. Aw, shit."

"Maybe they won't go there."

"Yeah, sure, Sul. They just cruisin', huh?"

The police car pulled over to the front of the building. The stickball bat had long gone. The players crowded around the car from across the street because one of the cops had sneered something at someone. The girls that had been jumping rope, the others who had been sitting on stoops talking, they came down and stood around. The kids in front of the painted red store came over, too. Except the two who had been reading still read. The twenty kids who had been playing Four Corners came over and stood around watching, whispering as the two cops went into the hall and disappeared into the black shadows.

Gina looked with great interest at the police car, wondered if that was the reason Sully had been watching that hall with such a consuming curiosity?

"Well, he's busted now. Whadda jerk, Jesus Christ, he could do nothin' for the guy anyway."

"Maybe they'll let 'im off, Jim."

"Aw, shut up, Sul."

Sully's brow furrowed as he looked at Jimmy for a while. Then his fingers tightened a little around Gina's ankle and his gaze went back to the blank hall where the sun hotly glared at the black shadows that would win out in the end anyhow, so the shadows did not bother glaring back, but sleepily ignored the sun. Younger kids about five and six darted into the hall right up until they met the shadows, then zipped back out very fast and glowing as if they were very brave and had dared death.

"Wonder what they're doin'?"

"Smokin' the shit outta him, what else?"

"Think so, yeah I guess so."

Sully's expression changed to one of injury as he thought of the two cops smacking the shit out of someone he knew. Tippy pushed his buttocks against the fireplug, put his hands in his pockets and looked down at his shoes.

Jimmy drummed the fingers of his right hand against his left wrist in a silent tattoo. Sully kept banging Gina's heel against his chest, looking over at the hall, empty, blank. They said nothing for ten minutes. Gina gave up looking at the hall and was looking up at all the people that were looking out their windows, many of them with their arms folded on pillows, pillows that came from all over the world, pillows that read *California, To Mom Your loving son Tony 101st Airborne Division, Washington D. C., To my loving wife 1st Armoured Division France 44, Coney Island, Hawaii, Puerto Rico, World's Fair 1939, Tokyo Japan, Times Square New York,* and *Worlds' Fair 1965.*

And pillows with pictures in horrible colors and pillows with flowers in horrible colors and plain old pillows from Blumsteins on 125th Street. And people, people, people, fat people, skinny people, pretty people, ugly people, plain people, fancy people and just people, millions of them. They all looked and watched the police car. They watched some more as their lagging curiosity picked up when a lone policeman came from the hall and snapped at the kids and mumbled something into his radio. He sat in the car and wiped his balding head, put his cap back on, snapped something else and went back in the hall. Jimmy said cynically, as if to himself, "Huh, now they'll send the friggin' thing."

Tippy, who did not look up from his shoes answered glumly, "Yeah."

Sully said nothing, just seemed sadder and sadder. Gina kept looking around at the people, at the block, at the oars, at the two kids still reading, then at the police car. Some kids were watching from the roofs where she was not allowed to go. She could never go up there until she was older. Another car drove up but this was just a plain black Ford. The two men in it wore everyday clothes, they went into the hall and left the door of their car opened.

Jimmy said, "We better get the hell outta here. That's O'Mally an' Keith."

"Yeah, damn right. Comin', Sul?"

"Naw. I'll wait awhile. Maybe they'll let 'im go?"

Jimmy did not look back. Tippy shook his head and walked after Jimmy. Sully stood and watched the hall. An ambulance came up the street and parked, blocking all, if any, traffic that should want to go by. Two men in white disappeared into the hall. The driver with the blue grey cap on his head went in after them.

Sully waited, stoically hitting his chest with the heel of Gina's shoe very softly, as if in the middle of prayer.

A brown canvas body bag came out then, and Sully winced because he had not seen it go in, just the stretcher. The attendant and the driver with the cap dumped it into the open back of the ambulance, slammed the two doors and went back into the hall.

Ten minutes later, the stretcher came out, and he could just see Mary's face and some of her long hair. Then she was dumped in between the two doors. The two men in white hopped in, slamming the doors after them. The driver got in up front and drove off back to the hospital two and a half blocks away.

Five minutes later, Bob came out between the two

men who wore everyday clothes, was thrown into the car between them, and they roared off. Then the two uniformed cops came out, snapping at everyone, and got into their police car and drove off.

Sully put Gina down. His big soft womanish eyes seemed softer and sadder. He kissed her forehead and walked away, clumping down the street in the direction that Jimmy and Tippy had gone. Gina watched him walk, then turned, wondering what it was all about and wishing she knew how to speak English so she could ask Sully.

The two kids who were reading the *Super Boy* comic looked at one another, grinning secretly. Then everybody went back to what they were doing before the police car came and Tony had died.

Chapter 5

Music, Mary and the Old Man's

It was dark and it was cold when he got off the subway station that night. He walked down the street for the room when he saw Nancy ahead of him, walking with her head down. So he hurried, placing his hands around her waist from behind and kissing her neck. She jumped and he chuckled saying, "Nervous, Shoulders?"

She turned to him, her arms going around him, and he saw the tears that were a different kind of tears, as if she were an angry young lady.

"What's the matter, babe? You look mad. Why are you cryin'?"

Her hands were on his arms now, squeezing hard, one pinching with enough pressure to make him want to wave it away. But he waited as she said, "That ... I hate him. He's filthy. He's not even a friend of yours."

Smiling, taking her hands in his because the pinch

was no longer a minor pain, "Who? Stop cryin' first. Tell me."

"Frankie. He touched me."

"Where?"

Her hand went down, indicating her stomach.

He said, still smiling, "Go upstairs. I'll be right back."

"No."

"Yes, go on."

"No. Are you going to fight with him?"

"No."

She protested for another five minutes, but he insisted by remaining silent, so she went up to the room. When he came into the old man's, Jimmy and Alice were sitting in a booth with Rosey and Mary, who was looking pretty high, but pretty. Frankie was sitting in a booth across from them, reading a paper. Alice watched him when he came in. Then her glance went to Frankie, who still did not see him, but did when he took the paper out of his hands and said, "I wanna talk to you."

Frankie grew a little pale as if he were sick or about to become sick. "Why? What's a matter? Hey man; I was only kiddin' with the broad."

"Stand up, Frank."

And the fool did, saying, "Aw, man. Bobby, she ain't all—"

His fist swapped hollowly into Frankie's jaw. Frankie fell back into the booth, his head a spinning blackness, almost closing down. Jimmy started up and the old man came running back. Frankie began to get to his feet with Bob standing there calmly, as if in the middle of a conversation. Frankie was almost on his feet, standing straight, when he hit him with an upper cut that caught him under his chin and in part of his throat. He almost doubled backwards back onto the seat, then falling to the floor under the table.

Bob turned away, passing the old man, walking for the counter. He poured himself a cup of coffee. The old man came running back behind the counter for a wet rag, growling at him as he passed, growling nothing, just making a noise.

He sipped his coffee as Alice came over, standing next to him, her arm going through his.

"I'm glad you did that."

"Mm, go away. "

Alice was a little upset. "Why?"

"Just cause I want you to."

At about that time they were getting Frankie to his feet, so he put his cup down and walked over and zapped him again with a goody that sent Frankie flying into the jukebox, then sprawling out on the floor. The old man stepped back, his eyes on Bob.

Jimmy turned to him, wailing, "Whadda you doin? I jus' got the guy on 'is feet again. Whycha tell me you was gonna hit him again? You gonna hit him if I get 'im up again?"

"Yeah."

"Well go 'head."

Bob turned away and went back to his coffee, Alice seeping away, her brown wrinkled eyes on him.

Jimmy said, "Well frig it. Leave him there. I ain't getting' him back up sose you can knock him on is ass again."

The old man knelt beside Frankie, his eyes on Bob as he patted the wet rag on Frankie's face. Mary, sitting in the booth, was studying him without expression. He turned, looking at her and grinned, "Hi. How you feelin', slim?"

She smiled and nodded. He walked over sitting beside her. "How's the kid? Whad you name her?"

"I just named her Mary. I couldn't think of anything then."

"Mm. She look like you? Is she pretty?"

"She's cute, Bobby. She has black hair and blue eyes, but I don't know if her eyes are going to stay the same."

Frankie was almost on his feet again, hanging soggily between Jimmy and the old man, who was throwing furtive glances at Bob. Rosey was standing back, watching, as was Alice, waiting.

He got up and walked over but Jimmy, stood in front of him, leaving Frankie hanging limply on the old man. Bob shoved Jimmy out of the way and in the same motion bopped Frankie back into the jukebox that rocked, then began playing.

The old man, still holding his arms in mid-air as if he still had Frankie in them, started to say something, then shook his head and walked for the counter. Jimmy sat in a booth, his chin in his hand, talking to himself. Rosey gasped near tears. Alice started to grin, tried to hold it back, couldn't, so turned, facing the front.

Bob walked over to Mary, bending, kissing her cheek. "Meet me an' Shoulders here tomorrow night; we'll go out."

She said, "Yes, all right. Thanks, Bobby."

He turned, looking at Frankie once more, but he wasn't moving, not a little bit, so he walked out.

Nancy was standing on the top step of the steel stoop, her arms crossed in front of her, wearing only a light sweater, so he took the steps three at a time frowning at her.

"Whadda you doin here, Shoulders? It's freezin'."

"I was scared, Bobby. What happened? What did you do?"

"Nothin, come on upstairs. Hell, Nancy. Do you know how cold it is?"

She rubbed her arms together. "Yes I know, I feel it. What happened? What did you do? Bob, don't lie to me."

"Nothin', honey. Come on."

She walked up the stairs, turning for the second flight. She said low, "You could have at least punched him."

He laughed, grasping her from behind, his face in her hair. "Shoulders, you sound angry. You mad at Frankie?"

Stopping, her head nodding, not turning. "Yes. He didn't touch you there, right in front of everyone, Bob, as if I were one of his—"

"Ssh, Nancy. He won't touch you anymore. He promised."

She pushed his hands away, walking quickly up the stairs, saying with her head low, her hand at her eyes, "Oh you. You don't know what it feels like for someone to do something like that, in front of everyone, with everyone looking."

"Hey, Shoulders. Wait."

But she ran ahead, when he came in the room she was standing at the window with her back to him, stiff, one arm crossed in front of her, holding the other. He went over to her and her eyes closed. She stood coldly, moving her body away from him, still within his arms.

"Nancy, stop. Believe me, he won't even talk to you anymore."

"No, oh no. You didn't even do anything. All you did was warn him and you did that before. I know. Alice told me."

"This time he'll listen. Hey, you feel cold, like you're still outside."

He was grinning when he said that but she ignored him.

"No, take your hand away from there. Stop, Bobby. I'm not fooling."

She moved farther away from him. He sighed,

sitting on the bed, taking off his shoes. She asked. "What are you doing, are you going to bed?"

"No. Take a shower, change."

"Are you going down to eat?"

"Mm."

He knew what was coming, taking off his other shoe slower, waiting, "I'm going to go home. I–"

He stood taking her arms, holding her tightly. "No, Shoulder's. That's enough. I've had it. You're not going home. You're comin' with me, down to Marie's an eatin'. Nancy, Frankie isn't going to bother you. I'm tellin' you that now, not Alice."

Her big eyes remained on him as she said softly, "You're hurting me, Bobby."

"I'm sorry."

He let her go. She rubbed first one arm, then the other, her eyes still on him. "I'm sorry Bobby, I don't want you to be mad at me anymore."

He fell back on the bed his eyes closed. "I'm not. Shoulders, you're sorry again. Don't be."

"What did you do, Bob?"

He sat up, yawning, shaking his head, "Nothin', nothin'." Then he smiled, "Hey. Come sit by me. I didn't get any lovin' yet."

Squinting her eyes, speaking through her teeth gruffly. "And you're not going to get any unless you tell me."

He laughed, reaching for her as she tried to dart away, his arm around her, laughing.

"Oh no, let me go. Bobby, that's cheating. You're stronger than I am."

"I'll only use one hand."

"Ow, you're such a liar. You're using two, now. Stop! Oh, if you ... ummm."

He kissed her, holding her tight, pressing against her, her arms going around him.

"We shouldn't. You didn't eat. Don't, Bobby. Wait till later, please?"

Winking, going to the bureau for a towel and clean underwear. "All right, babe. Put you in the mood later."

She chuckled softly as he walked out.

Baloney was a new kid around the neighborhood. When he walked in the old man's that night, he could hardly believe what he saw taking place. This guy Bob was punching this guy Frankie, and when Frankie would try to get up, just get up, he would knock him down again. He kept saying softly to himself, "Holy shit, holy shit, holy shit."

Charley came in then, standing next to him, watching Bob kiss Mary and walk out after checking Frankie once more. He walked past them without saying anything, so Charley went back taking Rosey by the arm. But Rosey didn't want to go. She wanted to help Frankie until Jimmy told her to "Get the hell outta the way, you dummy."

Because she got in his way as he was trying to hold Frankie's head up so the old man could slap him with that rag.

Rosey got huffy and walked over to sit with Charley and Baloney, who hit her with questions as soon as she sat down. "So what happened? What the hell did Bobby hit 'im for?"

"Because he felt up Nancy."

Baloney, unbelieving, "Whadda you mean, for just a feel?" Baloney couldn't understand that; all that action over one little feel. So he said again, "Holy Christ. Just cause a he felt her?"

"Yes." To Charley, "You know, Nancy, as if she's some precious virgin. The phony bitch."

Alice, who was standing close to them, watching the old man and Jimmy working on Frankie who wasn't saying a word until he was sure, glared at Rosey and asked sweetly, "Hey, you little slut.Who are you talking about?"

Rosey's mouth clamped shut, but Charley got a little shook.

"Ey, don't talk to my ole lady like that."

She dismissed him as a nonentity with a, "Shut up, you," then glared a warning at Rosey, turned back to the old man and Jimmy who had Frankie finally up, in a booth, limp and ragged.

Chapter 6

Twelve Feet High

Baloney and Charley were walking down the street, Baloney with a big lump under his shirt. Baloney was disgusted with Charley, because he felt Charley was a chicken and he knew he was right.

But Charley felt his displeasure keenly. He felt it unmanly that Baloney should think he was chicken and he was afraid Baloney might say something to Rosey, who he was going to punch in the mouth as soon as he saw her, because he knew she was with Frankie last night,because Frankie had told him, laughing at him.

Charley swung around standing in front of Baloney saying, "Gimme the fuckin' thing."

Baloney stopped."Why? Whadda you gonna do with it here?"

Charley growled. "Gimme It."

Baloney peered around, but saw no one, so he handed Charley the biggest pistol either of them had ever seen.

Charley took it and shoved it under his shirt, then looked around. Charley felt powerful, confidant. It was a thrill having a pistol on him. He thought about hold-ing that pistol and shooting Frankie through the eye.

Feeling brave and wanting something brave to do, quickly then, before the feeling evaporated, he saw the candy store four stores down and said, "Wait here. I'm gonna be back."

Baloney laughed nervously, the laughter corning out in a jerky expulsion of breath.

"I'll come. Wait, I'll come wit you."

The candy store they headed for was painted an old brown color ten years ago. It had a large plate glass window and a dusty display of goods put there ten years ago, and a door that was twelve feet high.

Charley marched resolutely for that door. The store was small. The wooden floor creaked when customers walked on it. There was a glass case with penny candy in it, and beside that, the cash register.

The proprietor was a thin old man with a white fringe of hair who had just had an operation on his eyes. He saw only shadows and relied on voices for identification. He had a large heart.

Charley pulled out the big pistol and pointed it at the old man, who asked, "May I help?"

Perhaps if Charley's voice contained more maturity, perhaps if he had not suddenly half-realized what he was about, perhaps the old man would still be alive.

But Charley said, with hesitation, "Money! I wan some fuckin' money or I'll blow you out!"

The old man turned toward the cash register, but

not for it. He reached under and came up with a little league bat and ran in a fast shuffle around the glass penny candy counter with the idea of batting Charley over the head.

Charley yelled at him, "Whadda you doin'? Whadda you think, I'm kiddin? I'm no kid. I'll kill ya!"

But the old man kept coming, breathing fast because he was mad, saying with a wild anger, "Yoou young bastids! Awwl bust yer goddamned heads in! Money? You wan' my money?"

That's when the bat came down on Charley's head and Charley howled and got dizzy. He heard Baloney scream the way he had, because the old man was about to go for him after he knocked Charley one more good one.

"Shoot the old son of a bitch! Shoot 'im!"

When Charley pulled the trigger he never in his life heard a louder explosion, a roar with a metalic ping to it. He smelled the sweet odor of a spent bullet, a rich acrid smell.

Baloney was gone by then. Charley had fired five times, each time bringing a greater degree of terror to Baloney, who fled.

The old man was crumpled up in front of the penny candy counter.

Two bullets had ripped through his cheat, the first killing him, blowing up his heart within him. The other bullets had zinged around the store wherever Charley had pointed the pistol.

Charley dropped the pistol quick and began running as a police car roared around the corner and drove straight for him.

A cop jumped out of the car while it was still moving. Reholstering his pistol, he took off running after Charley, tackling him down to the ground with a few punches.

The cop was more than just disgusted with Charley. Now he felt he should have shot him. After Charley was up in the joint awhile, he would-agree.

But then, he was crying inside himself, pleading with himself, saying to himself, "I didn't even know the old bastid. I didn't even know him."

But he didn't believe himself, so he kept pleading with himself.

Chapter 7

On the Rocks

Bob and Jimmy were sitting on the rocks, sunning themselves now. They had been swimming than the water turned cruddy, so they pulled up on the rocks and sat for a while, drying before dressing. It was chilly; the water still held winter.

Nancy was up in the room. In two weeks, bail ran out, and it was all over. They would go to jail.

Jimmy sat there smoking, his fingers trembling the way they always did, squinting across the river. "I'm getting' sick a this shit."

Bob knew what he meant. He played with some blades of dry yellow grass, nodding, "Mm," then smiled. "Almost over now."

Still looking out across the river, the cigarette between his fingers jumping, "No, it ain't; just the time we do. That's what's over. Then it just begins some more. It ain't endin', man."

It is for me; no more. I'm doin' the bid an' getting' the hell out."

Jimmy glanced at him, then away across the river

again. "She ain't gonna be waitin', Bobby. Whadda you gonna do then?"

"Not goin' back."

"You think she's gonna be waitin', don't you? Talk straight, ace. You really do?"

"Maybe."

"Boy, man. Come on, the broad's too good-lookin'. Ain't nobody gonna leave their hands offa her when you go." He chuckled, flipping the cigarette in the water. Bob watched the cigarette's short arc and thought he heard it hiss out. He watched it bloop down then pop up, float in a circle a moment, then let itself be carried upriver edging for the rocks. He stood, picking up his underwear, stopping before putting on his pants, looking at Jimmy staring out across the water.

"I don't know how I know, ace. But she'll wait. She's gonna be there when it's over."

Jimmy turned, looking at him, then away back at the river. He threw the rock he was holding, watching it land with a fat splat, skip and splat again. He believed him, because he did. But he did not feel so good. There was a little blip in his mind hoping he was wrong.

When they finished dressing, they walked slow for Broadway.

"Whadda you gonna do when you get out?"

"Don't know, Jazz, just try to get the hell away from here."

"Not me, man. This neighborhood's been good to me. I'm gonna get my own crib aroun' here an stay."

"Mm, yeah."

"What the hell. I'll make parole, probably the second go round."

Bob felt that Jimmy would make it, but he was going to go out of his way not to, whatever the time he wanted to do it all then. It would be too much the way it was now if he didn't.

He did not know why, but he could not tell Jimmy that then. He had almost told Nancy last night, but he had thought it over and found no way to explain it to her, no way that she would be able to understand it, no reason she could accept.

He felt Jimmy would find parole as distasteful as he felt today was. Then he thought of Nancy and what he was going to do and was ashamed, as right as he felt it was it was shameful because of her.

Then Jimmy asked for the second time because he had not heard him the first time.

"Hey, man. Whadda you gonna do when all you can do is write her, not screw her?"

He turned to him. Jimmy touched his shoulder, smiling, "Come on. Don't get shook. At's all you're gonna be able to do."

When they got to Broadway, Jimmy started for the Uptown Bar. Bob waited on the corner a moment.

"I'll see you, ace. I'm gonna go up an get some sleep."

Jimmy's expression soured.

"Come on, man. Have a couple a drinks first."

"No."

"Hell, come on. I don wanna be by myself."

"No Jazz. Shoulders is waitin'. She probably ain't been to sleep yet."

"Holy Christ. The broad can't wait a hour?"

"I'll see you."

When he came in the door, Nancy was curled on the bed in a half slip and blouse, reading a book. Her eyes went over to him, and with a slow grin, let the book fall in front of her. In a husky welcome voice, she asked, "Hi. How do you feel?"

He shrugged. "Greaasy, me, an Jim went down for a dip after it was over."

"Are you tired? Did you have a nice time?"

"Yeah. Patrice came down about one."

He grinned.

"She's good people."

"You like her, don't you? When you say that about people, you like them."

"Mm, Mugs said to say hello. 'Hello.'"

"He's nice, isn't he?" She sat up, sitting back on her ankles, on the bed. He answered tiredly, "Yeah, Mugs is a good boy."

He sat next to her, kissing her lips quickly, then started taking off his shoes.

Her head cooked to one side as her hand went to his neck, "If that's all, you really must be tired."

He turned to her as his shoe clunked to the floor and laughed, gathering her close. At first he merely caressed her, softly peeling the slip from her waist, more clumsy with his own clothes, at one point standing in only his socks, his lust aiming up and outward, causing her to giggle, "Now, you're awake."

Later, after he had showered, she lay on the bed next to him, watching his eyes close and him falling to sleep. She watched him, wondering what would happen in two weeks, and if he were afraid. He gave no indication one way or the other, as if he were going to accept it in that a low impassive patient way of his, waiting for it to be over, waiting for it to be gone.

She wished she could sleep, waking only when it was all over, when it would not come back. She watched his chest fall and rise slowly evenly and she knew how much she would miss him.

She placed her head carefully on his chest, closing her eyes, listening to him breath and feeling his heart beat with her cheek. This, she felt, was going to be one very long time, because she was young and the future was too far away to feel. The two weeks left would pass, she knew, in a breath, but the rest of the tine would ooze slowly, indefinitely. It would seem to her that she was forever contained within it.

Completely frightened now, her mouth opened as she sighed. She thought of Charley and Baloney and all the time they had to wait to contemplate the death of old man which they were directly involved with. She wondered why they had killed him and knew they themselves did not know, and how little it mattered now to the man that was dead. At the same time, she thought how much it really did. Then her closed eyes cried her quiet warm tears.

She touched him, wanting him to wake, because sleeping was a waste of time and he had so much to waste later. They both had. But he did not wake. He just moved his arm, coming around her and for a while she slept too.

When she woke later, his hand was in her hair. He held her close, but he was still sleeping. She slipped out from under his arm, put on some clothes and slipped down to Marie's for food.

The small diner was crowded, well, to Nancy, Marie's was crowded. She had never been there before when there were four other customers. She smiled when Marie touched her arm, kissing her cheek, asking half seriously, half humorously, why she had not been in lately and where Bob was.

"Oh, no. I just came from home last night. I was gonna come talk to you tomorrow. Bobby's sleeping. He just came back from Mug's bachelor party. Do you have something he likes to eat?"

"Sure, don't worry. Did you meet Patrice yet?"

"Patrice? Do you mean the girl Mug's is going to marry?"

"Yep. She's lovely. Meet her as soon as you can."

Marie turned to the coffee urns behind her, pouring two cups, placing them in front of Nancy, folding her arms, resting her elbows on the counter.

"Now, what were we talking about the last time you were in?"

"No, I want to wake him. He's slept long enough. I'll talk to you tomorrow. Please give me something to take out for him."

Marie nodded, pouring milk in her coffee and sugaring it. "Don't worry. Jimmy was in about nine this morning. He said he just left him. Let him sleep a while. How old are you now, Nancy?"

"I'm eighteen. I'll be nineteen soon."

"Yea, drink your coffee."

Obediently, she sipped at her black coffee, no sugar, the way he had taught her to drink it. Sometimes it did taste bitter. At the old man's, it did. But in many restaurants, it tasted horrible. Marie's coffee was not the best. She wondered if it were as bad as her own. Sometimes she was sure it was.

"Did he say anything about Patrice to you?"

"Oh no. Just that she was good people. That means he likes her a lot. That's an odd name, ain't it?"

"Why? What's odd about it?"

"I don't know. It just seems a funny name. I've never heard it before."

"It's not such a strange name, Nancy. I had a daughter by that name."

"Oh, I didn't know that. Is she married?"

She sang, walking toward the kitchen.

"No, no. Bobby knew her. Ask him."

"No. You tell me, please?"

"Nope. He's getting spaghetti. Tell him I said so."

Nancy was going to protest that she was sure he did not want spaghetti for breakfast, especially Marie's, because he always teased her about it. But Marie was too far away. She would have to shout, so she just sat.

She took the box that the food was in, after protesting. But Maria just smiled, nodding, telling her not to worry. When she went up to the room, he was still sleeping on his stomach, now his face in the pillow. She placed the box on the table, shaking his foot, because she did not want the food to cool. He rolled and coughed and looked up at her.

"What time is it, Shoulders?"

"Almost one. Get up. I have something to eat. Come on, Bobby. Please get up."

"Yeah, yeah. Lemme look at you. Come over here," he laughed.

"No, no the food is hot. Get up now."

But he was already in a sitting position, his bare arms outstretched toward her. She laughed, bouncing beside him as he hugged her.

"You want to eat. I went all the way down to Marie's."

He kissed her, then asked her not to speak, not to say anything at all. She thought of the two weeks and held him because even now they were going by too fast.

Later, when they were through and had eaten, she watched him sitting on the edge of the bed, polishing his shoes with a handkerchief that he kept dipping in water.

She was sitting on the floor wearing wine-colored slacks and pull over that fitted to her body so snug and that she knew he liked.

"Your shoes always come out so brilliant. Will you shine mine for me?"

"Mm."

"Bobby? Who is Patrice?"

"Kid Mug's is gonna marry."

"No. That other one."

He looked at her a moment, then away. "Why? Where'd you hear about her from?"

"Marie and I ware talking about her."

He looked at her carefully. "Oh?"

"Who is she, Bobby?"

"Just a broad." Softly not looking at him.

"Were you in love with her?"

He laughed shortly, dropping to his knees on the floor, taking her in his arms. "No, no, hell no. We've only been in love once, Nancy."

"Oh, yes. Thank you. But who is she?"

"Let it go, honey, You don't want to know."

She watched him a moment, looked into his eyes, then said, "Oh no. Tell me."

"Give me your shoe."

Then her eyes flashed and she said, "Well, keep your damn secrets. I don't care."

He smiled when she turned away, looking out the

window to the brick wall, assembling a very angry pose. He reached over, taking the loafer off her foot.

And it came to him then. He dropped the shoe and grabbed her by the arm, hard, bringing her close.

"No, not now. We don't have the time. When I come back, then it'll be over."

"Let me go. Bob, I forgot."

Their bodies banged together firmly, kissing strong a long time. When he had her laying on the bed again, he thrust into her, holding himself close, as if any time would be the last.

Later, with her curled in his arm, she asked again. He sighed saying dully.

"She was Marie's daughter. She was a junky."

Nancy squirmed in his arms, throwing her head back to look at him. "Bobby! No!"

"Why no, honey? She used to hustle on Eighth Avenue. Marie's husband was dyin'. She asked me to go find her. I don't know. The old guy wanted to see her, so I went over an told her. She came back in time for the funeral. Are you happy now?"

In a hushed whisper. "Oh, no."

"Why?What's the matter?"

"I spoke to Marie about her."

"So? Nothin's wrong with that. She knows you weren't tryin' to hurt her."

"Is she still a dope addict, Bobby?"

"I guess."

"Don't you know?"

"Yeah, honey. She's dead. I don't know what

happens then. Maybe God gives her all the junk she wants, or maybe he got a make-believe Harlem that she's still hustlin' in."

"Oh, you stop that, Bobby. God's not like that."

He smiled, bringing her close."

"Nancy, I'd like to go to your hell."

She laughed.

"But just you and me would be there."

Chapter 8

Day Before
the Last

They had spent most of the night whispering, her crying, wishing she wasn't, of making promises both hoped neither would keep. When he woke later that morning, she was sitting up beside him, her eyes on him, her hair falling on him as she bent close whispering, "It's still early. Are you tired? Don't go back to sleep, don't leave."

"No. I'm awake; move a little."

She moved away slightly as he turned then lay her head on his chest her eyes up at him. "Are you afraid?"

"For you."

"Don't be. I'll be all right." Her hand went up to touch his face. He took it in his, holding it.

"The time won't go quickly, will it?"

"No, it'll seem longer than it is. Don't wait, Shoulders. Things will be different when I get out."

Calmly, they both still whispered. "No, I told you

I was going to. Don't tell me not to. You said you wouldn't. I want to do it, what we promised."

His eyes were on the ceiling, holding her hand to his ear.

"It's going to be a long time, longer for you. You'll have changed your mind."

"No, not longer for me. Let me do it. Don't try to talk me out of it. I won't change my mind. Bobby, I love you. I want to go where you go."

"Will you do me a favor?"

"Yes."

"Will you go home to your people's house tonight?"

"No."

It seemed to him as if her body became heavier. He felt her hand tense at the side of his head.

"Your mother called Alice. She's worried about you."

Meekly, frightened. "Please don't ask me to do that."

"We have all day tomorrow, until three."

"Could I go home this afternoon and come back tonight"

"No, I have to see my lawyer tonight. Go home, Nancy."

"Not now, though?"

His arms went around her, bringing her up to him. "No, no. I couldn't let you."

She held back, her hands on his chest looking down at him.

"Don't make me go, please."

"It's better, Shoulders. Do it for me."

"I will, but I don't want to. I wish you would let me say goodbye. I know what you're doing, Bobby."

"Will you go?"

"Yes, I'll leave about twelve, not earlier. Bobby, don't say anything to make me."

He rode up with her on the train to the bus station. They sat on a bench. She was sniffling, trying not to cry, trying to control herself. Bob felt sick, his head ached and his body was sluggish. Nancy tried to keep her eyes from him, holding a hand over them. He whispered to her for a long time, she kept shaking her head no.

Her bus pulled in and left. He continued whispering. She was no longer shaking her head, but listening. A ten-year-old kid with early morning newspapers walked by with a cigarette cupped in his hand as if he were hiding it. He asked them if they wanted a paper. Bob said no, but the kid didn't hear him. So he stood there with the papers under his arm and one paper extended to them with the cigarette cupped in his hand. Bob gave him a quarter and took the paper, then turned to her, whispering again as the kid walked away.

Nancy cried, her voice thick. "I don't know now, Bobby, we couldn't."

But he persisted and she listened, then asked. "But why then?"

He whispered the reason, all the way over to New

Jersey they whispered, Nancy nodding because she agreed again.

Alice walked in the door about eleven, just as Nancy threw the sheet over the bed, holding it as it lowered, slowly covering the bed. Alice's eyes went to the window as she said, "Shoulders, he's gone."

"I know, I knew what he was doing. I want to leave the room neat. I knew he had to go down there this morning. He was afraid he wouldn't be able to say goodbye to me. I hate it, but it's better."

"Come on, Nancy. Let's get out of here. Let's go up my house."

"No, I want to let the mouse go."

Alice made a face. "Oh, that damned thing. Do you have all of your clothes?"

"Yes. He made me take them home last week. I'm going home in a little while, Alice. I want to be alone."

"Why, to cry?"

"Yes. I haven't yet, not the way I'm going to."

Alice went over to her holding her arms. "Ahh, Shoulders. Why you ... dammit." She blinked back tears, then let her go, going out the door quickly.

Nancy started tucking the sheet in place.

"Hurry home, love."

Chapter 9

R is for Rehabilitation

Moe sat in the shade under the awning with Law. They called him Law because he had a legal unintelligent opinion of everything concerning the law, his name being Law made it better. He believed himself possessed of a divine instinct for the law, the correct application of such interpreted as needed.

Jesus wandered by, talking to himself quietly. He always spoke to himself quietly because he thought of himself as a quiet person who should always be spoken to gently.

"There goes a bug. Facine's a bug, you're a bug. The only one that ain't bug is me."

Law took in and considered what he thought was a very outstanding lie just uttered by Moe.

"You are wrong. I ain't bugs. Ain't crazy either."

"Sure you are. That's why we hang aroun' Coffin for."

"Is he bugs?"

"You better believe it."

"Why do you say that for? I think Coffin has a very stable mind."

Moe gazed at Law as if thinking, then, "What's a stable mind mean?"

"I really don't know, but they always say it about people that ain't bugs."

"You ever hear 'em say Coffin's not bugs?"

"No, no. I really haven't. But that doesn't mean he is. Besides, he's always inna box so they might think he's bugs due to circumstantial evidence."

Moe waited awhile, then, "You sure you got that right?"

"I'm sure I got that right."

"I think he's bugs 'cause he's always inna box, too. He does hard time."

"Your opinion carries no weight."

"You really do think you're a lawyer, huh, Law?"

"Not yet. I will be."

"You will not. They won't let you be."

"Sure they will. I'll tell 'em I was insane but I ain't now."

"So, you plead insanity an' they'll still say you're insane."

"Nope. I'll prove I ain't."

"How in hell are you gonna prove it? I thought you didn't like no bug doctors."

"I don't cause a they're liars."

"So?"

"I'll marry the most beautiful broad inna world."

"Oh, hell, you funny-lookin bastard. No half-ass-lookin' broad's gonna have anything to do with you."

Ponderously, with a sage knowledgable expression, Law turned to him and said, "No millionaire's ugly."

Moe said, "Uhh?" Thinking, then, "How in hell are you gonna become a millionaire? Christ, whadda idiot you are."

Adamantly; "I'm gonna be a millionaire when I hit the streets."

Moe gave up, looking across the yard. Law stared at him with his mouth opened. Law had a very big mouth. He never closed it, not even while sleeping. He dribbled a lot. His eyes were deep-set and penetrating, though he saw very little. He was a pudgy guy, about five foot ten, but he had two beautiful punches, a right and a left that he used indiscriminately. He was mostly in the box for zapping people in the mouth.

A psychiatrist once told Law that he was a socio-path. Law then zapped him in the mouth. The doctor then told him he was a son of a bitch as they were forcibly placing him in the box. Law had plans about knocking Emile Griffith out as soon as he got out of the joint, so he started training and found out how long a three-minute round was and how much work and endurance had to go into, lasting six or seven, and said the hell with it, Griffith could keep his title. But Law had faith. He believed someday he was destined to become a millionaire someday.

Moe asked, "Hey, what the hell's you marryin' a good-lookin' head got to do with you not bein' bugs?"

"Cause everybody knows Joey Heatherton wouldn't marry no bug."

Moe was laughing. He could hardly get the words out, he was laughing so hard.

"You crazy son. Mahn, you ... like ... wow."

Jesus walked over then, standing in front of them, not looking at them.

Law asked, "How come you always talk to yourself for, Jesus?"

"Because," he answered without turning to him.

"That answer ain't no good. It wouldn't hold up in court."

"Why?"

Law hesitated, searching his legal mind for an opinion, then, "Cause it ain't plausible."

Calmly with a faint supercilious air, "Give me the definition of the word plausible."

Law frowned, then found it. "It means, somethin' that ain't good, a lie."

Jesus turned further away. Facine came up on the other side of him, smiling. "Whadda ya say? Where's Coffin?"

Moe said simply, "Box."

"Ahh, shit."

Jesus whirled suddenly. "Hello, Facine."

Facine jumped. "Whad you do 'at for?"

"What?"

"You scared me, you yoyo."

Facine sat in front of Law and Moe asking, "Whad he get boxed for?"

Moe shrugged but Law said sanctimoniously, "Because he broke the rules."

Jesus glared down at Law, then rasped, "Law, you are a plausible."

Law's head came up trying to figure out if he had just been insulted in courtroom terminology. He knew he had as soon as he saw Jesus's feet pointed in the other direction, the direction he would flee in before Law could grasp him around his long skinny neck and bang his skull like face into the dusty dirt of the yard. Law was sure he could not catch him but he did love to watch Jesus flee, the way his body would lead his head, his long neck precariously holding them together as if at any moment they might part and best of all, his face, contorted in fear as if he were already in great pain and the jerky movements of his body as he fled in fast zips that belonged to past seconds. So Law made a grab for him and Jesus flew, whee, splat. He stumbled over Facine and Law stumbled over him, battling him all over the yard until later when they were boxed.

Chapter 10

One Lonely Wife

Jesus walked over and sat next to Bob. They were inside the prison gym along the wall watching the basketball game. The gym smelled of sweat and stunk.

"How long do you plan to stay in population this time my friend, my one wonderful friend?"

"Don't know."

"You could never not go back, could you? That would be asking too much. You could not stay out of trouble that long, could you?"

"Don't know."

"Coffin, do you know that even the hacks look at you, treat you with a king of special care because they know you are one nut, one wonderful nut. Did you know that?"

"No."

"Take it from me. I am one expert on such matters."

"One wonderful expert?"

"Surely."

"Where'd you get the surely from?"

"My favorite hack says that a lot. I like that word. I

like many words, but that word has sex in it, doesn't it?"

"Surely."

Jesus snapped his head up to see if he was being put on, but Bob was expressionless, watching the game.

"Do you know who my favorite hack is, my one wonderful hack?"

"Yep."

"No, my friend, my one wonderful friend, you do not."

"I give. Who?"

"Beaton."

"I knew it."

"How did you know that? I never told anyone."

"Because of all the special attention he gives you an' you give him."

"That's how you knew?"

"Yep, that's how I knew."

"You are correct and right."

"Thanks. Are you still goin' to murder him?"

"No. I am going to kill him but not murder him. Do you know who is back?"

"No I don't know who is back."

"Would you like to know?"

"Not really."

"Yes you would."

"If I would, tell me."

"Our one wonderful friend, that's who."

"Who's our one wonderful friend?"

"You know him. He even knows you."

"That's nice."

"Are you interested? Do you want me to tell you?"

"Jesus, my one wonderful friend. If you want to tell me you can. If not, don't."

"I can never trap you. I can never bait you. Can I?"

"You keep workin' on it, you can."

"If I tell you, will you help me?"

"No."

Crestfallen, heartbroken, "But they hit me with another year, a whole year more."

"Frig em. Do the full bit. Don't ask those pigs for nothin'."

"But my wife won't wait. Please good and smart friend, just figure a way out for me and Facine."

He chuckled low, still watching the game.

"Facine's back?"

"Yes. Now that I told you, you have to come with us and help us."

"Not me. They'll hit you with more time."

"I know. But I have to see my wife."

"That's the first place they'll look for you."

"I just want one night."

"I can't help you."

"Why?"

"You're both givin' away to much. It's not worth it."

"I haven't had her for three years, Coffin; three years."

"You got two more, an' you don't owe anybody anything. Stay. Do it."

"I can't. I can't make it."

"I'm not helpin' you, Jesus. They can hit you with too much time."

"Very well, my was-one wonderful friend. I will do it myself, all by myself. Me and Facine will do it."

"How long Facine got?"

"Just two."

"If he goes with you, he'll have more. Don't ask him, Jesus."

"But I need help."

"Don't ask Facine."

"Will you help me if I go alone then?"

"No."

"But why?"

"Cause I don't wanna have anything to do with you dying, that's why."

"I won't die; give you my word."

"You will when they apprehend you an' you get hit with more time."

"But they might only hit me with a little more time."

"No. Moe's hustlin' again. He's got a package ridin' on this one."

"Yes, he is one cheater, one horrible cheater."

"Why, 'cause he don't clue you in?"

"Yes, he should. I am the best basketball player in population and the whole world. He needs me."

"But he don't use you."

"No, he doesn't use me, but he needs me. Coffin, tell him he needs me."

"None a my business."

"It is. I am your one friend, your one wonderful friend."

"So's Moe."

"Then you should tell him, that adds to my argument."

"You sound like Law."

"Where is Law?"

"Box."

"Again? He is getting as bad as you."

"Mm."

"You are hmming. I've asked you, I've asked you repeatedly not to."

"Jesus, go away from me."

"I would like to. I would like to go away from you and to my wife. Do you know she was a virgin when I married her, did you know that?"

"Nope; thought she was a prostitute."

"No. That was a lie. Why do I lie so much for Coffin?"

"Because you're a liar."

"Yes, but why am I a liar?"

"Because you're afraid to think of her out there all alone."

"Yes, it is a big world full of many, many evil degenerate people who will try and seduce my virgin wife."

Bob's eyes came away from the game to Jesus.

"Didn't you bang her when you married her?"

"Of course not."

"Jesus, get outta here."

"But, Coffin, listen. I couldn't."

"Why couldn't you? An' you give me a smart answer, we're both in a box tonight."

"Because we were married in a church, one wonderful church. And everyone loved me, even her family loved me, a little while that day."

"So, what happened?"

"Nothing. We went to our apartment after the party, such a wonderful party, one lovely party it was. We had a bed; what a bed."

Turning to Bob, holding his arm.

"Coffin, that bed was almost as big as this gym. Well, not as big, but it was one large bed. Then I undressed her. She had a white wedding gown on. She looked lovely, what a lovely young lady she was that night. At all times, she was lovely but that night even more. I love her dearly."

Jesus saw Bob's interest start to wane as he looked around.

"But wait, Coffin. Her zipper got stuck."

"And that's why she's still a virgin?"

"Of course not. Do you think I'd let a zipper stop me? No. But it did take a long time to unstick that zipper. She was so beautiful naked, lovely, and she seemed to want me very much. I felt the heat from her body. We got into bed and started, well you know, but then she cried, she cried and sobbed and said I was hurting her. If love her very much and did not want to hurt her, so I stopped."

Bob looked at Jesus, who was deep in tears of self-pity.

"Are ... You mean that?"

"Yes, yes. I'm sorry to say I do."

"How long were you married to her before you got knocked?"

Jesus brightened a little.

"One day, the police rang our bell the next morning and as I was going out the fire escape window a policeman smiled at me and asked me nicely to go back inside. He had a gun, it was pointed at my head. Naturally, I complied. As nice as he was, I think he would have shot me dead."

"Mm, guess he woulda. Didn't you get out on bail?"

"Bail? Oh, no. You see, I spent all of my money on the wedding because I wanted her to have one lovely wedding that she would remember for all time."

"Mm, she will."

"Why. Oh yes, yes I suppose she will. I did not bother to ask my family because they no longer loved me because I married her. You see, my grandfather has black skin and a white Caucasian person insulted him, so my whole family does not like white Caucasian people. They are very biased, since I would not marry the girl they wanted me to marry. No one would, I think. They would not have anything to do with me. She asked her family, I'm afraid she begged them, but they too are biased. They did not appreciate my being Puerto Rican, but they came to the wedding because

I paid for it and they all got drunk. Three times I had to run for my life when some of them tried to kill me. So naturally, they would not put up the necessary money for bail. Her father even told her he was very happy and he would pay for the divorce immediately. She loves me. She said no."

"She has less than a year to go."

"But now I am afraid. The last visit, it was not a good one, Coffin. She needs me."

"Not for one night, she don't."

"Maybe, with luck, we could make it a week."

"Even then it's no good. You'll blow everything, Ace, for her, too. Do your bit, get rid of them. No matter what happens while you're in. If you want it enough, you can get it back."

"Yes, but perhaps she doesn't want it enough?"

"Change her mind."

"Are you going to do that?"

"That's not up to me. You're the one confessin', not me. Let it go, Jesus."

"You, my friend, are very good for my morale. Perhaps I will change your mind and we will all escape, wheee, like a Batman."

"You're outta your mind. Forget it, Ace."

"But why will you not?"

"I won't."

"But if you did, I would have my wife, for perhaps a whole month."

"Perhaps. But I ain't helpin'."

"But why? You must tell me why."

"I don't want to."

"This woman of yours, what is her name?"

"None a your business."

"I know her name."

Bob was looking at the game again.

"Is she beautiful?"

No answer.

"Very well. I won't speak about her again. But that's how I feel about my wife."

He ignored him, watching Moe come off the floor, wiping perspiration off himself with his handkerchief. Moe was grinning. He had just won himself a package. He sat on the other side of Bob.

"A party tomorra, a party."

"You should be ashamed of yourself, Moe. You should have let me play."

"If you played Jesus, he wouldn' a beat me."

"But I can cheat better than you can."

"No you can't."

"Why do you say that?"

"Because you're stupid. You forget about the bet when ya playin' an' try an' make every shot, an' you make every shot."

"But if I remembered the bet every shot?"

"Then you'd blow it, cause you wouldn't make any."

"Moe, I do not think of you as my friend any longer."

"I'll send some stuff from the package over to your table."

"Moe, you are truly my friend, my one and only wonderful friend."

Chapter 11

Trying

Jesus and Bob were playing checkers. Bob was moving his pieces slow in order to prolong the game. He did not want to play another, but felt he did not have enough of this one, so he moved his pieces slowly.

Jesus was going to win with much celerity as soon as it was his turn. Bob saw the greedy impatient expression on his face and watched his tongue dip out between his lips as if in agony. So he deliberated without thinking.

"Coffin, my friend. You should move or capitulate."

"Mm."

For five minutes more, he sat there deliberating.

"Coffin, my friend. Have you ever heard of Proust?"

"Hm, what team is he on?"

"I don't know. He is a writer, one wonderful writer. All others are children."

"No, Ace. I haven't. I've never read a book in my life."

"Everyone has read a book of some kind. You must have read a book, one book?"

"Nope; none."

Jesus could not swallow. His throat would not react. A statement like that one that had just fallen from the lips of his friend, fallen from his lips accompanied by such a vibration of truth was hardly comprehensible. It was unbelievable, a statement said truthfully to his momentary horror.

"I am trying not to believe you."

"If you don't wanna, don't."

"I have to, but I don't want to."

"Do whatever you want to."

"I like neither alternative. I wish you would read. No, I do not."

"Um, move, Jesus. You won."

"I know. You have never read anything, not even a school book?"

"Nope."

"Why?"

"Just never did, that's why. Whadda you settin' up the checkers for? I don't wanna play."

"Fake it. We'll play Kings."

"Don't even wanna fake it. Is Law outta lock-up yet?"

"Yes, he's hiding in the corner so no one will see him."

"Why?"

"He didn't finish the poem he was making up."

"What's his poem about this time?"

"I don't know. He won't speak to me. But it must be very good. He was in three weeks and did not finish it yet."

"Maybe you shouldn't have told him about that pastorial art or whatever the hell you call it."

"Why, my friend? He believes in himself now."

"Yeah, I know. He thinks if he creates a work of art, he'll get a pardon."

"That's right. He probably will, if he creates a work of art."

"Know what's gonna happen, don't you? He's gonna spend the rest of his life in the box tryin' because you told him to get inspiration he gotta be alone."

"Yes, I know. I wonder why he believed me?"

"Because you lied to him, Jesus. You told him that's how Tennessee Williams got his start."

"Well, he shouldn't have bounced my head against that basketball."

"He told me why he did that."

"Why, my friend, my one wonderful friend, why did he do that?"

"Because you wouldn't pass him the ball all night long. You kept tellin' him he wasn't on your side."

"Yes, yes. I did do that."

"Why did you do that?"

"Because before the game, he said he was going to punch me if I didn't pass him the ball sometime."

"Why didn't you just pass him the ball?"

"Because, Coffin, my friend, my one wonderful friend, he loses it all the time. He's clumsy, like a fat woman."

"So you made out he wasn't on your side."

"Yes."

"Oh?"

"Don't look at me like that, Coffin. I'm not crazy like Law."

"I know. Why don't you just go over an' tell him you were kiddin'?"

"Never, not until I am released. Then I will laugh at him as I am on my way out and he is on his way back to the box."

"That's a pretty nasty thing to do, ace."

"I know, naughty to. It's rancorous, vengeful, disgraceful and nasty. But he'll never speak about my virgin wife again will he?"

"Guess not."

"You won't snitch on me, will you, Coffin?"

"Nope; none a my business."

"Thank you."

"I'll never talk about your virgin wife either."

"You never do, Coffin. Do you want me to release Law from his delusion?"

"Up to you."

"Do you believe in God?"

"Mm."

"I have never been able to fathom your way of communication. What does that 'Mm' mean?"

"Yes."

"You do!"

"Mm."

"But you never attend church with the rest."

"Move your checker."

"I thought you were faking it."

"I am."

"How could you be? You just jumped my king. My board meets soon."

"What again?"

"Yes, they are interested in me. They want to see my progress. I will make it this time. Will you write me a character reference?"

"To who?"

"The board."

"Are you outta your mind?"

"But, Coffin, my friend, my one wonderful friend, just because it is unusual does not mean it can't be done. You write it, give it to me, and I'll present it to the board when they interview me."

"No."

"Why?"

"I won't, that's why."

"Then I'll ask Moe. He will."

"I don't think he will, Jesus. No, I know he won't."

Jesus turned in his chair, yelling across the large room filled with inmates playing cards, ping pong, checkers, chess and others just talking. Moe turned at Jesus' call, saw him waving and nodded, playing the cards in his hand. Jesus grinned confidently.

"He will write one for me, then I will get Law to write one. Are you sure you will not write one for me?"

"If you get Beaton to write one for you, I will write one."

"He already has."

Bob's smile froze, then continued, "You mean he wrote a letter for you?"

"Yes."

"Did you read it?"

"No. He put it in a sealed envelope and told me not to open it until I submitted it to the board."

"Mm, well that's what I'll do with mine."

"You are truly a good man. You are my friend, my one wonderful friend."

"I am, Jesus. I am."

Moe came over, sat at the table with them smiling. "Whadda you want, Jesus?"

"I want you to write a letter for me."

"To who, your virgin prostitute?"

"Moe, I don't want you to write anything for me. Moe, you are not my friend. I am not going to speak to you again. I am going to move up your death date."

"Good."

"He wants you to write a letter for him, a character reference so he can give it to his board."

Moe smiled, thinking Bob was joking, saw he was not, turned to Jesus and laughed loud, "Whadda ya want, you wacky bastard, a letter? Can I write anything I want?"

"Yes, if it's true."

"Okay. I'll write a letter an' tell 'em you're bugs."

"That would not be true."

"Tell 'em they should send you to a bug house."

"That would be untrue and a lie. I cannot accept

your letter if you include such completely false state-
ments as that."

"You written him a letter, Coffin?"

"Yup."

"Then I'll write you a letter, Jesus."

"A good one?"

"A true one."

"Very good. I am going over to speak to Law. He will
write one for me, too. I'll be on the streets soon."

Jesus got up, heading for the corner where Law was
sitting in the shadows with a hack watching over him
with a wary eye.

Moe asked, "You really writin' him a letter?"

"Mm, jus' puttin a blank paper inna envelope."

"Is he really gonna give them to the board?"

"I don't know. Jesus is Jesus, right?"

"Yeah, yeah."

Jesus crept over to Law, who was sitting in the
shadow of the main building, wishing he were on the
streets. Jesus snuck over silently and carefully, as if
he were going to kill him. Then he whispered loud
enough to cause Law to jump, "Do you like authority?"

Law was at first shocked, then fuming, "You crazy
spic bastard! You wanna gimme a heart attack?"

Jesus gazed into Law's face benevolently. "I just
asked you a question, Law."

Law wondered how fast be could get his hands
around Jesus' skinny neck and choke him to death.
His eyes squinted and his hands formed claws. Jesus
dared him because Jesus was far enough away to get

away and Law knew it, so he stated honestly, "I'd like to kill you."

"I know. You would like to choke me."

He answered with great relish, "Yeah."

"You can't."

"Cause I can't catch you."

"No, not only that. If you did, they would keep you here forever."

"'At's what they doin' anyway."

"No, they just overlooked you. You probably did your time and everyone knows it, but they let it go so long that if they let you out now, they would owe you time."

"So they're gonna keep me forever?"

"Yes, they more than likely will keep you forever."

"I wanna kill you more now."

"But you can't."

"Why now?"

"Because they will keep you forever."

Law screamed and jumped at Jesus, who was long gone, running across the main yard in his silly long frightened jerky jump, his body going so feet that it seemed his long neck would detach itself and he would leave his head behind. Law laughed, then it turned to giggles that brought him to his knees.

Jesus made it across the yard in new record time and flopped next to Facine, who was reading a dirty book.

"You're a slob, Facine."

Facine did not bother to look up, just nodded his

head in agreement and said, "I never tried that like that, I'm gonna try it when I get out."

"Then you'll be back up here again."

Facine looked at Jesus, eyeball to eyeball, and said, very vindictively. "Uh, uh. Gonna try it with your virgin prostitute."

Jesus stared hard and would have liked to kill Facine, choked him to death. Then he plopped foot before foot around the yard, crushed. Not all the way around the yard, he detoured away from Law, who was still laughing at the funny way he ran. After about the nine-hundreth time around, he sat beside Moe, who had just finished a game of horseshoes. Moe grinned and slapped him on his back.

"Hello, you goddamned idiot."

"Do you like authority?"

"Who the hell's that?"

"Authority. Authority. The backers of social order."

"You mean the creeps 'at locked me up?"

"Yes, they are part of it."

"Well, I don't like that part."

"Do you know Coffin is in the box again?"

"Coffin's always inna box."

"Well, that's the reason."

"What reason? Whatta hell are you talkin' about?"

"Coffin fights authority. If he didn't fight authority, he would never go to the box. He would never be up here in the first place. Did you know that?"

Moe asked nicely, "Whadda you up here for, Jesus?"

Jesus groaned and walked away. He could solve the

whole world's problems if they would just stay still long enough, give them to him one at a time, if they would just be gentle.

Chapter 12

A Big Wedding

The crowd erupted suddenly from the wide opened doors of the church, breaking in all directions like feathers, going to the left, the right, crossing streets, getting into parked and double-parked oars, some gathering in knots, talking.

The kid with the paper under his arm, the other arm extended, a paper hanging limply from his hand, screeched as if in anger, "*Cat-lic News*! Eyy, getcha *Cat-lic News* 'ere!"

Sully came out into the bright sun and stood a moment on the top step, gazing around at the people. This was the second mass he had attended today, and again later he would attend another.

He started down the steps, walking for the old man's. The old man's wasn't far and it was a pleasant day. The bright sun was melting the first snow that had fallen last night. Some spots still looked fresh, bright and gaudily new, completely out of place. Two kids who had just gotten out of church were throwing snowballs at one another.

Sully felt they were wrong because they had just come from church. They whooped as they ran and he felt they were wrong. He walked along, trying to keep out of the puddles that were forming from the melting snow.

When he got to the old man's, Alice and Dicky were there sitting in a booth eating ham and eggs and drinking coffee. They were happy with one another, laughing at each other. They seemed tired and a little pale. They had been out all night and were slightly out of focus.

He sat in the booth after greeting them, Alice asking, "Hi, where'd you come from, home?"

"Church. I just came back. Later on I'll go again."

"Wasn't once enough? Why go twice?"

"It's a high mass, this one I'm goin' to."

She bent her head saying quickly, "Ohh?"

Dicky looked at him as Alice's shoulders shook.

"Whadda you mean, a high mass? You went to one, didn't you?"

"Nahh, two. I wanna go again. "

Dicky pushed some ham around his plate, saying flatly, "You're a jerk."

Sully said, "Hey. No, I ain't. Why?"

"Cause I said so. Whadda you think, it makes you more holy than anybody else 'cause you go to so many?"

Sully's eyes remained on Dicky, brooding awhile, then, "I don't think 'at. Hey, I jus' like church onna Sunday."

Dicky regretted calling him a jerk.

"Yeah, you eat yet?"

"Uh uh. That's why I'm here for."

"I'll buy. Whadda you havin'?"

"How come you're buyin' for me?"

"Cause I feel like it."

"Oh, okay. You got some red stuff all over ya neck. What's it, lipstick?"

Alice peeped. "Yes, he's wearing it there now."

"Oh yeah, you put it there, huh?"

She smiled wide. "Yes I did. You look handsome, you can kiss me. Dicky asked me to marry him, Sull."

Slowly. "Oh yeah? You gonna?"

"Should I?"

Sully thought it over. Dicky winked.

"Yeah, I guess so. He's a good guy."

Alice turned to Dicky, winking.

"All right, love." He placed his cup on his saucer, frowning a little.

"I wasn't kiddin'. I meant it."

"So'd I."

"You sure?"

"Sure. Sully said you were a good guy."

He grinned.

"Hell, I got you for a breakfast?"

She pushed her plate away.

"Ha. The expense will come later, lover. Nancy's going to be my maid of honor. She'll look lovely."

Dicky was unsure. "You really mean it, don't you?"

"You did ask, love. If you don't want to, forget it."

Speaking quickly, holding her by her upper arm, he was excited now.

"No, holy shit no. I mean it. When?"

Sully watched them both.

"When do you want to?"

"Today, tomorrow; hell, as soon as possible."

"Don't be silly. Later, after Christmas. We do have to have money, you know."

"What? Christmas? The hell with Christmas. I have money. Next month, that's long enough."

"Nope. Christmas."

Alice raised her voice to the old man. "Frank. Bring some eggs for Sully."

He growled. "Yeah, yeah. What the hell ya think I'm doin' anyhow, huh?"

"I don't know."

She turned toward him, "You have such a sweet disposition, love."

"Aw, shaddap, fer Chrissake."

She chuckled, turning back to Dicky.

"I'll put him in a good mood. I'll get us more coffee. You better go home and get some sleep, lover."

"Like hell I better. Why not next month?"

Still chuckling, standing, taking their cups. "Because I said Christmas. Don't go home. Come home with me, you can sleep in my room. I'll sleep out on the couch."

"Why not with me?"

"My mother and father wouldn't approve until it's legal."

She walked away. He turned to Sully and punched his arm, his voice merry, unable to express the joyous feelings in him.

"I'm getting married, you fat bastard."

Sully smiled low, unimpressed.

"So what, that's not so great. All people get married. Yeah?"

"But they ain't me, hoople. She's gonna marry me."

"Yeah, okay. Hey, I'm really hungry."

"You're hungry, sheee."

"Yeah, an' I gotta headache."

"That's from bein' in church so long, smellin' incense."

"Nah, it's one a them bloody kind."

Dicky's eyes snapped over to him. There was compassion in his tone when he inquired, "Those kind that hurt the worse? You takin' them pills?"

"Yeah, but it's little yet. I don't like any pills. They don't do no good."

"You should take them, Sull. That's why the doctor gave 'em to you for."

"Yeah. Nahh, he ain't so smart. Ain't nothin' wrong, I jus' get headaches alla time. Some people are like that, no?"

Dicky looked around, feeling uncomfortable, nodding his head.

Alice came back with two cups of coffee, smiling at them. She went back for another, placing it before Dicky. Sitting across from him, she said, "I have to call Nancy. She'll want to know. I'm beginning to be tired now."

"I'm not. Let's go to a motel an' sleep."

"Umm, no. You better not come home with me. I'll have to tell my mother and listen to her reasons why I shouldn't marry you."

"Why? What the hell's she got against me?"

"I don't know. She doesn't think you're respectful enough."

"Hey, tell 'er I'll get down an' kiss her feet."

"I will not. You will like hell. Let's go down to Nancy's apartment. I bet she cries."

Dicky laughed.

"That broad's something. I love her."

"Platonically?"

"Yeah. Sully, you better take them pills."

Alice asked, "Do you have a headache again, Sull?"

"Yeah. I'm hungry."

Louder, "Hey, Frank! I'm hungry."

"Yeah, okay; a minute."

Sully finished the six eggs and half pound of ham with two rolls and a dinner plate of home fries. Alice and Dicky had gone down to see Nancy, so he sat there wondering when the ringing would start inside his head.

Frankie came in then. He hadn't been around the old man's in a long time. The old man smiled when he saw him. Frankie nodded.

"Whadda you say? How's it goin'? Coffee's still good, uh?"

"Yeah, yeah. Where you been? Ain't seen you in a long time."

"You know me, Ace. Any phone calls this mornin'?"

"Wha, fer you? No."

"Whose inna back?"

"Just Sully. His head's botherin' him now."

"Aw, fer Chrissake. When's his ol' lady gonna stop playin' with him? When's she gonna put him in a hospital?"

"She don't know. You know, Frank, them head operations, they ain't so easy. Ya gotta be careful."

"It's easy lettin' him walk around like he is. She should have a friggin' operation.

He walked to the back. Sully was leaning with his head against the wall, his eyes closed. Frankie sat next to him, asking quietly, "How you feelin', Sull?"

He opened his eyes, grinning. "It's okay. Where you been? I been lookin' for you."

"Shackin' with some broad. When you goin' in a hospital an' havin' that operation?"

Sully's features changed. He spoke defensively. "I dunno. It's not like that. Besides, a doctor just wants a look inside. There might not be nothin' there."

"You're lyin' to me, Sully. What the hell do you think the X-rays he took were for?"

"They ain't so good."

"They show you gotta lump inside your head that gotta come out don't they?"

"Ahh, naw. That coulda been somebody's finger or somethin' that got inna way."

Frankie sat back saying, "You're fulla shit. Who you tryin' to snow, Dad. I was there with you."

Sully's eyes came down, looking at Frankie. "You know you gotta be careful inside your head. Somethin' could happen, an' I'm scared."

Frankie said blankly, "If somethin' happens, you'll never know it."

"How come?"

Palms of his hands up; "You're dead, pal."

"Yeah, but 'at's what I'm scared of."

"Don't be. A lotta people are dead."

Sully grinned. "Yeah. Hey, Frank, if you go, you gonna come wit' me to the hospital that day?"

"You know it."

"Yeah, I don't feel so bad then."

"So I'll come with you."

"Yeah. That girl Marcy, she was around lookin' for you."

"Frig her. She's a nothin'."

"Nah, she's not. I like her."

"She bangs for niggers. She ain't a broad anymore. She's a animal."

"Who does? Aw, she don't do that."

"Don't tell me. I know."

"Aw, not her. Come on. Who does she do it with, then?"

"Your buddy Blood."

Sully straightened his shoulders, frowning. "Hey, he's a friend, he ain't no nigger."

"Bullshit he ain't."

"An' we know him alla our lives. He's a good guy."

"An' a nigger."

"No, he ain't. That girl Marcy's pretty."

"Maybe, but she bangs for mooses. Any white head that bangs for niggers is nothin' one."

"But she likes you."

"Hell, she's onna long line."

"You ain't even gonna talk to her or nothin'?"

"For what, Sull?"

The wedding came off near Christmas. It was cold that year, without snow. Dicky caught Sully in time, right before he went to the hospital. In order to do this they had to move the wedding date up. Sully was the best man. It seemed incredible that anything could debilitate this massive healthy-looking youth who stood solemnly in a dark tux, white shirt, its collar about to choke him. He appeared as big as Ernie Ladd coming at a quarterback caught flat-footed. He was robust, full of vitality for that day, imperious in size and amiable in nature, yet he was awed by the ceremony.

At times that day it could be warm in the sun that was clear and bright. Alice appeared lovely in virgin white, hating Nancy for a few moments after seeing her in her gown after they had finished dressing, then holding her close, wanting to cry.

Dicky was calm, without anxiety, feeling he was being justly rewarded for something he had earned.

Freddy, who was one of the ushers in a tux, remained in the outer vestibule, picking his nose, reading the bulletin board. The church smelled of incense and sweet stale flowers, grim in its gravitas, and it bothered him.

Tippy stood with Frankie within the inner doors, escorting people to their seats. Kip was in the wedding party. She looked pretty, pregnant and pretty. Her pregnancy, everyone told her, was hardly noticeable, but Freddy told her, "You look like a fancy knocked-up whore."

That was after the girls had finished dressing at Alice's house. Freddy and Frankie had come up to drive them to the church. They had all laughed. It seemed a relief, the rest make-believe. All laughed but Kip, who blazed after him, screaming, "I'll kill you, you idiot!"

Freddy nimbly scooted behind Frankie and out the door down the stairs. Freddy had not wanted to be an usher, but was happy he was when he saw Frankie turn away in distaste as Mary came in. She wanted to stay near the back because she was all junked up, but Freddy hustled over to her, escorting her to a seat, whispering to her until he had her smiling. She was pale and thinner. Her hair wasn't combed right, and the adventure of junk was all gone now because there was no more youth, only Mary, because by then she could think of nothing but Mary.

It was a big wedding; the hall the reception was

held in was jammed. Since the week Alice had been born, her father had promised himself that his daughter was going to have a big wedding, and he had saved faithfully each week for that wedding. He paid for everything, including their trip to Bermuda.

Dicky watched everything with hooded eyes, not appreciating it in the least, feeling it a waste. Dicky wanted to be married in City Hall and have a beer party up at their apartment after it. Alice, who had been brought up with the promise of a big wedding, did not consider for a moment any other kind of wedding.

So it was large in volume, a combo similar to the one that played the lounge, it was as loud, played for them. The people, almost all that anyone could recall, were invited. And they enjoyed the booze, beer and food.

Dicky and Alice did not stay at the reception long. They had rented a room at a hotel that night until their ship would leave for Bermuda the next day. They left, Alice in tears because it was all over and she was not sure, now, for the moment, what was to begin.

Nancy left while the fading sun was still up because Frankie tried to get close to her. She was fading into herself when he asked her to dance, feeling lonely. More than ever, she wanted someone, when Frankie asked her to dance, she knew she had better because right over a rim were ruthless thoughts that petrified her in dread trepidation.

He held her close and whispered to her. She pulled away in panic, shaking, screaming low, "No, no. Let go of me, Frankie. Ohh, how ugly you are."

Then she fled out the door, almost upsetting a waiter who was on his way to serve a table. Freddy, who was near the exit, went after her, speaking calmly as she moved hurriedly down the street. Freddy felt correctly that she would seem sort of out of place going home alone on the subway in a gown. Besides, she might catch cold. She agreed, feeling Freddy to be harmless. He was a friend, so he drove her home.

That night she prayed to God to kill Bob Coffin, then horrible little images started, so she stopped.

Chapter 13

One Beautiful Woman

Jesus whispered confidentially, hardly moving his lips, the way he knew it was done in very tough prison movies, for no reason, since they could speak to each other if they wished.

He was sitting next to Bob, Facine, Moe, and Law.

"Do you see him, my friend?"

"Who?"

"That hack."

"Beaton?"

"Yes. I am going to kill him."

Facine: "When? Beaton? How come? He's a queer. You tole me."

"But I must kill him because he makes fun of my wife, my lovely wife. He makes a derisive mockery out of her childishly immature letters of love. She is one lovely wife."

Law: "She ain't nothin' but a whore."

Jesus' mouth froze shut. Moe was chuckling.

"Jesus, you crazy spic bastard. They hear you talkin' like that, they'll box ya."

"But he reads my mail. He reads my mail, then makes fun of my mail."

"So, go ahead. Kill the silly bastard."

"Thank you, Moe. I shall. Coffin, my board meets soon. Is there anything that you would like me to do for you from the streets?"

"Nope."

"I could go see your girl for you."

"Could not."

"But why, my friend, my one wonderful friend? I would tell her to wait, that you will be out someday."

Bob ignored him, yawning up at the frosty sky. Law gazed at Jesus, his lips puckered in slow thought, then, "Have you read your own fortune, Jesus? Answer yes or no."

He pointed his finger, almost jabbing Jesus' eye out.

"I cannot read my own fortune, Law. I have told you that many times."

"I know. I read it for you. Know what?"

Jesus asked fearfully, "What is that?"

Smiling fully, as if the condemnation that would follow were true and he was happy, "You will not make the board. They will hit you with more time. How's 'at?"

Jesus slouched away, hands deep in his dungaree pockets, his spirit deep in gloom.

"Shouldn't a told him that, Law."

"Why not, Coffin? The son of a bitch is gettin' out. I ain't."

Moe: "Yeah, but the poor bastard believes you."

"Maybe I'm right."

Facine: "You are right, Law. He ain't makin' the board. He been inna box too much, jus' like Coffin. He ain't never gonna make his board neither."

"Mm."

Moe's hand slapped down on Bob's shoulder. "I like the way this man does time. He just says, like, boom, 'I'm doin' the full bid' an' he goes an' does it."

Facine, in amazement: "You really gonna do the full bid."

"I don't know. Up to the board, ain't it?"

"Hell, Coffin. You better than halfway now, aincha?"

"Mm."

Facine: "Yeah, but he could make it out on parole if he was careful."

Law, sanctimoniously: "Yeah, but he was sentenced to a specific amount a time an' he should do the full bit."

Moe: "Shud up, you asshole."

Facine: "Law ain't never gonna get out anyway. He been here forever and's gonna stay, too."

Law flopped back against the fence, his chin on his chest, heartbroken now that his secret was out. Jesus must have told them. He leaned back against the wire link fence that was there to keep the other fence of concrete from pushing its way into the rec yard.

The concrete fence was there to keep the weeds from growing in the rec yard.

They were quiet for a while, just looking around the cold crowded rec yard. Over in the far corner were the queers, hundreds and hundreds of them. They stayed in their corner.

Off to the side were the Negroes. There were hundreds of them, too, and they stayed in their section. The Puerto Ricans had their section, too. Jesus was the only Puerto Rican that hung around with the Caucasians. He did not eat at their table because he ate at another. That was the way it was when they came, and they all accepted it.

Facine was snuggled up against the wire link fence, forming bubbles from spittle on the tip of his tongue, then blowing them away hoping they would hit someone. He was concentrating hard at this creative endeavor, which was why he did not see her until she was very close.

She wore a tweed suit under a black coat that was open. She was lanky, thin, resembling both a woman doctor and a lesbian. She was a psychiatrist interested in penology. She was making a study of some kind that was important and highly thought of by someone. There were two others with her and a chaplain, two hacks, a member of the parole board who was going to vote to deny Jesus parole because he thought Jesus was crazy and also thought it pretentious for anyone to go about with a name like Jesus.

The broad wore glasses because she was a doctor still attending college. They were heavy black-rimmed glasses. Her hair was brownish and thick but cut too short and combed with too little imagination.

When she spoke, she pronounced her R's and her diction was beautiful. The two guys with her Facine immediately thought were queers. But then, he thought anyone was a queer that spoke with such fine diction and pronounced their R's so much. He would dearly have loved to find out whether the broad was queer.

Facine dreamed nightly of making love to a lesbian or watching a Negro in bed with a white woman. Facine was a little queer, too. But right then, all he was looking at was the broad's belly, her tweed belly that just barely made a slight rise, and he began whispering slowly, feverishly, earnestly, "Ooooooooohhh, oowwwwwooooohhh!"

Moe looked at him with a furrowed brow, then followed his gaze and said, "Oh, no. God, no. Don't make it like it is."

Jesus, who had returned to tell Law how absolutely wrong he was, swayed lightly, making feeble sounds such as, "A woman, one woman, one wonderful girl woman. Ohh, five minutes."

Law frowned at them all, then followed their eyes and shock set in as he stared at a thing called woman.

Bob looked at where they were staring and closed his eyes.

Then Moe bravely came out of his hypnotic trance that had put dirty thoughts in his dirty head and moaned.

"Alls you can do is look."

Facine groaned softly, near tears. He sniffled.

Law was not sure he was breathing. Jesus just stared panting. Bob kept his eyes closed, because even this dull dumb broad could make him think of Nancy and he knew he must never do that.

The broad gave them a matter of fact glance and started by. The two hacks glared warnings. The parole official was going to bring this to the attention of the director. It disgusted him that these animals should look upon this young woman the way they were, in such an indecent manner. They did not even try to hide their hunger.

The chaplain's eyes were on the young lady's ankles for a reason the chaplain could not understand. He was sure no sexual desire lay in him, but he did not consider this until he could no longer see her ankles or the drooling, simpering faces of the impeached.

The two others wore blue suits, white shirts and ties. They kept glancing at the five, then away as if embarrassed. They were speaking about, of all things, how shiny the silver fence was. It did gleam in the cold sun.

Jesus struggled out of his deep trance mumbling, "They are cruel, sadistic, fanatically harmful dirty bastards. We have all qualified for release through torture."

Moe bowed his head because the broad was almost out of sight now. "Yeah, it's worse than lookin' at short-arm pictures. Ohh, man. I wan' out."

There were tears in Facine's eyes. "Oh, I gotta have at broad."

Bob grinned without looking up, "Ace, you wouldn't buy her a drink onna streets."

"Yes I would, man. I'd buy 'er anything she wanted. I'd kill for her."

Law was sighing, looking toward the corner she had turned.

"Oh, man. If I could only squeeze one tit," Facine said fervently.

"She's the greatest lookin' head I ever seen."

Jesus nodded and spoke philosophically, even poetically. "Yes, just then she was the most beautiful girl in the world. She may never be again, but then she was. Then, she was worshiped, I know that will never happen to her again. Still I would love to screw her just once more."

Six eyes hit him. He pointed to his head.

"I only did it here. It was one wonderful screw."

Facine: "Ah, shit. I did 'at, too."

He got up and walked for the queers' corner, Law following.

Chapter 14

A Quarter a Piece

It was a warm pleasant sunny Saturday morning, the second day since Jimmy's release. He rubbed his shoulders against the warm brick he was leaning against and smiled at the sensual feeling that flowed through him. He wondered what time it was and guessed it must be after nine. There was a thin sardonic smile on his lips as he thought of waking her, her in a robe, hair in those big lumpy curlers, her eyes heavy with sleep and her smelling warm, like a bed and her mind dumb. He wondered if Nancy was beautiful then and thought not.

He pushed himself from the building, walking for the hall and the locked street door. At first he was puzzled when the knob did not turn, then he fumed.

"Aww, now, will ya lookit this. Son of a bitch. Shheee."

He pressed a bell that he figured would ruse someone on the top floor. A minute later there was a ring near the knob. He pushed the door in, still cursing it and whoever was responsible for putting it there.

He climbed a flight of stairs to the first floor, still muttering, glancing at the doors on either side of the stairs that continued up, saw 1-D and bammed it with his fist in a non-rhythmic knock. He heard the buzzer sound again downstairs and grinned.

"Yeah, sure. Be right there."

No sound came from the other side of the door, so he rang the bell he just noticed, rang for a long time. Then he saw the three keyholes, one under the other, and his hand came up and banged his forehead.

"Wha? No. What the hell's this broad think she got?"

He laughed, knocking again, hearing snapping locks. The door opened fast. Nancy's expression was far from pleasing. His eyes skimmed down her body and to him then, that was. In her large dark eyes at that moment, there was nothing but annoyance.

She snapped, "What is it? What do you want? I was ... My God. Jimmy!"

Smiling. "Yeah, Jimmy. Listen, somebody clued me I could get a piece here for a quarter. That right?"

She stepped back, taking a deep breath. He saw her stomach move in and out, then she shook her short radiantly dark hair, running to him, throwing her arms around his neck with a soft scream and he felt touched.

"You're home! Oh, I'm so glad for you. Let me look at you. Oh, Jimmy, it's wonderful to see you again."

Her arms were around him. To him, she felt very soft, very feminine and warm. She smelled fresh, soapy, a flowery perfumed scent was there, tangled with that of a woman. It excited him.

His hands held her waist. Two fingers touched flesh that gave under pressure where her sweater came away from her form-fitting tight slacks. His body warmed.

"Hey, Nancy. You feel good. Lemme go, babe. Lemme look at you."

Her arms dropped from his neck, her hands going to his around her waist. She moved away some, there were tears in her eyes.

"Jimmy. Jimmy, I can hardly believe it's you. You look, oh, you look just wonderful."

The sweater defined her breasts clearly in delicate spongy tenderness. The tight slacks helped allow the sensuality to flow unimpeded through him. His fingers stiffened about her waist. His voice was lazy, heavy.

"Nancy, like I never saw you before, you wan' more than that quarter?"

She laughed, embarrassed at herself and for him, not unaware of the pressure around her waist or that had been in his voice.

"Oh, stop that, Jim. Not me. Come inside. You couldn't have changed that much."

Taking one hand from her, holding the other, leading him into the three room apartment, he walked into the bright room as the morning sun poured in. The bed was folded into a sofa when it wasn't used for a bed. The flowered sheets on it gleamed from the sun's touching. Toward the end in a tumbled pile was another sheet of flowers with blue and pink blankets.

There were flowers on the pillows at the other end. Two Danish modern chairs were near the window.

On the wall was a large painting of a giant black bull with muscles outstanding and eye bloodshot, bandoleers hanging out of its back with some streaks of blood, the ground was being puffed away from the force of air coming from it's nostrils. Away in the background stood a miniature figure of a matador and a cape. In the matador's hand was a silver line, obviously meant to be a sword. Further in the background were cheering faces in an arena. Jimmy did not feel the painting to fit Nancy, but then he thought he never knew her that well. It just did not seem to fit her, so he said, "If I was that fool, I'd run."

He motioned his chin at the picture. She laughed, saying in a quick voice, "Wait. Don't look. The place is a mess. I just woke. Here, sit here a minute."

She led him to one of the chairs, nearly pushing him down, then went to the sofa bed, dropping pillows on the floor saying, "Let me fold this. Wait, don't say anything til I'm finished."

"I want to look at you, I have so much to ask."

Her back was to him as she worked, bending, stretching, kneeling.

He groaned to himself almost loud. "Oh, Christ, this woman. "

She finished with the sofa, flopping on it, her eyes completely interested in him.

'When did you come home? I saw Alice Wednesday."

He didn't say anything.

"Jimmy, you're so tall. Are you home for good now? You won't have to go back, will you?"

"No. Got home yesterday. I saw Alice. Hey, you really are beautiful. I never thought about you like that before; I mean, me tellin' you."

She bent forward slightly, uneasy as she tried hiding her breast from his view with her arms crossed in front of her, her elbows on her knees.

"Don't talk like that. How long will you be on parole?"

"A while. What's happenin' with you. What's new?"

"Oh nothing, really. I guess I'm just the same." An expression came to her eyes as if just realizing him then. "Jimmy, you're wonderful. I can't tell you how happy I am to see you. You look so, well, you look so much the same, as if we're sitting having a cup of coffee in the old man's." She laughed. "Any moment I expect to hear Kip yell at you to leave her alone."

He grinned, not thinking much of Kip.

"Yeah uh, how's she? You see much of her?"

"Who, Kip? No, she married Freddy. They have a baby boy now."

He sat up in the chair, not believing her. "Who married Freddy? That right, they got a kid?"

"Yes, her and Freddy have been married a while."

"Holy Christ. Freddy?" Then he laughed. It hardly seemed possible. "Alice an' Dicky got married too, uh? I saw them yesterday. How bout you? When you gonna?"

She shook her head once. "No, not for a while yet."

"Hey, I'll marry you. When?"

"Nooo."

She watched as he got up walking over to her. "I want you next to me, Nancy. Ain't hadda broad sittin' next to me in a long time."

Her hand went to his shoulder as he sat. "I'm flattered." She asked softly. "Did you see him, Jim? Bobby?"

"Umm, little bit but they separated us after reception an sent us to different joints."

"Ohh."

"How come you don't write him?"

"I don't know, he never wrote and Dicky said that the letters I wrote when he first went there were just held for him until he would be released, so I stopped. I don't write anymore."

"Yeah?" Jimmy threw away a soiled feeling that had started to build in him.

She asked brightly, standing quickly, finished speaking before she was through the kitchen door that was in the same wall the picture of the snorting bull was on. "Do you want some coffee? I'll make some. Wait."

She walked out. He sighed down in the chair, allowing himself to dream about her on that bed with the flowered sheets under her and him on her. She came back as he was starting again. He had a hard time fighting feelings that he did not want in him because he knew she had been crying. It seemed to him as if she were forever crying. She tried to make believe she hadn't been.

"Alice is coming up about eleven. She's going to have lunch with me. Stay, please? We have so much to talk about. You will stay?" She stood in front of him, her hands on his knees, then bending close. "You will won't you? I still can hardly believe you're here."

He laughed to himself, knowing damned well he wasn't about to leave.

To her, as his hands covered hers, "Okay, but I need a broad. I didn't know how much til I saw you." She laughed, hugging his head to her chest.

"Oh, Jim. You're the same, but I thought you didn't like us so much?"

He pulled her down on his lap. "I grew up, up there. Sure you won't take that there quarter?"

She giggled. "No. I'd have to give you change. I'm not so good anymore."

"Yeah, uh, maybe Alice will."

Her eyes widened as she said with serious humor, "Yes, but she'll charge you much more than that."

She laughed with him, he watching her as she did, then saying, "Come on, get offa me before I start thinkin' how great you'd look layin' on that bed soon."

She stood quickly. "Oh, you're silly. You just feel that way... Well, you'll get over it."

"Yeah, I know, soon's I get my first piece."

"Don't say that. Can't you make out as if I'm a man, you know, just a friend?"

He smiled large staring at her. "Uh uh, not really."

They walked into the kitchen that was very small, the one window narrow and short, a half table with three chairs small enough to be childrens', a four-burner gas stove, a sink and a refrigerator lining one wall. The other wall was mostly a closet for dishes. It was dark in there after the bright light of the living room.

Nancy clicked on the light in the ceiling saying, "I always need a light in this room, even in the middle of the day. The cups are in the closet, Jim. Will you get two, please?"

He placed the two cups on the table and sat. "Man, this joint is little. How come you don't live with your people anymore?"

"I don't know. I just wanted to live alone."

"How long you been livin' here?"

"More than a year." She lowered the flame under the coffee pot as it began perking. "I make terrible coffee, but say it's nice anyway, okay?"

She turned from the stove to him, saw his expression and asked with a plea.

"Aw, Jim, stop. Please don't look at me that way. You never did before. Well, after you meet some other girl you won't feel that way."

"Yeah. Got anything to eat?" She rose, going to the refrigerator.

"Did you have breakfast? How about eggs? I don't have any ham. Would you like bacon?"

"Naw. Got any corn flakes?"

She turned, a little surprised. "Corn flakes?"

"Yep. Got any?"

"I don't know. I think so, but they might be stale."

"Naw, they don't get stale."

She took a small package of cornflakes from the closet that she had bought over six months before. She had no idea why she bought them.

"Are you sure that's all you want? I could make bacon and eggs for you."

"No this is great. That's all I ate up there. I like 'em."

She placed a bowl before him with sugar and milk then sat at the other end of the table, smiling.

"Jimmy, you remind me of Bob."

"Uh, why?"

"I don't know. He always ate the most unusual things. I suppose a lot of people eat corn flakes for breakfast, but I always thought only children did."

"They're good. Want some?"

"No, I've eaten all ready."

He watched her awhile, Nancy turning away from him. Then he said, as if just making up his mind, bluntly, "I'm gonna lay you, Nancy."

Her intake of breath at the unexpected statement was sharp and she blinked. "You're what?"

He glanced around the table after pouring milk and sugar on the cornflakes, "I need a spoon."

She was now blinking rapidly. "Did I hear you right? I know I did. What did you just say to me?"

"Said I was gonna lay ya. Gimme a spoon, uh?"

She laughed because she did not believe he could mean it. He was just kidding her.

"Behind you in the closet on a tray. Jimmy, you're crazy. "

He leaned back in the chair, took a spoon from the bright orange plastic tray in the closet, saying, "No kiddin', I'm gonna." Then he set to eating.

Her head fell on her arms that were on the table as she continued to laugh. Jimmy was a funny guy. "You really are crazy. Oh, God, you're funny."

"Yeah, I know. How's that coffee?"

"I don't know. I guess it's ready."

She turned off the flame. Taking the pot, she moved to his end of the table to pour. His hand touched her buttocks.

Her eyes narrowed. "Get out of there. I'll pour this on you. Stop Jim, take your hand away."

He smiled. "In a minute."

She put the pot down, standing stiffly.

"Aw, please stop it. It won't be any good, really I don't want to. Jimmy, I'd like to help you, but I can't. Please, don't." The last was a whine.

His hand dropped. He imitated Bob, winking and chuckling, "Sure, kid. Put you in the mood later."

She did not know if the imitation was real or feigned, but she moved away from him. Jimmy then, was not sure either.

"Pour your own coffee. You have to stop that."

"What, feelin' your ass?"

"No, don't talk like him anymore. I don't want you here if you do."

"Did I sound like him?"

"Yes, just like him."

He poured the coffee in the cups.

"You still takin' it straight?"

"Yes."

She took the cup from him, forcing a grin. "You could have used saucers, you know."

"Yeah, didn't think. You been goin' out with anybody, Shoulders?"

"No, not really. Don't call me that, okay?"

"Why not?"

"I don't know. I just don't want you to."

"Should I call you Nance?"

She smiled laughing softly. "Yes, if you really think you're going to lay me, you can."

Her laughter died when he said, "Okay, Nance."

Then it came to her that he was going to try to do exactly as he said he was. It amazed her. It seemed so fantastic. She tried reasoning with him.

"Jimmy, I'm not going to let you. I don't know whether you're insane or not, but I'm not whatever you think I am."

"I know, but I'm gonna lay ya."

She stood. "I think you better leave now. I don't want you here anymore."

He ignored her, asking calmly, "You see Frankie lately?"

"Yes, I've seen him. Jimmy, don't try anything."

"I'm gonna. You're gonna let me. When you see him last?"

"About a month ago. He tried the same thing you're trying. Just what the hell do you guys think I am, some kind of frustrated slut that goes around begging?"

"Uh uh, sit down."

She did, then popped up as it came to her, asking loudly, "Did he say a thing like that? Did he say that I'm letting him ... Did he?"

"Take it easy, Nancy. I ain't seen him since before I went upstate. Nobody told me nothin'. I wanna screw you all by myself."

Her head moved up and down. "Oh, you do? How nice. And what do you expect me to do, prostrate myself so you can?"

"Somethin' like that, whatever the hell that means."

He munched. She sat.

"Jimmy, I'm sorry, but I'm going to disappoint you. I want you to leave when you've finished that."

"Uh uh."

"Oh, damn, this whole thing sounds so foolish."

"Yeah, that was pretty good. Tell me about Frank. What's with him? He really try an' make you?"

"I don't want to talk about him. I'm just something Bobby once had and he wants, that's all."

"Did he?"

She asked warily, anger mounting greatly. "Did he what?"

"Get in."

"Jimmy, you–"

He laughed, holding his hands up.

"I'm kiddin', I'm kiddin'. Don't get shook."

"Well, you just stop kidding. Do you want more of those damned cornflakes?"

"Nope, I jus' eat one bowl. Don' wanna get fat."

"Let's go out to the living room. I don't want to stay here. I think this room goes to your head."

She walked past him and grimaced when he touched her, singing coldly, "You better stop that, Jim."

When she sat on the sofa, he sat next to her. She growled, "Oh, hell," and started to stand, but he held her arm.

"Don't. Stay here. I ain't gonna bother you yet."

She was completely out of humor then. "Thanks. Is that a favor? Really, don't try anything. Alice will be up soon."

"Yeah, what time is it?"

"A little after ten."

"Aw, not enough time. I'll wait'll she leaves."

She smiled, at ease again. "You're leaving with her. But I am glad to see you. Aren't you happy to be home again?"

"I didn't know. I mean, when I first got out, it was okay, but I didn't know how glad I'd be until I saw you. I didn't ... well, not just cause I wanna bang you. I don't know, when I first saw you I felt like I was home again."

She was startled, deeply moved. "Did I make you feel that way?"

"Yeah, Nancy, I never wanted a broad more in my life than now."

His arms went around her. He brought her to him. She fought, digging her elbows in his chest, keeping her head back and her face turned away.

"Don't, don't. Let me go, Jimmy. Let go of me."

He forced her arm back holding it behind her then cupping her breast kissing, working up her neck, forcing her head back, kissing her lips, his lips were on hers when he said, "Open your mouth, Nancy."

She twisted her head away, saying fiercely, "Let go of me, Jimmy. Let me go. You have to stop. Oh, stop. You'll hurt me, dammit."

His hand was under her sweater. She felt the strap of her brassiere give. She got her hand free, slapping at Jim. But now she was breathless, fighting, trying to squirm her body. She began feeling weak. The buttons at the back of her sweater began popping because he was holding it, pulling harder when he felt it giving.

She screamed, "Jimmy!"

Her hand slipped from his shoulder. He brought her closer, his leg between hers, she cried as the sweater came away.

"No! Oh, no. Stop. Let me go. Let me alone. Go away, Jimmy, please."

She sagged limp, not fighting anymore, even when he tore her underpants, bringing them down her legs. She cried, not looking at him, his finger irritated her when it went inside her, his mouth at her breast hurting. She tried to move away, but he brought her back and lay on her. She moaned because she enjoyed it then, the release that came without her will, moving her body against his without his urging, gasping at the force of her own desire. She felt strong when he moved from her. He was panting slightly with his hand still covering her breast, his body beside hers.

She urged him to his back. Her head went to his stomach because she wanted more then. Jimmy's hands played in her hair, then she moved and he lay upon her again, pulling clothes away as he ground himself against her, then a dull stab as he entered her, humping and grunting softly.

Later, she put her robe on and would not look at him. He dressed slowly, smiling. "Sorry it was like that, Nancy."

"Just go. I don't ever want to see you again."

His smile grew. "Why? You enjoyed yourself."

Her eyes flashed as she said loudly. "Do you think so? You were only a ... a... you weren't even there. I tried something, it wasn't worth it."

Jimmy threw the shirt on the sofa that he had just picked up. "Whadda you talkin about? You were moanin'."

"Oh, for God's sake, Jimmy. You were ..." Softly as she walked for the bathroom, under her breath to herself, "... just a shadow. I think I used you."

He sat on the sofa, trying to bring himself back together again. He felt shame, not because he had raped her, probably because he hadn't. He was sure he had just lent himself to an act he had no part in. He was still sitting, looking blankly ahead of him, when she came out of the bathroom, just putting her robe back on. He looked at her lovely body and again wished he could place her on the sheet of flowers.

She said quietly. "I'm sorry for what I said. I didn't mean it. I'm sorry if I hurt you, Jimmy."

"Yeah."

"Honestly, I didn't mean what I said. I was angry at myself. I did enjoy you."

He picked up his shirt again, shook it, his head nodding.

"I know, Nancy. I know. You wanna do me a favor?"

"What? Yes."

"Tie your robe an' get me a glass a water."

"Uh, water?"

She tied her robe, blushing, a pinkness forming from her ankles up through and under her eyes. She backed away from him.

He put his shirt on, smiling at her as a thought came wandering up from the rear of his mind, wishing he had a knife so he could cut her stomach open.

She went into the kitchen. He went out the door. When he opened the downstairs door, Alice was coming in. She grinned, asking gruffly, "Hiya. Whadda you doing here so early?"

"Nothin'."

"What's the matter, Jim? You look sick."

"No, I ... Yeah, I'm tired. Tell your ole man I'll see 'im tomorra'."

"Yeah, sure, love."

He walked away from her. She wondered what the hell was going on as she went up the stairs. When she came in the door, Nancy was sitting on the sofa, brushing her hair listlessly.

"Hi, Shoulders. Was Jimmy just here?"

Nancy answered hollowly, "Yes, he was, Alice. I tried to make love with him. It didn't work. It frightened me as if I had masturbated the way an animal would have, as if I were an animal."

Alice closed the door, her outward expression not the least effected. She smiled wide, walking for the kitchen saying, "That's nice. I see you made coffee. It must be love if he drank yours."

Nancy said dully, "Yes."

Alice ran water in the sink and began to make a new pot of coffee, placidly saying to herself, She looks as if she wants to jump out the window. If she does, I'll call an ambulance before I go down to her.

She thought over what she had just said to herself and dropped the coffee pot in the sink, going to the living room quickly. Nancy was still sitting on the sofa brushing her hair. Alice spoke with angry authority, "Come in to the kitchen with me, Nancy."

Turning to her, placing the brush on the sofa arm, "What's the matter? Are you mad at me?"

"Yes. Come in here."

She pointed toward the kitchen. Nancy stood, trying to smile, but it was almost as sickly as Jimmy's had been when he smiled at her before he left. She walked into the kitchen, Alice following.

Nancy sat at the table asking, "Are you making coffee?"

"Yes."

"I don't see why you're angry, Alice. I think I got the idea from you. Yes I did. You almost told me to."

Alice said quickly, "That's not what's bothering me." She turned from the sink where she had gone when Nancy sat down, asking, "Shoulders, tell me the truth. Are you going to try to kill yourself?"

"Uh, what? Alice, where did you get an idea like that from?"

"Your medicine cabinet, those pills you have in there, and just now I thought you were going to jump out the window. I'm afraid for you."

She was a little indignant. "Those are sleeping pills to use when I can't sleep."

"Yes, but you've had them over four months and haven't used one. Don't lie to me, Nancy. No doctor prescribes that many."

Adamantly, "They're sleeping pills, Alice, prescribed by a doctor. Your imagination is bubbling over. I said what I said when you came in the door because I was ... well, I don't know, disappointed, I suppose."

Alice turned back to the pot of coffee she was preparing, had prepared, slamming it on one of the burners, turning on the gas jet, forgetting that the pilot wasn't working, muttering, "You were almost hysterical. You're becoming more childlike as you grow older."

Nancy gasped, her mouth dropped, momentarily stunned, then, "Why, who do you think you're talking to? Alice, why are you speaking to me like that for?

What started it? Why do you think I'm going to kill myself?"

Alice sat next to her. "Stop, Nancy. You're turning white. I'm sorry if I upset you, but you upset me when I came in. No, not what you said, just the way you appeared, as if you wanted to be any place but here. I'm not mad at you, I'm just afraid for you."

She was bewildered. "Stop it. That's enough. Is everyone supposed to be sane but me? And I suppose you are the sanest?"

"Yes, thank you, love."

Angrily, "You're welcome. Would you do me a favor?"

"Of course, what is it?"

"Turn the gas off before we blow up."

Alice whirled around in her chair as the thick sweet smell came to her then. "Oh my God."

She turned the burner off, looking at Nancy who was watching her, then she laughed. "Talk about suicides. I almost killed both of us."

She opened the window, sitting again, still chuckling. "I'm glad you saw it."

"Yes, Alice, I hope you never speak to me that way again."

"I won't, hon. Why didn't you enjoy Jim? He seems like he could do a good job."

She was grinning but Nancy wasn't. "No, I tried, but it wasn't the way I wanted it to be. Oh, it was disgusting, to be truthful. I felt more animal than human."

Still grinning, she mocked. "Really? When I feel that way I enjoy myself most."

"Stop, Alice. No."

Grinning wide, "Shoulders, sometimes you're a little too delicate."

"I am not. That wasn't the way I meant to describe it. I meant, yes, like that. But I don't know."

"Nancy, love; someday you're going to have to come down from your tower."

Annoyed; "This morning you seem to have pockets full of advice. I wish you wouldn't try out your Freud or whoever you've been reading lately on me."

"All righty, will you do me a favor?"

"Yes."

"Give me those pills."

"Oh, you ..." Then Nancy said with finality, "Oh, go to hell."

Chapter 15

A Token

Jesus sat there and thought about his wife, the streets, about his wife, about Billie Holiday and how beautiful she sang, about his wife and the very good time they were going to have together when and if he were ever released. Mainly, he thought about his wife.

He watched Facine, who was the best baseball player in population, Jesus considered himself the best basketball player in population, in the world, simply because he was. Everyone in population agreed except Moe.

Jesus watched Facine hit a long high one over the fence, over the fence that was there to stop the woods beyond from growing into the rec yard.

Bob Coffin, his Caucasian friend who was playing left field, did not look up when the ball was hit. Facine rounded the bases smiling, happy. Jesus could never understand how Facine could be happy. What had he to be happy about? He had not been back on the streets a good year when they had bounced him back up again to this lovely country, God's country, one of the hacks had told him; his favorite hack, Beaton, the queer he was going to kill, not murder, kill, he had told him that.

Law limped over and sat next to him. Law had a sprained ankle. Law was sickly pale. Law was going to die soon. Jesus knew this because he read it in Law's fortune when Law hurt his ankle. Law had just gotten out of the box again, Coffin had just gotten out of the box again, Facine had just gotten out of the box again, Jesus had just gotten out of the box again.

The only one that never went to the box was Moe. Moe never was in and never would go. Law had told Jesus the only thing that Jesus had made any sense out of anything Law ever said.

He said, "Moe is adjustable. He can adjust himself to punitive correction. He is a model prisoner, a regular ass-kisser."

Jesus had added, "One wonderful ass-kisser."

And Law had agreed. But Moe had made up his mind before being sentenced that he would get out, get out of prison as fast as possible, anyway he could. After that snap judgement he thought it over and amended it. He would not try to escape because he was afraid of being shot.

Law sat on the grey bench with the green legs next to the person he thought the greatest chicken he ever knew, Jesus. He wasn't even ashamed of being a chicken, he reveled in it. Jesus's lips were moving and Law asked him.

"What?"

"What what?"

"What were you jus' whisperin'?"

"What was I jus' whisperin'?"

He asked the question because then he honestly did not know.

"Yeah, that's what I jus' said. What was you jus whisperin'?"

"I don't know what I was jus' whisperin'."

"You have to know what you was jus' whisperin'."

"Yes, but I can't tell you."

"Do you wanna invoke the fifth?"

"Fifth what?"

"The amendment."

"To what?"

"Whadda you, stupid?"

"Yes. Amendment to what?"

"To what? How in hella I know to what."

"Then why did you ask me?"

Through clenched teeth, Law said very vindictively, "Jesus, I think I'll punch you right in your mouth."

Jesus said complacently, "An' I'll kick you in your ankle."

Law winced. Something was happening. What Law was not sure of, or truer, did not want to believe. His great cowardly chicken was turning. He could not bring himself to punch him.

How could he? Suppose Jesus really meant exactly the act threatened. His ankle pained him so much he was afraid to talk about it, not think of what would happen if Jesus kicked him. But he was sure Jesus would not kick him. Not because of any compassion on Jesus' part, simply because Jesus' eyes were darting around. Jesus would be to busy running. He knew he was still chicken because his feet were moving already, running in midair, not touching the ground.

So Law said, "Okay. I won't punch you. Don't talk about my ankle or I'll kill you."

Jesus watched him carefully, still, not sitting completely.

"I won't talk about your ankle. Does it pain you very much?"

"Yeah, yeah."

Law was stretching his lips the long way as he grimaced in pain.

"Does it pain you a lot when you're in bed?"

"Yeah, yeah, yeah."

He gasped. "Do you sometimes wish they would cut it off?"

"Yeah, oh yeah." He was close to tears.

"Do you grind your teeth?"

He sobbed. Jesus tsk-tsked.

"I told you you shouldn't think about it. You should do things to keep your mind off it."

"I know, but I can't help it."

"Why don't you ask them for some pills?"

"I did. They won't give them to me."

"Jessie the queer has pills. Maybe she'll give them to you."

"No, the creep wants a pack a cigarettes a piece for them, an' you won my last carton last night."

"Yes, I did do that. I will let you have it back if you'll give me two cartons on your next visit."

"What? Are you outta your skull? Two cartons for one?"

"No, I'm not. Two cartons for one and you can sleep tonight."

"That's thievery, Jesus."

"No, it's usury. But you want them?"

"Yeah, but I don't think I'll ever punch you again. I don't think I'll ever talk to you again. You're cheatin' a sick crippled man."

"A sick crippled dying man."

Almost crying again, "Yeah, a sick, crippled, dyin' man. How could you do it, Jesus?"

"Very easy, my friend, my wonderful sick crippled dying friend."

"I'm not your friend anymore."

"Then I won't lend you my carton of cigarettes."

Quickly; "Okay, I'll be your friend."

The game was over. Then the players lined up to drop their gloves in a big wooden box while a fat smiling hack stood by, counting. Bob, Moe and Racine came over and sat on the bench along side Law and Jesus.

Facine asked happily, "How's yer leg, Law?"

"Don't talk about it." Law had glared that ominously.

"Okay, okay. Jesus, did you see me hit that ball? It made Moe cry."

"Moe, did it really make you cry?"

"Yeah, it really made me cry. Facine is as stupid as

you. He gets carried away with the game instead of the bet. He chokes in the opposite direction."

Facine peeped softly, hoping Moe wouldn't hear. "You shoulda bet on us. "

Moe heard and yelled, "Ahh, you shit bird. We were the favorites."

"Oh."

Jesus asked, "Facine, why do you smile? How can you be so happy?"

"Why not?"

"Why not? Why not? They let you out. They let you go. You were walking the streets, women all around you. How would you let them take you back? Why didn't you kill yourself?"

"Cause I ain't got no virgin prostitute I gotta worry about. That's why."

In a hurry, Jesus ignored Facine. "Bob, you are going out soon, won't you help me?"

"No."

"Coffin, you are selfish. One selfish bastard is what you are. A man who has done all his time and will not help relieve those of his fallen comrades can be nothing but one selfish bastard."

"I am one selfish bastard."

"Will you go see my wife for me?"

"No, I will not go see your wife for you."

"Why will you not go see my wife for me?"

"What for?"

"To ask her, no, tell her to wait for me, that I love her, that I need her, that she is my life."

"She knows that by now."

"No. Women have to be reminded."

"You write her a letter every day, don't you?"

"Yes."

"That's enough. Nothin' I can tell her will help."

"Coffin, you are a hard man, a man of basic cruelty."

"Jesus, are you gonna play bench five inna tournament?"

"No, Moe. I am not going to play bench five in the tournament."

"I am going to hang myself so bet with bench five."

"I'll wait til tomorra mornin' to make sure."

"I'll bet you all of my cigarettes against one of yours that I do."

"Okay."

Jesus had roughly about ten thousand packages of cigarettes, owned, owed, stolen.

"All except one that has been lended already."

"Yes, but you have to pay him two cartons on your next visit."

Law was mortally wounded.

"Why didn't you shut up?"

"Because I don't like cheaters."

Facine asked religiously, "Are you really gonna hang up tonight?"

"Yes, I am."

"But, why?"

"I cannot go on any longer. Life has come to be too much of a burden. I am tired. Facine, I am one tired young man. I will write one last letter freeing my wife so that she will never have to lie to me explaining how she broke her membrane while riding down a rocky icy hill backwards on a sleigh that slipped out from under her. I am tired, one wonderfully tired person, so I shall die."

Facine, as if he were talking to a ghost, "Dead?"

"There is no other way."

"Jesus?"

"Yes, Coffin, my last friend on earth?"

"If I go see your wife, you will not hang up?"

"No, I shall not hang up."

"Not kill yourself in anyway, an' not try getting' out?"

"I will do everything you say if you will go see my wife."

"I will go see your wife."

"Do you mean that?"

"Have I ever lied to you before?"

"No, you have never lied to me before. You never lie, do you?"

"Everyone lies."

"Are you lying now?"

"No, I am not lying now."

"Then let me believe you never lie."

"Go ahead."

"Thank you. Do you want her address?"

"I have her address. You gave it to me forty-seven times."

"Oh, was it that many? Yeah, startin' forty-seven days ago. Yes, I did give it to you this morning, didn't I?"

"Yes, you gave it to me this mornin' just like every mornin'. An you'll give it to me tomorrow mornin'."

"Yes I will, I don't want you to forget."

"Thank you."

"You are a humanitarian, Coffin; a philanthropist, a do-gooder, an up-lifter minder, a Florence Night-ingale."

"I know."

"Do you know how truly grateful I am to you? I shall always and forever be in your debt. My life is yours and I love you."

"Thank you, Jesus."

Then the queer runner came over and told him he was wanted up front and Jesus went up front and they sent him to Matteawan State Hospital for the Criminally Insane.

"Coffin, what you gonna say to her?"

"I don't know."

"Then what the hell you go in for?"

"I'm not."

"Oh."

Chapter 16

Home Again

Jimmy walked up the street angrily because he was in a hurry to go no place. He wanted to think of what had happened but was afraid if he found out he would kill someone.

He was disgusted with himself because he had fucked his best boy's girl and outrageously appalled because his best boy's girl had fucked him.

He was afraid to let his thoughts go any further than that.

So he walked fast, going nowhere for two hours. Then he felt chilly because the shirt he was wearing was thin and a wind was blowing, so he walked along Broadway to his grandmother's apartment. Turning into her building, he promised himself he would not think of Nancy any longer.

The apartment door opened to a large old-fashioned kitchen of gleaming white brightness that was part of a long six-room railroad flat. His grandmother was a woman touching eighty who almost weighed ninety pounds, was hard of hearing at times, losing her hair as well as her eyesight and, his mother loudly thought, her mind.

She thought the sun rose, set, and if he liked, would stop burning, for Jimmy. In her sight, he sometimes thought so, too. She loved the loud vulgar humor he employed when speaking to her. To her nine children she showed not one smidgen of affection. Jimmy she would have fawned over had she thought he wanted or would allow her to. He never showed he did, so she never did. Eight of her children were dead. Only Jimmy's mother remained and she hated her daughter as dearly as she loved her daughter's son.

The insurance from her eight dead children, her not loved but neither hated, hardly remembered late husband, lay hidden in weird places, such as television sets. She had three holes gouged out in walls, tiny tin boxes hidden throughout the apartment and in stocks that paid her quarterly and bank accounts under her daughter's name, without her daughter's knowledge. Her daughter never knew any of this, did not know her mother was comparatively well off, as she collected social security checks with a fond smile and a seemingly uncomprehending mind when ever questioned.

Her laugh, or giggle, was closer to a high-pitched cackle. Jimmy could have her cackling for an hour by simply greeting her with, "Hello, ya old whore."

Which is what he said when he walked in the door. She had been sitting at the old-fashioned wooden table, sipping long cold black tea from a bowl. Her eyes danced, her head shook and she cackled. He watched her and slapped his forehead with his palm.

"Whadda you laughin' at, you silly old bitch?"

The cackles came faster, louder and seemed merry. He laughed.

"Come on, you ole slob. Gimme some a your tea."

She went quickly for the porcelain teapot that was steeping on the stove, cackling all the while, with Jimmy's eyes on her as she took a bowl from the floor-to-ceiling wooden dish closet attached to the wall. Johnny had carved all their initials there one day when they had played hooky. He, Johnny and his grandmother had listened with large smiles as the truant officer banged at the door, promising he would call the police if they did not open up. He didn't, they didn't, he gave up, bewildered.

One of the happiest moments in his grandmother's life had been the night the police had knocked upon her door, informing her that her grandson was wanted for questioning about an attempted robbery and completed murder. One of the most annoying was when they apprehended him, absolving him of that crime, that one. She had entertained visions of an Earl Rogers defending him and proving him not guilty, leaving only a small stigma of doubt. She had been about to lay bare her secret hideouts and bankbooks to obtain the services of a mythical Clarence Darrow or John Napolitano.

She had not been just a little put out by the police deciding he had only held up one man. Still, her faith in him remained unshaken, her aspirations knew no limits. She called him gangster, thief and murderer even when she was not fooling, because she wanted him to be just that. She was a lovely little old lady.

"Come thief. Sit, sit." She pounded the table before an empty chair. At times she was hard of hearing so she imagined everyone else in the world was. But Jimmy knew well enough that if a whisper were important she would hear it, could hear it through walls.

He plopped on the chair saying in a sarcastically sweet voice, "I need some bread. Gimme some money. I'll buy you a present if you gimme the money."

She shook her old grey head, holding her middle finger before her, moving it up and down in an obscene gesture she had seen him use so often, then poured his tea. He slapped his head, speaking low.

"Come on, will ya? I need it. Gonna go out an' get drunk as a bastard an' come back an' beat your ole ass in."

She cackled, almost pouring the tea in his lap instead of the cup.

"Watch it! Watch it! Whadda you wanna do, cripple me?"

She cackled some more, finished pouring, and shuffled her way off to her dark bedroom that was the last room in the apartment.

He sipped the tea, made a face at how darkly strong it was, looked to see if he could see her. When he could not, he poured it down the sink. He sat back, lighting a cigarette, thought of Nancy, then tried not to. He thought of Kip married to Freddy, thought of when he had her. He had been the first one to have her and she had cried. He laughed at her and was sure she never forgave him. He wondered if Nancy had been a virgin when Bob had her, then damned her because he knew she had been, still could be and wished her dead, her and her mystical virginity. He damned her again, wishing he could drop the complex she had wrapped him in.

He turned as he heard his grandmother's shuffling feet. She grinned with her false teeth, plopping a folded wad of dollar bills in front of him.

"Here, gangster. Get good and stoned," she hee-heeed, sitting in the chair she had left, sipping her dark strong long cold tea. He began counting the one-dollar bills. She screamed, "Fifty. That's enough, yes?"

Had he said no, she would-have given him more, but he nodded his head yes. She cackled at him and went back to her tea. He put the money in his pocket, then got up and left without saying goodbye.

After the door closed, she slammed the bowl of tea on the table, the bowl broke, tea slopped over her, the table, and the floor. She shuffled to the sink for a rag to wipe it up.

He walked slowly, still not sure where he intended going, feeling a nauseous type of guilt in him now. He was sorry he had taken the money from her, wondered why he had not said goodbye. He knew she would brood over it.

He stood on the corner, not knowing which way

he was going to turn. It occurred to him then that he wished he was back in the joint. There, it seemed he did not have to worry about other people or how they felt. He had not been afraid to hurt anyone's feelings or was he bothered by wondering where the hell he was going. Last week it seemed he had wanted to go to so many places, had wanted to meet so many people again. Now that he was out he did not want to go anywhere or meet anyone. He shrugged, muttering, "Frig it."

He headed for Marie's. At least he could lay her and the five dollars he would cheat her out of would make him feel like he was doing the laying.

He woke Sunday morning with a slight hangover, his mouth dry yet sticky, his head throbbing high in the rear and above his eyes. He felt feverish, holding his head in his hands speaking aloud to himself, softly.

"Whadda great day. Maannh, I feel rotten. Son of a bitch, whad I do last night. Ohhh, the friggen Uptown, sat in there an' drank whisky. I hate whisky. Whad a shitty taste it got. Yesterday what the hell 'id I do?" Then, "Oohh, Christ. That broad Nancy. Why in hell I fool aroun' her for, friggen big-eyed bitch. Same as she always was. Cause a them big eyes she thinks everybody's gonna feel sorry for her. Ahh, frig her."

He let his feet fall from the bed, sitting up, his head feeling worse. He stood walking through the living room and kitchen, taking the salt cellar from the kitchen table as he passed, uncapping it, pouring some in his cupped palm, then adding tooth powder, he took his brush from the rack above the sink and began brushing vigorusly.

"She's some broad, I gotta give 'er that. Man, whadda body, man. I wonder what's wrong with her? She acts like she's about to melt any minute, like somebody's gonna bite her. Ahh, frig her. She's bugs one. Send 'er to the whacky factory see if one a them psychs can fix her brains. If he could keep his friggen hands offa her, I couldn't if I was one."

He laughed, straightening from the position he was bent in over the sink. Seeing himself in the mirror, the pasty foam around his wide mouth made him scowl. "Sheeet. Look like I gots the rabies or somethin."

He rinsed his mouth, hunted the shelf for his razor. Wetting his face, he applied lather from a spluttering pressurized can. His small bright eyes searched his face.

"I'll never be a handsome bastard, I'll tell me that. How in hell come I got such a big nose? Nobody else inna family got it?" His fingers traced along his nose, now even more outstanding because of the lather below around and touching.

"Aw, frig it. Even without it, I'd be a ugly son of a bitch. The hell with it. When I get rich, I'll get some kinda plastic surgery or somethin."

He went down to the restaurant on the ground floor of the building he and his mother shared an apartment in since he could remember, going in through the side door rather than walk around to the street entrance. In the hot sweaty kitchen, he waved to Bill, the owner.

"Cornflakes, ace? Hurry up, ah?"

Bill glanced up from the table he was mashing food on.

"Yeah, yeah, okay. Got some good crumb buns. Wan' some?"

"They're stale, you lyin' bastard. Yeah, gimme one."

Bill laughed. Jimmy walked out front to one of the tables, waving to Luz who was behind the counter, serving customers. She ignored him immediately. She was a young short good-looking Puerto Rican girl who spoke with an accent. The night before, Jimmy had taken her to the Uptown bar and drank whisky. Later in the evening, when everything was falling into him, or him into it, he tired of her, or thought he had. He told her he would be right back. He had not returned and Luz right now was not a little bit angry with him, she was a whole lot.

When Bill told her to take the bowl of cereal over to him. She wanted very much to refuse, but she needed the job. So she brought the cereal, bun, and coffee over, placing them before him, neither looking at him or speaking, so he grinned.

"Smile at me 'fore I spill coffee all over your white dress."

"Goda hell, you beetch." This she said as she started away without looking at him, his hand clamped over her wrist.

"Come on, baby. I was all juiced up las' night. I went

an' fell asleep inna park. Just woke up a couple hours ago." He kissed her hand, laughing to himself as her haughty expression began to fade, watching him.

"You liah."

The innocent lines long since mastered fell into place.

"Straight talk, like I'd never have left ya. Believe me, it's been a long time since I been drinking, it got to me." He spoke the last with a sad shrug of one shoulder.

She capitulated, believing him completely, bending over, leaning close. "You seeck now. Go essy. Too mouch one time no good."

"Yeah, I know. Meet me there tonight. I'll be there about eight, an' I'll go slow. Like you can teach me that dance you was teachin' me last night. Whadda you call it? The marenga. Will you meet me?"

"Outside? I cannot go inside without you."

"Okay, babe." He slapped at her buttocks as she walked away. He had no intention of meeting her that night or any other. He had lost interest last night. Why should he try to regain it tonight? He finished his cereal, bun and coffee, paid Luz, after again making her promise to meet him that night.

He walked down the street. It was a pleasant day. The sun was high overhead and warm. There was a clean winter smell in the air, impregnated with a sweet smell of carbon monoxide.

Somehow he felt himself to be a foreigner to this neighborhood. He no longer felt it a part of him, no longer did he feel he could call it home. There seemed no more safe corners to rest. It was a strange place to him now. He turned, walking up Broadway. The sun on his back felt good. He saw Ralphy with a girl on his arm. Jimmy did not like Ralphy. To Jimmy, Ralphy was a bastard.

There were too many times that he could recall when Ralphy would whisper in a cop's ear and a friend would be bounced up the station house on charges and charges against Ralphy would be dropped, and there was a girl named Joan who was dead from an O. D. because of him, because he turned her on the first time and it killed her, because Ralphy chickened out when she started to go under and left her.

But Jimmy soon would have more reason to dislike Ralphy, because he recognized the girl on his arm, thinking about her silly-colored hair that stood out anyplace, so he stopped, laughing, pointing at her.

"Hey, lookit you. Miss bitch all growed up."

Liz's eyes squinted, then lit as she recognized him, yelling, running ahead of Ralphy. "Jimmy! Jim you're out. Howja do it? Are they after you? Whenja come out?"

He met her as she ran to him, picking her up, whirling around with her.

"Yeah, yeah, I'm out. Hey, lookit you, missy. Lizzy, honey, I love you. You grew up, uh?"

Her head jerked up and down her arms around his neck.

"Sure. Whatcha think I did? I'm a woman now. Where's Bob? Is he home with you?"

"Uh ungh. They keepin' him a while."

They kissed, breaking and laughing.

"Lizzy, comere. Come on with me. We'll have a party."

"Yeah, ohhh yeah."

Then she halted her exuberant laughter, turning to Ralphy, who was standing back warily. He knew Jim did not like him, not at all. The last thing he wanted to do was fight him, which if Jimmy thought about it he would have to. Ralphy did not want that, Jimmy would damn near kill him and he knew it. Ralphy did not consider Lizzy worth a slap, much less a beating.

Jimmy looked from her to Ralphy, asking her, but staring at him. "Whadda you doin with that creep. He's a nothin. I'll bust 'im in half for ya."

He took her hand and started away, but she did not move, shaking her head, saying faintly, "No I can't. Ralphy don't wanna go."

He growled.

"Frig him. You owe that bum one nothin. You know what he is? He'll make a junky outta you. Besides, I'd like to kill the S.O.B. anyway!"

Then to him; "You leave her alone, creep, or it's all by ourselves, me an you."

She loosened her hand, backing away. "Don't say things like that, Jim. I'll see you again, huh?"

He watched her walk over to him and take his hand, then warned.

"Like now you got me on you, punk. She's one a mine."

"Hey, take her."

Ralphy pushed her towards him. She whirled, clutching his arm.

"Nooaaw, wait."

Then Jimmy walked away.

He met Tippy, who was still tall and pale with hair that was almost white. They shook hands, laughing, slapping one another on the back. They went up to Tippy's house, smoked marijuana while watching a basketball game on TV. Tippy and his girl Margaret were going to a gathering at Eddie's house that night, so Jimmy met Luz and brought her along.

Then he watched Tony kick Ralphy's head until he was sure Ralphy had died. He heard Eddie tell Pete that they should jump Tony, but if they had they would have had to fight him, so they didn't.

The expression on Tony's face when Liz refused to go with him made him sick and he left. It was all disgusting, the whole life he was involved in was disgusting. Because Ralphy was pushing, handling weak ounces, he was a big man. Eddie and Pete were both addicted, Tippy flirted on weekends and Ralphy was the man.

Jimmy walked home and sat in his room with the lights out and cried.

Chapter 17

Consummation

The big rock that they were told to roll up to the top of the big hill with the two big crowbars of black steel lay turtle-like, lazy in the sun that was beaming down, beating down, clubbing, crashing, pounding down on them.

The rock was a malevolent lazy killer that promised them that it would indeed malevolently, lazily, kill them, squeeze them to death if it possibly could, at least crush an arm, leg, rib, skull if it could, if it had the slightest chance, if allowed the minutest opportunity. It would dearly love to crush them both, would readily settle for less if this were disallowed, like a finger, a toe, even a bruise. It would settle for anything that would cause and lend them pain. That was why it lay there, fat and unmoving. This was not a punishment detail. It had nothing to do with punishment. This task was asked for and immediately given.

The head of the institution had come to the idiotic conclusion that a very great rock at the very apex of the institution would serve as a symbolic reminder to all that entered and made exit that God's justice would always be done, served, somehow some way, attempted. So he ordered the rock to be placed at the top of the hill, which would not be for a while yet.

Facine and Bob being in no great hurry had not moved it six feet after five hours of trying, then the head wanted it painted, in his words, "Virgin white."

Facine, hearing this wild and weird request, order, for volunteers for the asinine task which would serve no purpose whatever except to put a rock on top of a hill, thought the director had finally gone stark raving mad, parading before himself, allowing himself to show himself that he was mad, seeing himself as Facine thought everyone saw him.

So Facine had stepped out of line with his hand up, a brave tight little smile on his silly-looking face, and declared that he and Bob would raise the banner of the precious virgin atop the hill –no, mountain– which is what they were beginning to consider it for sometime, now, at least the last hour.

It was very hot, the sun was disgusting him the way it sat on his head, shoulders, back, legs, even behind and in his eyeballs. This ugly big hill, mountain, was the tallest point of the whole institution. From nowhere else would the rocky banner wave so sightlessly. And Facine wanted so much for it to wave sightless. He ughed and huffed with a mighty heave, which moved the rock not at all.

Bob looked at his grimy face with sweat running

down, caking the dust in runnels, as if tears. He leaned on the hot crowbar, head shaking. The guard was sitting on another rock numbed by the sun, not looking at them but at the fence beyond.

Facine sat on the big rock looking at Bob grinning, "We ain't movin it."

"Nope."

"You should try harder, Coffin."

"You're in my way, Facine."

"That's 'cause I'm restin'. It's hot. You shook cause I volunteered you?"

"It's all the same. You're dirty, Facine; cruddy."

"So are you. But that's from workin' so hard."

"When?"

"You're gonna hit the streets soon, huh?"

"Mm, Facine you're in my way. "

"Will you miss me when you go?"

"No. Move."

"It's nice to be onna streets inna summertime."

"Move, Facine. Lemme get a bite."

"You won't even have any parole, will ya?"

"No. Move your foot."

"The last time I was onna streets, I didn't have no parole neither. It was nice."

"Move your foot, Facine."

"Now I ain't gonna have much either, cause a I been inna box so much. You think they really did bug Jesus?"

"Don't know. Are you gonna move your foot?"

"He's not so buggy, no more 'an me or you. Yeooooww! Whatcha do 'at for? Ow, ooohh, ow, how come, owww?"

"So I could get a bite, now you get a bite."

Facine moved listlessly, shoving the tip of the bar under the rock. "This is your last night. Whadda you gonna do?"

"Not a damned thing. Will you getta better bite than that?"

"What for? It ain't gonna move anyway."

"Try it, just for kicks."

"No, Coffin. I don't think so."

"I'll wrap this bar aroun' your head. Getta bite."

"No, you wouldn't. You'd spend your last night inna box."

"Bet?"

Facine made a face, peering closer at him, then quickly sent his bar deeper under the rock.

"How come you're so nasty sometimes, Coffin?"

"Cause I got idiots like you volunteerin' me, that's why."

Facine was stricken, dropped the crowbar, arms wide, head up. He spoke more to the sky than Bob. "Owwie, man. I did it cause a I'm your buddy. Coffin, I did it so we could be close 'fore you left an' you wouldn't forget me."

"You did it 'cause you're a ball-breaker. Now pick up your bar an' getta bite."

Facine stepped away. "No. Go over an' ask the hack if we could get a drink a water."

"No. Pick up your bar."

"Come on, Coffin. If I go over, he'll tell me no. He'll let us if you ask."

Bob dropped his bar, took out his handkerchief, wiped his face, then looked around the yard at the silver-wire linked fence that surrounded it, fragile and black against the bright light of the sun, up at the big hill, at the rock that would never reach the top.

Then he looked at Facine, whose bushy hair was jutting out in all directions with his T-shirt plastered to him and the sweat rolling off him. Shaking his head, breathing deep, he said, "Yeah."

Chapter 18

Once Upon
a Time

On the ride down to the big city in the train, he stared at his reflection in the window. He thought about how silly it was, that it was long over. Then, if anything was silly, the last thought had to be.

He had never written her because he hoped that by not doing so she would have more of a chance at changing her mind, then too, it was easier for them both because at times, few times, they had almost been able to believe neither had ever existed. Many times he had almost been able to convince himself that they had been two frightened children that night, but it was gone when he thought about it too long; it couldn't last.

The old man's was still there, it seemed to him then that it would forever be there. It was still ugly and cruddy and the paint was still peeling off older paint and the window still read cigarettes in gold leaf. The door was opened, held there by the old iron. It was dark inside because of the bright sun outside. It was a quiet empty summer day.

Flies buzzed around the old man's head as he bent over the sink, washing glasses in dirty grey-colored water, speaking softly to himself. There was a faint lingering scent of yesterday here, sweet the way flowers smell in a close room, flowers sent to memorialize the dead, overpowering. It was hideous and sweet, but it was far away.

He stood before the old man until Frank noticed him, glancing up asking quickly, "Wha, whadda you wan'?" Then a squint and a longer look. "Ahh yeah, yeah, yeah, it's you. Hah. Hey, Bobby, Bob. Ahh, God, boy. Yer back again, uh? Yeah, yeah lookit you."

He chanted his way around the counter with a heavy hoarse voice. He came around with a dirty spotted apron around his waist, head nodding, repeating his name over and over. Then Bob held him and pulled the old man to him in a strong affectionate embrace that he had not thought about. He held him and blinked back something like tears, trying to speak to him.

"Frank. You've been here a long time. How long you been here, Frank? How are you? Everything all right? Are you all right, now?"

Frank nodded, head bouncing in short jerky nods, his eyes light under the heavy bushy brows that were brown and white, his hair thick and dirty with a lot of grey now. He was wearing an old yellow shirt and blue pants. "You good, Bobby, you good."

Then the old man cried with little rocky sobs and Bob held him. "It's been a long time, Frank. The place looks the same. You still makin' good coffee?"

"I'm good. Yeah, they cuttin' me up, but I'm good. 'Ey shoulna did it to you, them other guys. It was okay, but not you." He grinned.

"Why not me?"

"Nahh, nahh. Not you."

"Who's cuttin' you up? Why?"

"Ahh, 'em doctors up in Knickerbocker. 'ey think I'm dyin'. I ain't."

"Whadda you mean, Frank? What's the matter?"

"Cancer. Ah, it didn't kill John Wayne. It ain't killin' me."

"John Wayne."

"Yeah. 'at's right. It didn't kill him, I ain't gonna die."

Bob was not sure he was still following the conversation. "Frank, you got cancer?"

The old man's hand went to his throat. "Ahh, they don' know nothin'. First 'ey cuttin' my throat. Now 'ey thinkin it's in my lungs. Ahh, they don' know what in hell 'eyre talkin about. They wanna cut my asshole out, too."

"Hell, don't sweat it. Can't kill a cowboy, it sure as hell ain't killin' you."

The old man beamed. "Hey, yeah."

"When do you have to go back to see them?"

"Ah, I ain't. They wanna keep me awhile."

"Where's everybody? Why's the place empty for?"

"Nah, they don't come in no more. Only junkies

what's left. Everybody inna whole neighborhood's usin' junk, Bobby, even the girls. Ahh, it ain't no good, no more kids, only junkies. That Jimmy. What's a matter with that kid?"

"I don't know, Frank."

"Ahh, fer Christ sakes; goin' an takin' an O. D. wid Mary."

"Mary? Was Mary there?"

"Yeah, yeah. She's inna bug house now."

"Why? What happened to her?"

"Ahh, she tried to take a hop outta a police station winda, cryin' about bein' a little girl again. Ahh, fer Christ sakes; 'ey all belong inna bug house."

"Mm, yeah. What about Shoulders, Frank? Where is she?"

The old man turned away. "She ain't no junkie."

Bob's grin was quick. "I know."

The old man turned back to him. "I dunno, Bob. She's a good kid but ..."

"Frank, I don't want you tellin' me nothin', just where she is."

"No, no. I don't mean 'at there what you think. She's a good kid." The old man's hand went to his head. "Jus' kinda, yuh know, lightheaded, cause she's scared a everything."

"Yeah. Have you seen her?"

"No. Nah, she don't come down here no more. I don't know where she lives. She got her own place down by Alice an' Dicky. They got married you know?"

"Oh?"

"Yeah, that Alice, she's some kid. Nancy, she hangs around with her still."

"You know where Alice lives?"

"No. No, you gotta call 'er mother. She'll tell you. Hey, Bobby. I mean, you an' that kid, you two belong together."

"Mm. What happened to Sully?"

The old man started walking toward the back. Bob followed. The old man sat in a booth, his palms flat on the table before him.

"It's bad business what 'ey did to him, Bobby."

"Yeah."

"They sen' 'im to a hospital out in Brooklyn. Dey cut 'is head open. A nurse tole his mother later on she should sue." The old man rubbed his face. "His ol' lady don' wanna sue. What for now? They cut it outta him, an' is brains wid it. His ol' lady don' wanna make no money on somethin' like that. She can't, any-way. Them doctors are gonna take care a each other. Whadda you gonna do, Bob?"

Bob looked down at the table he had bought from the old man when they had been new. The old man said, as Bob saw Nancy's name scratched out, "That was Jim. He was in one day. He cut it out."

"Mm."

"He was a good guy, kinda a funny guy. Hey, Bobby, you ain't gonna use none a that shit, huh?"

"No."

"Yeah. Bobby, you know, when I go, I mean, you'll

come to my funeral, huh? There ain't nobody much around. I don' wanna die by myself."

He turned to him, grinning. "What are you talkin' about, you ol' bastard. You'll bury me."

"No. Don' say that. Jim said that, too. You gotta promise me you an' 'at kid'll be there."

"Nancy?"

"Yeah."

"We'll be there, Frank."

"Yeah, I knew you would. You're good people, Bob."

He went into the phone booth and dialed Mrs. Mallory's number. He was in the middle of wondering whether she was home when the phone was picked up.

"Hello? Who is this?"

"Hi, babe. How've you been?"

"Fine ..."

There was hesitation, he heard her breathe then, "Ah, wait a minute. Let me guess. I hope to God I'm right."

She whispered it and he wished he did not feel the emotion he felt when he heard his name.

"Bob?"

He answered gruffly, quickly.

"You win. How's things?"

"I don't know yet. I'm trying to think of something bitchy or sexy to say so my daughter will be proud of me. Are you all right? I'm sorry, that's all I can come up with."

"Yeah, yeah, I'm good. Where's Nancy, Mom?"

"I don't know her address. Alice has it. Go see Alice, Bob."

"I will. Give me her address. I don't know where they're livin'."

He wrote Alice's address down, then left, saying goodbye to the old man and his death, promising to see him again soon, almost running away. He was afraid of the reception he felt he would receive from Alice, worse than he had gone through. He did not want to hear about friends dying, dead and bugged, because he did not feel a relation with them any longer. He put off going to see her, walking along the river, dropping Nancy's letters there, ripping them into small pieces because he knew she would want him to do that, he watched them float away.

Later, when he could breathe better, he started for Alice's apartment.

The marble stairs he walked up were cool and dark. He felt relieved as soon as he entered the hall. He climbed the three flights slowly. Knocking on the door, he heard her voice from deep in the apartment somewhere calling, "Come on in! It's open."

He walked into the tan and white kitchen that seemed comfortable and clean, leaning against the door he just closed, looking at the doorway across the room that had no door, waiting. He heard her voice become closer as she said, "Who's in my house? I'll be right there. Wait a minute."

He dropped his suit jacket across a chair back, wiped his brow and hands.

"I'll be with you ..."

She came through the door, clean and crisp in a starched house dress that had to be put on while wet, her hair falling down informally to her shoulders. He laughed softly.

She grinned. "Hi. Uh, Bobby!"

"Mm. I'm hot, dry as hell. Gimme something to drink. Should I say please? You look good. You haven't changed."

She shook her head, as if clearing it, then laughed high, almost cracking.

"You ... You've been gone a hell of a long time. Where the hell've you been?"

"I learned a new word; rusticating. How's that sound? Come over here, Alice."

She ran to him with tears. They embraced as if lovers, holding one another, afraid to let go. Later, when they loosened, she whispered.

"Lookit you. You look beautiful. You dumb bastard, you have troubles. Why the hell didn't you write her? You should have at least written. She would have waited. She's waitin' but ... Bobby, she doesn't even know it. You should have written to her." The last she said flatly, with a feminine practicality.

"Where is she?"

"She has her own apartment. She's working now, She'll be home at six. Let me call her at work for you."

"No, I ... Christ, I'm shaking. Don't call her. I'll see her when she comes home."

She felt the trembling of his shoulders and arms tightening her grip around him. "Bobby, Bob. You do so many things so hard. You could have written the poor bitch. She would be right here now. Sometimes you're awful ignorant. Why did you take the chance you did with her? You damned near lost her."

"Yeah, I had to do it the way it was."

"Crazy Bobby. Yes, you are crazy. We all are. She has sleeping pills, a lot of them. Take them away from her."

"Mm."

He closed his eyes and buried his face in her hair. They stood that way for almost five minutes, then they sat down, and when they saw each other they both laughed, because there was a minute the whole world was still naked and clear and they still possessed a degree of understanding. So they laughed.

After, she remembered he was hot and dry so she swung to the refrigerator and came out with a pitcher of lemonade because there was nothing else except gin and scotch and she remembered he disliked both, so he drank unsweetened lemonade. She did too, though she did not know why, because any other time she would have sweetened it. She gobbled him up with her eyes, staring at him so hard he became self-conscious.

He smiled. "I feel lightheaded. I got ... I have so much, what? Tension, I guess. How is she, Alice?

Don't tell me anything but, I don't know, how she is, that's all."

She pressed her lips together, but her eyes, try as she might, were laughing.

"She is fat. Wow, is she! What an ass she's got now, and two teeth are missing. She doesn't take such good care of herself."

His small grin stopped her.

"Oh hell, Bobby, even more beautiful than when you left; a lot more scared, I think. I could call her, tell her someone was dead or something, tell her to hurry up home. Bobby?"

"Mm."

"You still mm, huh?"

"Yeah. Hell, more than I used to. Don't call her. I'll wait."

"Is that all you want to know about her, what she looks like?"

"She'll tell me whatever she wants."

Angrily, "Well, be careful. She'll tell you every un-virtuous thought that ever popped into her prudish skull."

He laughed then. It seemed like a helpless laugh. Alice had never heard anything like it before. It fright-ened her the same as a look had that Nancy had given her once. It frightened and angered her because she knew no reason. Still, she wouldn't ask him why be-cause she was afraid the same as she had been with Nancy, she was afraid she might be told.

"Stop it. Are you going to marry her?"

"I knew it, tell her I said so."

His eyes jumped over to hers.

"What, I'm not here, slim? What did you just say?"

Smiling, relieved. "Nothing, just tell her I knew it."

The four keys were lying in his palm flatly, two lying on one, another away near the tips of his fingers. They seemed to gleam with an outlandish meaning and were etched there on his fingers and palms with unearthly ridiculous reality.

All of their admitted and omitted dreams were now puffs of childish thoughts, wishes. They were sloppily wrapped in longings that were unattainable and to them now, long gone. Now it was that he had to leave them, step into a reality where protest fell on long immune ears that could hear nothing and pain could not be endured simply because eventually it would go away, and he could, within them both, no longer contend with. The romanticism had faded and bleached. There were no elixirs, it was all damned and so had to be this way.

He opened the door, stepping in, away from the hot sun that was still beaming down. Then he heard a woman call, asking him to hold the door for her because she had packages.

He did. She thanked him. She was old and wore fur around her neck in summer. She smelled of Chanel Number Five and wore blue beads. He nodded a welcome. Climbing the stairs without hesitating, he put the keys in the locks and turned them.

She was there when he entered. He saw her

immediately, sitting on the sofa that turned into a bed, brushing her hair without any interest because she was tired of being alone and was uncomfortable because of the weather. She felt perspiration forming at her temples and upper lip. She was wearing a half-slip and bra. They were whitish blue. Her eyes were dark. She had smiled when he entered because she thought he was Alice since he had used her keys. Then the brush fell and she whimpered and he began to feel again.

"Oh, no. You!" She bent, her hand blindly searching for the fallen brush, her wide purple eyes that were very wide, on him.

"Go away. You must. Please?"

Her hand stopped still, she brought her body up to a sitting position, her eyes on him still. They were fantastically wide.

"You've got to go, Bobby. I'm different ... not like I was. I'm afraid of you now. Go away, please. You waited too long."

He was standing close then. The keys were still in the door that was opened. He held her hand that was up in front of her as if warding him off. She stared at that rather than his face. She knew she was speaking yet having no control over what she was saying or knowing what it was she was saying.

"I have my ring on, the one you gave me. I'm going home, my mother's house. Please go away, Bobby. Please."

She placed her other hand on the one he was

holding loosely, as if going to help it escape from him. But she did not. She placed it on top and her head, fell on those and she cried.

"You don't want me anymore, do you? I'm not that way anymore, because I've changed. I don't want to, Bobby, I'm afraid now. We were wrong. Please don't."

He sat beside her, because if he didn't he would have fallen, because he was feeling all the emotions that had left him blank a while ago. He brought her closer to him, whispering to her, she sighed.

"Yeah, oh, yes that's what I want to, Bobby, now I do. Oh you, you're afraid too, aren't you?"

He nodded and she screamed, delighted.

"I have them, Bobby. I knew you would come. You need me now, because you're afraid. Bob, let's. I'm not afraid, not now."

Chapter 19

Bricks in a Wall

His hands were in his pockets as he stared at the brick wall five feet away from the window. He stared at the bricks and continued staring until he could not see them any longer. They were nothing, not even inanimate pieces of clay and straw, no sand and cement between, no rivers and jails no bridges and explanations because there were no reasons.

He decided to let her alone, let her stay. She did not belong here. She would recall it someday as an adventure, he could recall her someday when it was over, like a shadow only rarely coming to life with her pulchritude, luster, naked naivete.

He turned away from the glass tank and the simple schoolboy gesture that was its connotation. He was afraid he would hurl it through the window if he saw it.

"Ohhh, Christ."

He banged his shoulder against the wall and stayed there. It was dark, the sun was gone, two days had gone, she had come and gone, had been informed of his being in jail and left.

That was all. Let her go. Stop thinking of her, not to think of the way she ... Not then, there had been too much elegance in her movement, too much loveliness in her desire.

He opened the door and banged down the stairs. They were wood, they were dark, they were narrow stairs and she was afraid of them. That's why she whimpered when he pounded down so unexpectedly. She did not know it was him until he was just two steps away.

He stood still, holding the bannister and the wall, his mouth opened, his body stiff as if he were struck dumb.

She flung her arms around him, crying her eyes out in his stomach.

His hands touched her hair. He could no longer stand so he sat on the stairs and listened to her cry, because that was the only sound he could understand then.

He spoke hesitantly, holding her tight now, because he was afraid she might evaporate into an ugly dream.

"Nancy, ahh. Come on, kid. That's enough. No more. Shh, don't cry."

She was not about to let him go because she was afraid he might evaporate into a wish. She croaked, because she was hoarse, because she had been crying so long.

"You're here?"

"Yeah, I'm here. Let's go upstairs. I, aw, Nancy I thought you were gone. Nancy, Nancy."

Later, they finally wound their way up the stairs and into the room. They sat on the bed in the dark, holding one another, looking at one another, trying to carry on a conversation with mumbles grunts and half words. They would not let go of one another. When they tired of sitting, they stretched out across the bed. She whimpered and groaned, cried and bit his arm. He tried not to cry, because she was only another broad, another piece of ass. But that didn't work long. He held her and had a hard time finding breath.

Daylight came and they went to sleep. She kept waiting to see if he were alright and still there. He kept waking to see if she were there. That would have gone on forever, but they caught one another at it and stayed awake awhile, then undressed and slept.

Chapter 20

Overpay

The young man beside her was her husband. They had been married three years.

She had assumed she loved him then, now she loved no one. Three years ago she had not used narcotics, hardly heard of it. Six months after they were married, Georgie had introduced her to heroin. He had not offered it to her, just used it in her presence continually. The introduction had been slow, over a two-month span of time. Ellen accepted the wonderful dark, seemingly, safe world of heroin. The price of her life that night could be, and was, a five-dollar envelope of safe, dark white refuge.

Georgie did not think much of his wife, did not care whether she found a way of gaining the two dollars she needed for the purchase of one of the envelopes of heroin he had hidden in the hall of the building they were standing. He had already made eight sales; seven more and he would have enough to buy more. But then he would have to use three or four himself, so he would have to sell eleven more. He liked the number eleven. From seven he had gone to eleven. Then tomorrow morning he would purchase a new supply.

About Ellen, he thought, "I gotta worry about me, can't worry about no strung-out pig like her. Favors she wants, but when I got popped, what'd she do? Nothin; went out and hustled to get her bread. She got high all the time I was in the joint. Now frig her. Let her go out an' hustle some more. She wants my smack, she better have bread."

He watched Cory come up to the stoop with a wide grin. He knew he had another sale, maybe two. Cory always had money. He used heroin only on weekends. During the week he worked so Cory always had money and his voice was loud and Georgie knew he had been drinking, which was better.

"Hey man, whadda ya say?"

He took the extended hand, not shaking it, grasping it lightly and letting it fall. He smiled wider.

"Hey, ace. What's happenin'? Lookin' to cop?"

Cory's eyes moved quickly to Ellen, saw her looking at him hopefully and shrugged.

"I don't know. You dealin?"

"Yeah."

He saw the look, turning speaking disdainfully to her.

"Why don't you make it? Nobody's gonna turn you on."

Her eyes took them both in, one then the other, without expression. Then they closed and she walked away, hands deep in her coat pockets, shoulders hunched. She walked quietly.

Cory and Georgie talked while Georgie nodded a few times, then went into the hall a few minutes, later emerged. Cory looked around nervously, then walked along behind him.

They crossed the street, turned the corner, then into an apartment building halfway down the street. Inside the hall, Georgie bent, his hand going under the steaming spitting radiator, taking out a dirty bulk wrapped in a grey spotted handkerchief.

They both climbed the five flights of stairs to the roof landing. The landing on the top floor was dark. They could make out the metal-jacketed door that led to the roof. Georgie sat on the stairs, unwrapping the handkerchief. The light from the landing below just reached his hands.

Cory slipped off his coat and suit jacket, folded them over the banister. Unbuckling the belt from around his waist, he whispered very softly, "I'm first."

Georgie's head nodded as he carefully tore a piece of the white edging from a dollar bill. A glass eye dropped with a baby's rubber nipple fastened to the end by thread wrapped many times around to hold it secure. A bright small chrome needle lay next to a book of matches and an aspirin bottle containing only water next to that.

Cory rolled his sleeve up, fastening his belt around his biceps tightly. The veins in his arms stood out in thick dark lines. Still he kept clenching and unclenching his hand, moving his arm at the elbow repeatedly. Georgie opened the two small envelopes of heroin, peeling the cellophane cape, then discarded the envelope after extracting another and sniffing at it. The second had no tape. He unfolded it carefully, tapping it with his finger, until all the white powder was all in one corner. He glanced at Cory for a moment whispering, "I give a good count, lots a doogee, uh?"

Cory whispered, "Yeah, yeah. Hurry up."

Georgie emptied the contents of the bag into a bottle cap no larger than a quarter, then the other. He took off his shoe. From behind the tongue he ripped a small piece of cotton. Then he uncapped the aspirin bottle. Dipping the strip of dollar bill in the water, he folded it around the neck of the eye dropper, securing the needle by forcing it on tightly. He placed the tip of the needle in the aspirin bottle. Drawing up some water, he let it run out in an unbroken line smiling, speaking almost normally.

"Clean, good wares, eh?"

Cory was crouched down close to him. "Shhh. Yeah, come on. Cook up."

Georgie drew up water in the eye dropper, filling it to just under the edge of the rubber nipple, then let it run slowly into the cap, melting the white pile of powder. He lit four matches. Holding the bottle cap with his thumb and index finger he held the matches close, holding the bottle cap on an angle so the direct heat would not burn his fingers. The water and powder bubbled quickly.

He placed the cap on the step above him. No longer was white powder to be seen, just water colored liquid. He dropped the piece of cotton that he had taken from his shoe and rolled it into a tight ball. With the needle tip placed in the center of the cotton, he drew up all the liquid. Squeezing half back, he handed the needle and eye dropper to Cory, who sat on the step, watching as if hypnotized.

The religious sensual ritual went on as Cory placed his upper arm on his knee to hold the belt in place and held the long thin bump that was his vein. Holding the glass eye dropper with his thumb and forefinger, he tapped with quick jerky movements of his index finger at the top of the baby's nipple. Georgie watched as the needle went under the skin then seemed to find a hollow spot and sunk with ease, barely a movement. His eyes came up to Cory's face and he whispered, "You got it, ace. You got a hit."

Cory whispered back quickly and excitedly, "Yeah, I know. Loosen the belt."

Georgie's hand went to the belt around Cory's arm as Cory moved his knee from under it. The thin thermometer red line floated up the liquid in the eye-dropper. Cory squeezed it and the liquid disappeared beyond the needle in his skin. He relaxed his fingers and blood flowed back in the eyedropper, it looked now like all blood. Georgie whispered.

"Okay, come on. Don't boot. Fer Chrissakes, I wanna get off, too."

Twice again, Cory let the blood run out then back.

Then he handed the empty eyedropper to Georgie. He sank the needle in the water of the aspirin bottle, then drew up and squirted it back out, then the remaining liquid in the bottle cap. He wrapped the belt around his arm and repeated much the same ritual as Cory. Completed, he rinsed the needle and eyedropper in the water of the aspirin bottle and wrapped them with the bottle and cap in the dirty handkerchief.

Cory went out on the roof and vomited as he did each time he used narcotics.

They walked down the stairs, slower now, eyes bright, pointed, both quiet after asking each other how they felt and assuring one another that they were very high and it was good stuff. Silent heat played hell at the back of their brains, soft sleepy purple.

They walked slowly to Nick's restaurant around the corner. Nick was a fat old Puerto Rican with a wide flat mustache who mostly did not like anyone. He was behind the wooden counter in the rear. Booths lined the restaurant and some were occupied.

Both Georgie and Cory nodded to three men in a booth toward the front, waiting for a booth about half-way. They sat on either side of the table, not speaking as if very sleepy, their heads nodding.

Robby walked in a while later. He could not sleep again and wanted a cup of coffee. It was late. Nick's was the only restaurant open. He saw Georgie and Cory, noted they were trance-like, and walked to the counter, saying, "Good morning," to Nick, who grunted, poured him a cup of coffee.

He ordered a piece of pie and sat in a booth, glancing at his watch and grinning as he pictured waking Jean now at five o'clock in the morning. He knew how much she loved sleep on weekends. Even at eight he would have trouble waking her, and she would be growling for two hours after. But they were going skiing, and she would have to get up if he had to carry her.

Robby was a pleasant person, with light hair and broad features that were pleasant. He most always had a smile on his pleasant face. He had grown up with Georgie and Cory, but did not like what either of them were, and felt nothing for them but some form of understanding that was not complete in him yet. Toward Ellen, he felt a sad complete form of pity. Before entering he had made sure she was not here. Sometimes seeing her hurt him, touched something in him that for days he would have her on his mind.

Ellen was not beautiful. She was pretty, she was attractive, her short red hair demanded attraction. Her body was not ravishing. It could be sexy, he supposed. If she would wear the right clothes, it would help. But Ellen's eyes seemed to express what she felt how, about everything except her need and passion for drugs. They were devoid of life, as vacant as the truly insane, without life. The brown eyes that he could remember could look so frankly at you when she spoke no longer did. They no longer gave a damn.

Once, in some kind of idealistic dream, he thought of locking her away somewhere, to help her. No one cared; he would. Now, he knew better and it was gone. So many in this neighborhood were just that way; too many rooms. Now he thought of Jean and tried never of Ellen.

A thin man came in, wearing a jacket, and tapped Georgie's shoulder. He looked up without speaking. The man showed him a ten dollar bill. He said to Cory, "Right back, ace," then walked out, the thin man following.

A half hour later, Georgie came back, set in the same seat. His head began the repetitious nodding. Men and women came in. The next hour, motioning, nodding, touching, somehow signaling him. Each time Georgie got up and left with them.

She had never done it this way, never so cheaply, never for so little, never here in a hall on the ground floor behind stairs. She knew it was going to hurt her now but then without too much pain. She lay on her back on the cold marble small-diamanded floor. She did not remove her coat, only unbuttoning it. Her skirt was above her waist, underpants in her pocket, her legs bent at the knees, spread wide. She smelled herself but did not care. Neither would he, she thought. The tall fat negro in his late forties held his erect penis in his hand. He was very drunk, and she knew would be a long time in attaining his climax, if he would. Her eyes were closed as her hand directed him into her.

Robby watched as a young man came up to Georgie, the young woman he had left standing alone in the front of the restaurant. He could not hear what was said, only saw Georgie shake his head once, then shrug his shoulders and leave with him, the young woman following. He went and ordered another cup of coffee. Then it was after seven and he was going to start for Jean's house soon and damned himself for not going to the car sooner as his heart jerked and his stomach tightened.

Ellen walked into the restaurant slowly. She looked worse, worse than he had ever seen her before. He wished with emotion that came hard and alien, yet seemed always have been there. He wished clumsily for a way, something to help her. She stood next to Georgie, who looked up. They were not as high now. Soon they would use more.

She spoke softly. "Georgie, I got it, like the bread. Gimme a bag. I'm dyin'."

He spoke flatly without feeling. "You got a pound? Like all I got left is a ten-dollar bag. You in trouble, babe."

Ellen could not believe it. She knew down deep somewhere within her how disgusting she felt herself to be and how hypocritical. She hated Georgie fully while at the same time forgiving him.

But then, she was a condemned soul for that moment, for that whole moment when her eyes went round the small dirty restaurant without seeing it. Robby seeing her, the tears starting to fall from her eyes, the laughter of Georgie and Cory when they saw them and the one-dollar bills, crunched and squashed so they almost formed a perfect ball, lying in the center of the table that divided the seats.

It appeared to him then that the world Ellen inhabited now became for her one large empty vacuum that rushed down, and with all its deliberate might, crushed her. The loud deriding laughter of Cory and Georgie were her only requiem.

He sat at the table, unable to comprehend completely the look he saw on her face, as if all the cruelty in the whole world were there, personified in that expression of bewildered helplessness and allowed wanton cruelty for that one long blink of time. His stomach felt as if it were going to suffocate with his near comprehension of that one stark moment numbed frozen in his time.

Then Ellen's eyes gazed at the center of the table as if to see why her money was not good or enough. His shoulders started shaking, trembling slightly just beneath the skin, afraid now of all he would like to do to all of the politicians who allowed this and ignored her and this one moment that was allowed to happen to this one person. Then he waited to the table, placing a ten-dollar bill ahead of the balled up five that almost formed a ball. He took the ball and handed it to Ellen, who took it only from reflex because she was not there now.

"Give her that bag."

Georgie looked up, about to smile, but it died as he slid the envelope of dope across. Robby looked at

Ellen, who looked at the envelope for a half a second, then snatched it.

"Thank you ... Like, thanks." Then she walked out.

Robby never understood what he had done, whether good or cruel.

He looked at Georgie and Cory as if for help, then turned and walked out.

Jean would understand some of it, he would tell her someday, after Ellen died, soon. And after that, he would be able to live with himself. It would be soon.

Chapter 21

Hurry Home

The fourteenth of July that year was warm and pleasant. Adlai Stevenson died in London, two kids in Queens were murdered when no one was looking, and the day before, a chaplain at West Point died. Lollypops started growing again somewhere.

He walked out onto the dark roof, standing motionless, close to the iron rods that were for clotheslines to be strung on. He peered about cautiously for a full five minutes. He stood there, not moving. Then, sure no one was on the roof, he cut the four clotheslines of varied strengths and thicknesses from number eights to number twelves. The last refused to part with the small penknife's cutting. He growled, "Aw, come on. Come on. Come on, you son of a bitch, break will ya? Come on, huh? Please, come on."

It was wire-cored and finally parted, as if in answer to his plea of the last part of the growl that ended in a whine. He held them near the end, the four lines, and let them fall over the front of the building to the fire escape below. Then he wrapped the end he was holding around a vent pipe twice, and tied a bulky knot.

He looked over the building to the street below. It was deserted, only near the far end, a man was walking a dog in the opposite direction. Nerves played hell in him, because he was frightened while he wondered what would happen if he could not hold his own weight. But desperation overtook the fright, and he moved over the edging of the roof, grasped the rope in sweaty hands, and slid down. Using only his hands and arms rather than helping with his legs, he slid quickly to the fire escape, his fingers and palms burning. Holding his hands under his arms, he leaned against the building, praying feverishly to someone, asking that the people in the apartment on the top floor had not heard him.

He waited awhile, breathing softly, to hear every sound. Rubbing his lands slowly, gently, then quietly, he made his way down the steel steps. On the floor below, he went to the window on his right without hesitation. He tried to lift it. The apartment was dark inside. He could see nothing, except the twist latch on the window that was preventing it from opening.

Taking the butter knife from his waist, he slipped it between the upper and lower parts of the window between the latch three times and the window was unlocked. He lifted it slowly, hearing a low growling. From the intensity and sound of it, he was sure it was a small dog. He was just as sure the apartment was unoccupied other than the dog. He climbed in, closing the window after him. The dog, a small brown Pekinese, yapped angrily and made half a charge at him. He tried speaking soothingly. "Shhh, shhh, fella. Come on, take it easy. I ain't gonna bother you."

The dog made another charge, halting a scant two inches from him, warning him for the last time to leave.

"Aw, for Christ sake. There, idiot." He kicked savagely, catching the dog on the side and lifting him, sending him across the room, yipping in pain, slamming into the wall, then lay gasping, later wailing low.

This was a bedroom he'd let himself into. He went and felt for a bureau. His eyes accustomed now to the dark, he could make out objects around him. He searched carefully, unhurried. Finding a suitcase, he began packing things that he would sell quickly; two watches, a man's and a woman's. The man's did not work. Some assorted jewelry, most worthless, but a seven-hundred-dollar diamond ring. He did not know this and would not. Two cameras, a tape recorder, and a portable typewriter.

In the next room, obviously a child's, he found a three-foot-high bank of plaster, molded to an elephant's form, pink with a bright pink bow around its neck. He could not lift it from the dresser top.

He went over to the bed. Ripping the blankets from it, he placed them around the bank. Feeling the lamp that was beside the bank to be heavy and steel, he snapped the cord from the wall and smashed the blanket-wrapped bank. It crumbled with the blow.

He unwrapped the blankets, there was a great pile of change, crumbled plaster and paper money. He picked the paper money out, throwing the plaster chips on the bed. He took the suitcase to the other room and poured the change in. He snapped the case closed and walked out the door. It was all he could carry, and, he felt, enough.

He went down the stairs neither fast nor slow. At the same pace, he walked two blocks to the heavier trafficked cross street, hailed a cab and gave him an address.

He counted the paper money. There were three tens —that surprised him— two fives and eleven ones. Two blocks from the Greek's, he left the cab. Through this neighborhood, he walked quickly, chanting.

"Slow down, come on, man. You'll blow it. You're movin' too fast. Oh, man, don't lettem bust me. Come on, not after I'm almost there. It's just like you to do that. Please don' do it. Let me get to the Greek's. Come on, please?"

He walked down the nine steps to the Greek's store that was located below street level. The Greek was large and fat. All his features were heavy and he had dark shadows under his eyes even in sunlight. The skin on his face was pockmarked and scarred. The store was very small, tightly packed with racks of clothing with hand-painted paper signs with prices marked and in assured premise that all were bargain; most really were. There was no counter, only a cash register hidden behind high-piled boxes of women's shoes that were bargains, too.

When the Greek saw him, he walked behind some boxes where the sink was, where the water was dripping.

"What you got for me, Bill?"

He lay the suitcase on the floor, snapping it opened. "Look it over. Hurry, huh? I'm sick."

The Greek knelt, handling each object, looking carefully, then glancing up at him. "What about the coins?"

"Count them, weigh them, do something. I can't use them that way. Hurry up, huh?"

"I don't know, fella. Take me a long time to off this here stuff. Tell you what I'll do."

"Yeah, yeah."

He grunted to a standing position, breathing deep as he said, "I'll give you sixty dollars for the lot."

"No, you won't."

He smiled evenly. "Take it easy, take it easy. Look, you're sick. You can't off them no place else tonight. An' if you do, you won't make any more. Listen, if I get more on the stuff, I'll give you more. How's that sound?"

"Like I'm getting' screwed. Gimme the bread."

He counted out six tens from a large folded wad in his pocket.

"Now, don't worry. If I get more, you get more. You too good a boy to lose in steady."

"Gimme the money."

The Greek handed him the bills and he turned and walked out. Again, he hailed a cab.

At Eighth Avenue, he started walking slowly. At One-hundred-thirty-second Street, he saw Calvin, a slim, medium-sized Negro, who was standing alone beside a bar and grill. He hardly nodded his eyes, going away from him. When they saw him, they looked through him as if he were not there. Then he turned and went into the building that was beside the bar.

He walked two houses past, then climbed the stoop and hurried up the six flights of stairs to the roof. On the roof landing, he snapped the latch of the door, then stood silently trying not to breath, listening for footsteps he dreaded behind him, praying to something that he would not. After five minutes, he went out onto the roof, crossed two until he was standing beside Calvin. They whispered.

"Billy boy. Man, it's hot down here. You'll pull my cover, you keep comin' down like ya do."

"Yeah."

"Like, white studs gotta stay outta the valley for awhile. You call me, ace. I'll come to your place."

"I couldn't. I needed it right away. Joany's sick. So am I. You got smack on you?"

"How much you want?"

"Twelve."

"Oh, sheet, no. Man, I only got two bags on me. Come on down the pad."

"I got the three tens I owe you."

As Calvin walked down the stairs, he held his finger to his lips, smiling and nodding.

They went into an apartment on the third floor. The hall they entered was long, dark and narrow. There was a smell there that he could not identify, similar to Joany, he had smelled all of his life. At the first doorway of the long hall, Calvin motioned him to enter his bedroom. It was small and dimly lit. The double bed that Calvin flopped on filled half the room. To Bill, it seemed it would be dirty if the light were stronger, yet it seemed safe.

"Hey Billy, like ace, I know you good for the cash. You sure you wan twelve? That's a big load for a white stud to be carryin' around here."

"Same as one, ace. If I get busted for one, I might as well take a pop for twelve."

Calvin chuckled, reaching under the bed. A moment later, holding a tightly wrapped bundle of five-dollar envelopes of heroin in his hand, he counted out twelve and handed them to him.

"You wanna get off 'fore you go? I'm gonna."

"No, Joany's waitin'. Tole her I'd hurry up if I could."

"Yeah, but if you get busted, at least you're straight."

"Naw, she's waitin'."

"I'm turnin' you on. Like, man, you can have my stuff." He smiled, shortly counting out ninety dollars.

"I'll remember that when I'm sick, here."

Calvin shook his head, taking the money. "Man,

Bill. You're crazy. Where you gonna carry it?" He took a red rubber balloon from his pocket. "Put it up high enough. Maybe they won't find it."

"Yeah, sure. Maybe, but they will."

He unbuckled his belt after inserting the envelopes in the balloon. His hand behind him, he bent slightly.

"You better be careful, buddy. You put it up too high and you ain't never gonna get it back out. Some doctor will cut you open an' get it."

"I gotta get it to my place."

Leaving Calvin as he was preparing his heroin, he went over the roofs again, down the stairs and into the side streets, then into a park. Feeling almost safe now, few of the lampposts were working and it was very dark. He stooped at a bench and held the wooden plank, shivering a "Grrr" sound. "Wait, wait, please. Wait. Wait, will ya wait?"

He tried, but the hot cold nauseous gritty feeling compelled him to sit. It was cold and it was hot and the park was moving sickeningly. Then it started to fade before it got worse and he went on. Coming out of the park after climbing stairs, he crossed a street, then through the oval softball field across another street alongside Lewisohn Stadium and out to Amsterdam Avenue, he followed Amsterdam down a block, turning on One-hundred-thirty-fifth Street.

He hurried to the building where he and his wife Joan shared a three-room apartment. Once up to the second floor, he snapped the heavy police lock on the door, placing the lock to the floor, he called.

"Okay, babe. I scored. Come on."

Then he went into the bathroom that was on the other side of the kitchen he had just entered. He left the door open and heard her say, "What? I didn't hear you. What did you say?"

It was there in her voice, the inevitable warning of impending cruelty that forecast disaster. He slammed the door shut behind him, flipping the weak wire latch lock into its eye. Then he flushed the toilet twice before the two plainclothes policemen banged the door against the wall and stood before him.

"You think you're pretty smart, don't you, you son of a bitch?"

He was pale, his body was shaking visibly as he whined, "Come on, Carlson. I didn't have nothin'. I'm just sick."

The short stocky policeman named Carlson advanced on his after spying over his shoulder to his partner.

"Look under the tab. Look all over. This punk is a cutey."

The tall red-haired policeman bent without comment. Bill held his hands up as Carlson searched and Joany watched. He gave up after searching him half-heartedly, asking him to take off his shoes, socks, turn down his cuffs, then socked him, hitting solidly in the pit of his stomach and somewhere in his head, way back. Down.

He heard Joan scream, "Oh, God. Don't hit him in the stomach."

Then he let himself fall, gasping involuntarily, trying not to hear anything, not to believe that the pain
that was in him was his. Then maybe they would go
away. They would, did, after searching and disgustedly
watching Joan try to administer to him with a wet
towel.

He whispered later, "The door, the door. Lock it.
Hurry up. Come on, hurry up."

Joan left him, locking the door, coming back, kneeling beside him.

"Billy, I'm sorry. I forgot to lock it after you left.
They just walked in."

"Yeah, yeah. Don't worry. Whadja do with the
wares?"

"They're still here. They didn't find them. I told you
they never would in that place."

"Go get them."

"Why?"

"Will you get them?"

He was screaming and spitting in the towel. She
went to the kitchen, using a chair, she reached up,
took away a small chunk of plaster from the wall, and
extracted a needle, eyedrop, with a small baby's nipple
attached, then went back to the bathroom.

"Are you spitting blood? How's your belly?"

"It's alright. Don't worry."

His pants were off. He slowly extracted the balloon
from his rectum, unfolded it and handed the envelopes to her.

She watched, wide-eyed. "You didn't flush them?"

"Hell, no! Too much trouble. Cook up."

"Alright. Billy, are you sure you're alright?"

"Yeah. Come on."

She adjusted the needle to the eyedropper and went to the kitchen for a spoon after the powder had boiled. She drew it into the glass eyedropper, handing it to him.

"No, no. Goddamn it, will you get off."

"No, you went through so much. Honey, please."

"Will you get off?"

She held the sleeve of her blouse in her teeth. Inserting the needle in her vein, she mixed blood with water, allowed that to run into her, then cleaned the eyedropper under the water of the sink, emptied another envelope of powder onto the spoon, added water, holding the matches until it boiled, then drew it all into the needle.

Kneeling by him, she held his belt that he had wrapped around his arm. He still had the towel is his mouth, still spitting. She inserted the needle in his arm. He relaxed, moaning, "Oh, yeah, better. That's better."

His hand went to her shoulder, bringing her closer to him, his lips at her neck as he was crying, "We made it, Joany. Goddam them, we made it."

Chapter 22

A Mountain Stream

It was a warm muggy morning that would become hot later, and sticky. He was frowning, not just because he felt uncomfortable, but because he would not see Nancy until later that night. He was frowning because it was a stupid way to feel and he knew it but could do nothing about it.

He was frowning because he felt they were wasting time, a thing they had too little of. When he glared up at the El that roared overhead, there was nothing but anger in his eyes.

Jimmy came walking along in a gawky trot, smiling a lopsided grin. "Whadda ya say, ace? Where's your ole lady?"

"Home."

"Man it's hot. I'm sweatin' already. Let's go swimmin'."

"Where?"

"Down a river."

"No."

"Why not?"

"I don' feel like it."

"Whadda you gonna do?"

He pointed. "I'm gonna go over an' sit on that stoop."

He started walking, Jimmy alongside him, speaking, "Aw, come on. Tippy, Sully an' Charley are goin'."

Bob sat. "You go, I don't feel like it."

"Nahh, I don' wanna go wit out you. Come on."

"Jazz, don't start. I said I didn't feel like it."

"Aw, how come you're so touchy about everything lately?"

"I'm not, ace. I just don't want you botherin' me, tryin' to con me to go down the river when I don't want to."

"Yeah, bet if that head Nancy asked you, you'd go."

"Mm, yeah. I would."

"You an' her act like you're married."

"Our business, ain't it?"

"Yeah, hell. I don't care. I'll see you later at the ole man's, eh?"

"Uh-huh."

Bob sat watching him walk away with his long loping strides.

Jimmy walked a few blocks, crossed a wide busy street under the El station, then continued toward Twelfth Avenue and the river beyond.

He felt small and petty, envious and angry, all attending feelings directed toward Nancy. Since Bob met her, he never seemed to have time for anyone else. He spoke to himself in the self-suffering voice he used when speaking to himself.

"Me an' him are buddy's, one. Now he gotta go ape over that broad an' don't even know I'm alive any-more. She's a nice kid an' everything, but hell, he's supposed to be my boy. Long as I know him we been friends, an' at's a long time. Why in hell can't he treat her like he used ta treat dem other muffs, like Frankie treats his broads? I mean, she ain't nothin' but some-thin' ta fuck. I'm his friend. A good buddy, ace boy. You don' go throwin' friends aroun' like they don't mean nothin'."

He turned, crossed in front of the brick dayline dock, looking down the rocks that bordered the river, rocks Nancy thought belonged to her and Bob. Jimmy felt disappointment when he did not see anyone there. He turned and walked for the docks in the other direction.

"Hell. He said she was home. How come he didn't come with me? Even if he didn't wanna come here, he coulda came an' we woulda went someplace else. Aw, thas that stupid bitch who's aways makin' them big eyes at 'im, an' makin' him feel sorry for her. Wish the hell he never met her an' was still foolin' aroun' with them other broads. Maybe soon he'll get sicka her an' tell 'er to get the hell outta here."

Feeling better, he turned onto the wooden dock and saw a group of figures at the end.

"Yeah, he'll do it, 'cause he never got mixed up wit no broad this long before. He prolly did it already, ha."

He yelled walking up the dock. "Hey, ya bastards? How's a water?"

Sully, tall and naked, his hair darker now because it was wet, boomed, "Dirty! Shit tide's in."

Jimmy came up, taking off his shirt, smiling, happy to be among friends.

"So what? Jump in an' bust 'er up."

Frankie came out of the water, using the ladder they had built a long time ago. His dark curly hair was straight, sopping wet.

"Whadda you say, Jimbo. Gonna show us your skinny white ass?"

"Yeah. What's new? Water wet or what?"

"It's shitty."

"An' you're like a friggin' buncha broads."

He slipped off his shoes, socks, then his pants and underwear. Climbing for the last pilings, he screamed and dove in. Charley, Tippy and Eddie were in the water swimming out as a large tanker lumbered up river slowly out towards the middle.

Frankie slapped Sully's rump, pointing, "Come on, lard ass. Let's get in for the rollers."

He dove. Sully followed. They swam out, forming a loose bunch, watching the river ripple before the tanker, sending high wrinkling waves towards them. Jimmy shouted loud as they all laughed, the first wave carrying them nowhere but up then down, followed closely by another and still more.

Eddie, red-haired, freckle-faced, called loud over their laughter.

"Hey, the current's movin' like hell. We better get in."

"Piss on you."

"Get lost, chicken."

"Go to hell. I'm havin' a ball."

Jimmy cackled hysterically.

Eddie started back to the dock, pointing before he did at a tug emerging from the dock two hundred yards down.

"We'll be down by the boats, it's runnin' so fast."

"Go home, mother Eddie."

A small pleasure boat cut its motor, headed towards them. A man and two women waved.

"Hey," Frankie yelled, waving back.

"They're takin' our pitchers."

The man held a motion picture camera up to his eye. Tippy chuckled.

"Now we should moon 'em."

Jimmy laughed loudly.

"Hell, yeah. Hey, yeah. Come on! Ass to the sun."

They dove under water, only their buttocks breaking the surface. The man with the camera continued taking pictures, the women beside him laughing.

Tippy shook his head, scowling when he surfaced, treading water.

"Lookit them goddamned fools throwin' money. Chee, like we can see in this shit."

They waved scornfully and swam hard for the dock.

The six of them climbed the ladder sitting or lying on the creosoted smelly rotting dock.

"Where's Bob?" Tippy asked, sitting next to Jimmy.

"Ahh, he didn't feel like comin'. That broad's got 'im all jammed up."

Eddie spoke grinning. "Hell, I hadda broad like her, I wouldn't mind bein' jammed up like that."

Frankie nodded slowly. "Yep, that's right. She's a bit, alrighty. Like ta get into that bitch. She's warm."

Sully looked at him unhappily. "You don't let him hear you talkin' about her like that."

Frankie snorted. "Come on, Sull. All's I mean is, she's a nice head; healthy, got a nice ass."

Charley sighed.

"Yeah, that chick Ceily from Hun-forty-first is awright, too."

Tippy looked at him, grinning. "Why? You gonna get into that, little man?"

"Tryin'."

"What's Rosey gonna say?"

Frankie smiled broadly at Tippy, with friendship, saying before Charley could answer, "I wanna get in your sister Marcy."

Tippy's whole body turned bright fire engine red. He stared at him, hardly believing what he heard. Frankie smiled.

"You better watch your ass, Frank."

Frankie stretched out, unconcerned. "Umm hm, I will, like hers. Like to Greek her."

Tippy started up at him, but Jimmy held him.

"Let it go, man. He's only kiddin.'"

Frankie smirking now. "Don't get up, buddy. You won alright. Now lemme sleep." He turned his head to lay out and saw three colored kids walking up the dock on the other side.

"What them niggers want?"

Sully stood.

"Ahh, eh, jus' swimmin'. It's a hot day, yeah?" He walked to the edge and dove.

Frankie said, "Niggers can't swim."

He sat up as he spoke, watching them walk to the other side. One called over.

"How's a water?"

Jimmy answered. "Wet an' dirty; shit line's in."

Frankie frowned, turning to him. "Don' tell 'em bastards nothin'."

"Ahhh."

Jimmy stood, following Sully, cursing himself under his breath.

The colored kids started taking off their clothes, folding them in small piles, speaking amongst themselves, chuckling. Completely undressed, they jumped in the slack water that formed between that dock and the one across the way about two hundred yards.

"See that?" Frankie said. "They're stayin' close to the dock. Tole ya niggers couldn't swim."

Eddie stood. "Yeah, come on. Let's go back in," Tippy said. Charley went in with him. Frankie sat. Two colored kids climbed from the water, panting and laughing at the third, who still held onto a piling, his body submerged.

"Well, come on up. You ain't gonna stay in all day, is ya?"

He shook his head, laughing.

"Hell no. Jes makin' warm spots."

Frankie stood glaring at them as the third boy climbed to the dock. Then he turned, walking to the end, climbed to the top of the pilings, watching Jimmy, Sully, Tippy, Eddie and Charley.

Only the tops of their heads showing, they had swam thirty yards against the current and were now letting it sweep them back. Jimmy lay on his back, bringing his toes up to the surface, clasping his hands behind his head, elbows above water.

"Come on in. It's startin' to clear, Frank."

He nodded, diving, going deep down, opening his eyes beneath, seeing only a shadowy sickish green fading into deep gloomy ghost-like black. He kicked his feet fast, pulling with his hands breaking the surface, forgetting about down there.

Sully was climbing the ladder, motioning out to the center of the river, when he made the top.

"Here comes a ship. Let's get the rollers."

Frankie and the rest stroked for the dock, climbing the ladder one by one.

The six of them stood waiting for the rollers, the first wave came hitting the dock, the dock groaning from the force, then it washed over. They dove, swimming hard for the next swelling wrinkle.

Frankie growled when they were out between the rollers.

"Whadda them black bastards laughin' at?"

Sully smiling, watched the next roller corning at him. "Ah, they're only kids, yeah, Frank?"

Then the next roller came. They again sat on the dock, Frankie with his back resting against the pilings, Sully full out drowsing in the sun, Jimmy, Tippy, Eddie and Charley sitting together talking. Two of the colored kids were bouncing a ball between them.

"Thas seven."

The third called as the ball hit a stick. Frankie watched with an intense scrutiny of basic hate without dilution. Looking over to Jim, he asked, "Why don't you go over an' take their bell?"

"Uh, wha' for?"

"They nigs, ain't they?"

"Aw, go ta hell. Ain't even old enough to be out by their selves."

Frankie got to his feet.

"I'll go get it."

Walking over, he caught the ball that bounced between them, the three kids looked at him warily.

"What you want, man?" The tallest boy asked. Frankie looked at the pink rubber ball in his hand.

"This your ball, nig?"

The smile on the tallest kids face died. Frankie had addressed the question to all three, but he knew he would have to do the talking. He looked at Frankie and wished like hell he had stayed around his block.

Frankie felt he was big enough to smack the hell out of all three of them. No sense, he consoled himself, would it make to look over there, over there were five more of them.

Tippy, Charley and Eddie were grinning, Jimmy was staring away across the river at the palisades. Sully was lying in the sun sleeping.

The tallest kid's head bobbed as he spoke. "Yeah, 'at's my bawl. Why'nt yuh give it here, huh?"

Frankie still looked down at the ball in his hand. "Spaulding. That's a good one. How much you pay for it, or you rob it from some little white kid?"

"I payed twenty-fiy cents. I din't steal nothin'. Come on, why'ntcha give it here?"

"You wan' it?"

He shrugged, looking from the ball then out to the river.

"Yeah, you gonna throw it?"

Frankie was looking out to the river now. "You can swim, can't you?"

"Yeah, a lil."

He whipped his arm back and flung the ball, it landed with a small splash two hundred feet out, as he turned he said. "Now you better go get it. You don't, I'm gonna throw you an your clothes in."

The kid knew he should have shut his mouth and stayed home.

Frankie walked back to the pilings and sat. Jimmy said nothing, watching the kid. Tippy chuckled, Eddie and Charley smiled at Frankie.

The kid reassured his two friends who were watching him wordlessly, "Ah, I could get it. Come on, walk me to the end."

They waited beside him to the end of the dock. Frankie watched.

The ball bounced on the slight white caps as if undecided which way to go, with the breeze or the current. The tallest kid whispered quickly to his two companions when they reached the end of the dock.

"Ah'll swim out there. Then you grabs the clothes and run."

"Ah'll swim to the next dock an meetcha."

The smallest worried. "Man, Lee. Dat's a long ways out. Dey might ketch us."

"Uww, don' worry. You could run fast. You see, them white studs ain't catchin' nobody."

Then the kid jumped from the dock and began swimming. His two friends waited a moment, then walked slowly for the clothing.

Jimmy walked to the end of the dock and called after the swimmer.

"Hey, watch it. The tide's runnin'."

The kid continued stroking. Jimmy shrugged a shoulder half-heartedly and walked back, Frankie smiled.

"Ain't worried about the nig, are you?"

"No."

He sat. The kid stroked overhand, the tight feeling in his stomach becoming worse. It was the same he always had when he was afraid, so he kept repeating to himself, "Ah could get it, Ah could get it."

The hot fearful blind feeling did not come yet. It was only when he swallowed some water and feared he was choking that the panic started. He spit the water out with a gagging sound but the heavy salty taste remained in the back of his throat and on his tongue. He wanted to vomit. But he kept his legs kicking frantically under him and he kept his arms stroking until he saw the ball was nowhere nearby. It was far off to the side and the current was bringing him along towards the tugboats.

Then the feeling came to his head, came with such a force he could not see. Blindly he lashed out, lashed out and clutched water. He screamed loud, his two friends, Jimmy, Frankie, Tippy, Eddie and Charley heard the, "Oh, gawd, ohh muh god, hep me, hep me … Oaaaaooowwh." Then the last, as if angry, as if a demand, something he had a right to, "Gooawd, help me!"

They all ran to the end of the dock, saw him rise above water to his waist, his eyes wide, white and rolling. Water spouted out of his mouth and his hands flailed the air about him, then he popped under the water.

The seven youths stared, standing naked at the end of the dock. The spot they stared at became roughed over by the breeze, the white caps played and the ball bounced along. After some moments passed, the smaller colored kid asked in a loud piercing voice, "Where he at? Where muh frien'?"

They woke Sully and dressed quickly, leaving the two kids at the edge of the dock, one crying, the other gaping in wide-eyed unbelieving astonishment at the spot he thought his friend had gone under.

A tanker was pushing its way laboriously upriver, corduroying the water before and after it. The rollers that came from it were high and they washed over the dock. The two kids ran, both crying now.

Sully walked with his heavy motioning roll, he said slowly, as if brooding on it along time, "Shoulda let the kid alone, Frank."

Frankie whirled, angry, stopping.

"What? Aw, bullshit! How was I supposed to know he couldn't swim? Besides, I tole ya niggers can't swim."

Jimmy's head felt empty in the corners. He wanted to say something. His eyes fell on a broken milk bottle lying near the curb. In the middle, it was broken, its sides crushed in and there was mud on it as if it had rained the night before.

Chapter 23

Hail, Columbia

Bob lay in bed sleeping, his face in the pillow. Nancy was over him, a hand on either side, looking down, grinning, her breasts swaying faintly, humorous mischief bouncing a glint in her eyes. "Come on. Wake up, Bobby. Stop sleeping. Wake for me."

A threatening growl came from deep in the pillow.

"Oh no, stop. Wake up, please. I can't sleep. Talk to me."

Just his lips came off the pillow as soon as finished speaking, then went back again. "Get outta here, Shoulders."

"No. Wake up."

Again, he raised his lips from the pillow. "What time is it?"

"Seven. No, well, a little before."

"Nancy, we just got to bed."

"Yes, but I can't sleep, Bobby."

He groaned as she laughed. He turned her breasts a quarter inch from his lips.

"Get outta here, Elsie, before I kill you."

She sat back on her ankles as he turned back to the pillow, her lids closing to slits.

"Don't you say that, don't you call me that. Everyone will start calling me that if you do. Don't you say it anymore."

"Mm. Go away, Elsie, an' I won't."

Raging; "Ohhhh you!" Her raised fist came down and powed him in the small of the back. He groaned, surprised. Accompanying the sunrise, and to a much greater degree, was pain.

Nancy climbed off the bed, standing away, no longer angry, wondering if he would hit her back. He rolled over, sitting up, rubbing his back, beckoning to her with the finger of his other hand, ignoring how low the sheet had shifted, he denting it with his newfound aroused interest. She saw it, rolled her eyes, and did not like the anger in his eyes. She would have been very happy to dress and go home, as he said.

"Come over here. Come here, Nancy."

Shaking her head. "No, no, I'm sorry, Bobby. I was just fooling. Stop looking at me like that, please?"

She approached slowly, fearfully, carefully. He watched her and gave up, pulling her onto the bed with him laughing, then kissing her.

"Hoo, umm. That was nice. Why did you do that? I thought you were mad, would you have hit me, Bobby?"

"Mm, you don't know how close you came. Your eyes saved you."

Her nose wrinkling, "My eyes, they did not. Don't say that. Bobby don't go back to sleep."

"I'm tired." He moved away from her, rolling his face in the pillow again.

"Oh, you."

She lay out beside him, bringing the sheet up around them both, falling to sleep. Near eleven that morning, he woke, feeling warm, sweaty. She was awake beside him, smiling.

"I just woke up too."

"Ummm, Nancy get this goddamned thing off."

"But it's just a sheet."

"I'm hot, woman."

She laughed, pulling the sheet from them letting it fall to the floor her eyes wide and excited.

"Sexy hot?"

"Dirty hot. I'm sweatin'."

"You sound cranky. Are you mad at me?"

Softer; "No. I'm still tired. Got a headache."

"Ohh. I'm hungry. Do you want to go to Marie's?"

"No. I wanna sleep."

"Oh."

He pushed his arm across the bed as she sat up. "Where you goin'?"

"I'm hungry. Stop. Let me alone, Bobby, let go of me."

He held her, pulling her back down as she tried to stand from the bed.

"Wait a while. I'll go with you."

"No I don't want to. Please let me go."

"What's the matter? Mad cause I wouldn't get up?"

"No. You were nasty. Don't do that."

Laughing.

"Bobby, stop. I want to be mad, I feel like being mad at you. Bobby, don't. Oww, wait."

"I will if you'll open the window."

"No, the draft. Lefty might catch cold."

Laughing, holding her tight. "What about me, I'm dyin?"

"Oh, all right. But you'll have to move Lefty over to the table."

"Shoulders, I don't wanna move myself."

"You have to. You said you would come down to Marie's with me."

"Mm, yeah, all right. I wish Pete wouldn't get so drunk."

"Why does he send up so much steam when he's drunk for?"

"He told me cause then people don't know how blind he gets."

"Oh? He's funny, isn't he?"

"Yeah. I have to go downtown at three." He got up, naked, searched for his socks first.

"Oh, to that lawyer. Will you come right back?"

"Mm. Is it snowin' out?"

"No, it stopped last night. Don't you remember?"

"Uhh, yeah." He looked at her on the bed. "You look beautiful, Shoulders."

"Oh, I do not. I'm naked."

His expression froze a moment, then he laughed, going to the bureau for a towel, shaking his head, as he wrapped it around himself. She watched him, smiling.

Freddy sat a while on the fender of a white Chevy. It was late morning. No one was around. Everyone was in the old man's around the corner. The dirty snow, ice and slush melted, folding, squirming its way towards the sewer at the corner. He watched people walk by, staring directly at them, for no reason other than he was wondering if they could help him by their appearance only, perhaps they could give him an answer of some kind.

They dropped their eyes and turned their heads when they saw him looking at them like that, so openly as if he could see into them. A man walked by, dropping his eyes, turning his head, then when he was twenty feet away, he stopped, turned and stormed back angrily, demanding, "You son of a bitch! Cut it out. What the hell ya lookin' at?"

Freddy pointed his finger at him and gave him a little smile to go with it, the man yelled repeating, "You son of a bitch. Cut it out."

Freddy cut it out because the man turned the corner. But he kept staring at people as they walked by, and they kept dropping their eyes and turning their heads.

Jimmy came walking by, looking at him eye for eye. He slowed, stopped, then leaned against the car. He had a big overcoat on with a small-brimmed black hat, grey gloves and a scarf with a stick pin in it, thin-striped black pants and pointed shoes. "Whaddaya doin' here, Fruits?"

"Lookin'."

"At what?"

"Nothin'."

"Then what the hell you doin' here?"

"You made a big score, uh?"

"Maybe, why? You talkin' slow today, uh?"

Freddy squinted at him, frowned and turned away.

"Yeah I did. You like the coat?"

"Naw. Everybody's inna old man's."

"Why, don't you like the friggen coat?"

"It don't fit you. Nancy's in there. She's waitin' for Bob to come back."

"No kiddin. She finally went back in, huh? How come you say my coat don't fit? It does so."

Freddy looked at him, his eyes looking all over Jimmy's, as if searching for a speck of something that perhaps impaired his vision, then turned away from him, watching an old woman rock her way carefully up the street. In either hand she held an empty shopping bag, as if this were her ballast, her balance, and without either, she would fall.

Freddie no longer wanted to speak to Jimmy. Freddy, at that moment, no longer wanted to speak to anyone, no one in the whole world did he want to speak to.

"What the hell's a matter with you?"

Freddy walked away down toward the river to watch the ice melt and float away, break away from each other into smaller and smaller pieces until they were no more and another hot summer would come and the politicians would turn off the water.

Jimmy went around the corner to the old man's. Frank was sitting up front, reading a sloppy magazine full of pretty pictures of naked broads. The back seemed deserted.

"Where's everybody at?"

"They left. Went up to Sonya's place to hear some record she got."

"Just Nancy an Alice inna back there. "

Jimmy walked back, opening his coat, untying the scarf, dropping the stickpin in his pocket with his gloves and cursing Freddy in a mild way. Alice and Nancy were whispering with their heads together across the table, each absorbed completely in whatever the other had to say, becoming instantly quiet as soon as the other would open her mouth.

Jimmy sat across the aisle and watched. It seemed incredulous that two broads would stop to listen to each other with such regularity. He watched for a while and they kept it up. It went on so long that he tired of it and began brooding again on that crazy bastard Freddy Fruits. He gazed down abstractly at the long filled ashtray, his finger mowing the butts around, knocking them out. Putting them back in, then he began to separate the lipstick-tipped from the plain. It took him fifteen minutes to decide one case that seemed to have an almost, but never an honestly discernible, pinkness to it. He decided that it was then and forever more a shim. At the end he had twenty-one shims, sixty males, sixty-nine females. He mixed them all up again and dropped them one by one into the ashtray, putting the big ashtray into his pocket. He walked out. Neither Alice or Nancy had noticed him.

Freddy sat up on the pilings in the corner of the dock watching the pieces of ice moving away, crushing each other, smashing, grinding, squeezing. He watched until it was dark and he could hardly see, only an illuminated glow and dark separate lines, quiet groaning noises and the growl of water some-times hissing. He reasoned that since his teeth were chattering, his body shivering, that the temperature must have fallen, so he climbed down, heading back towards the old man's.

At that time, Tippy was sitting where Jimmy had been. The two girls were not as absorbed in conversa-tion now, smiling secret smiles at one another, drink-ing coffee; they were completely in agreement.

Tippy sat looking at Alice as if she were a little boy and she was a big bully who had taken some-thing from him and had no intention of giving it back to him no matter how he pleaded with her. Alice sat smiling at Nancy, having no intention whatever of giving anything back.

Bob came in about four-thirty, saying hello to Alice and Tippy in the same voice, reaching for Nancy's hand, and they left.

Tippy hated Bob then like no other human he

would ever hate the rest of his life. Alice got up and left a little while after them. Tippy thought about running up to her, throwing a block at her, knocking her down, then helping her up, kissing her better, feeling a warming in his breast as if he had just stopped crying. He sat there knocking his cigarette ashes on the floor staring at the door she had gone out.

Freddy came in then, eating a big hero sandwich, a quart bottle of beer in his hand, his mouth so full all he could do was nod to the old man who told him to keep the beer out of sight. He went to the back, offering a bite of the large sandwich to Tippy by holding it a half inch from his nose. Tippy shoved it away, sending a slice of tomato across the room where Freddy followed it, picked it up and ate it.

He sat down at a back table and began munching and slurping happily. Jimmy came back sitting next to Tippy. He began to whisper, though he did not see Freddy back there. He whispered anyway. In the middle of the whisper, Tippy pulled his coat away, peering in, then smiled and nodded.

A while later they left, Freddy smiled and shrugged then went back to his chow. After he finished, he began sucking his teeth and working up one giant burp that would need some nursing to come out loud, clear and satisfying. He sat there, contenting himself with the careful nursing, when a pretty girl came in, spoke softly to Frank, who grumped, shrugged and pointed to the rear then turned away.

She walked back very slowly, hesitatingly, her eyes

wavering nervously from side to side until they came
to rest on the only person they could come to rest on.
He beamed a happy smile and waved. The girl almost
turned and ran out. Freddy was sure he had never in
his life seen her, but he was just as sure that he would
very much like to see more of her. Because under that
big fat coat she wore were two rather healthy-looking
bumps where most women have bumps and her hips
were not to be denied even by a big fat blue coat that
went nice with her bleached blonde hair, if her brown
eyes would stay in one place long enough.

Freddy was ready to tell himself how lovely they
were. She stopped ten feet from him, whispering
Jimmy's name. He cupped his hand to his ear, shaking
his head, his eyes never leaving her. He looked like a
lecherous young fool about to pounce. She moved a
half inch closer, whispering Jimmy's name again.

And again, he cupped his ear because his hand
had never left that position and shook his head. She
moved a little bit closer, whispering in near panic, if he
knew Jimmy. He nodded his head, confirming he did
know a Jimmy, but honestly was not sure the Jimmy
he knew and the Jimmy she was inquiring of were the
same Jimmy. He bid her sit down, raised two fingers
to the old man, who glared a very obscene word at
him, but poured two coffees and plopped them down
in front of them, then scurried back up front behind
his beloved counter.

Freddy spoke slow, in deference to the fact that he
did not know the young lady, so obviously she did not

know him and he could speak as slow as he pleased. She did not touch her coffee and sat at the very tip of her seat as if afraid Freddy might pounce on her and rape her. Freddy had no such thought in mind. He wanted to con her into letting him lay her, so he said. " Jimmy who, honey?"

She described Jimmy, not at all like the Jimmy he knew, except for the big nose. He asked where she met him, if she knew his last name.

"Up in the pool last summer; there was a fight. No, I don't know his last name." She spoke so low that Freddy wished he had left his hand up, cupping his ear. But since he had taken it down, he did not want to upset her by putting it back, besides she seemed to be thawing some. He was not taking any chances, so he listened carefully when she spoke and nodded sagely, even when he did not hear what it was she said. But he did find out how they came to meet and that she had not seen him since.

Freddy hmmmed, thought about that, then said he knew where big Jim was, so they left together. Only she did not seem so interested in big Jim anymore, and since Freddy had not the slightest idea where Jimmy and Tippy were, or what it was they were holding up, burglarizing or persuading. He went off to the good old Columbia Hotel and his favorite room.

Jimmy and Tippy watched as the young woman came out of the factory with the little brown bag. Tippy walked ahead of her, close, Jimmy behind, catching up past a crowded corner down a way. He pushed her into a hall, holding the gun that didn't work, over her shoulder. Two inches from her face, he spoke kind and polite and soft.

"Take it slow, missy. I don' wanna hurt you. Just gimme the bag." The broad was cross-eyed, staring at the gun that didn't work.

He took the bag and fled; her not moving or resisting, only watching the gun. About four and a half seconds later, she let out a screech that stopped elevators.

They scooted away untouched, chuckling richly. Tippy felt very good, and did not hate Bob anymore, but he promised himself that he was going to get laid that night.

Jimmy somehow had a feeling that he was cheated out of something, but had no idea what. And Freddy never told him, not even when Freddy came back to the old man's and borrowed some money off him, then ran back to the good old Columbia Hotel and was not seen for a week because it was delicious, better when the broad told him she had never been laid before even though he knew she was lying, so did she.

Kip never would believe that his father was in the hospital all week on the critical list and to get even with him, she told him she was pregnant and damn near fainted when she found out she really was. Jimmy went uptown and bought a whole lot of heroin and hid away in a room on the top floor of the Columbia Hotel, sleepily nodding his head.

Chapter 24

Tarry a While

Dicky turned from the stamping machine and its hypnotic pounding. He glanced at the clock, wiped his face with a handkerchief, feeling a depressing dejection that the time was only three o'clock. It seemed so long since lunch and quitting time so far off. He entertained the thought for a moment of quitting then, just walking out, then grinned.

He took the round disk of cloth that had the steel circle his machine would stamp to hold in place. He thought about how little effect it would have on the world if this piece of cloth with its ring of steel had not been invented or discovered. No difference, none, he was sure. He did not even know what they were used for or why. He would just have another job in another factory punching something else. No one would ever know that he had lived or had punched these cloths, whatever they were used for, under duress. It would not matter either, not to him.

He clenched his teeth each time the machine pounded down. Then his hands would move quickly from right to left, right hand feeding left hand, retrieving the stamped disc.

He forced himself to concentrate on the work before him. Time, it seemed, would go faster then. At four o'clock, he repeated to himself, "Another hour, another hour, one more."

At three minutes to five, he was in a circle of workers with his numbered time card in his hand. All the workers were in the circle except the piece workers, of who Dicky disapproved of deeply.

There were twelve workers around the clock, most of them young, under thirty. He stared down the wide two-hundred-foot-long room disinterestedly. Half of it was in darkness now, just the middle aisle where the piece workers were still working under the new, seemingly out of place in the old room, florescent lights.

There was a clean, dusty, starchy some kind of oily taste in the air, mingled with an old decaying odor. He was half listening to the conversations going on around him.

He heard Jack the foreman saying to Phil Tolmound, "Ah, shit, you talk like a fool. Whaddaya mean, we don't need no union?"

"So what in hell's a union givin' us? Nothin'. Jus' takin' our money an' tellin us to vote Commie or Democrat."

"What's a matter with votin' Democrat?"

"That ain't it. My dues are gonna support anybody the friggin' union feels like, if I don't vote for them or not."

"Aw, you talk like a guy with a paper asshole. There gonna get us raises, job security."

"Aw, hell. Security. If the friggin' company goes broke, whadda they gonna do with their security?"

Dicky turned away, looking over to Hector and Mac. They were close to the time clock, speaking low, Mac laughing.

"Come on man. You're a spic, ain't you? Don't gimme that you never did."

"I'm tellin' you man. I never did."

Mac, chuckling hard now. "Bet you go home an' try it on your wife tonight."

Hector laughed. "Naw, naw, can't, not tonight. Like, she's gots the rag on, but I'm gonna try it."

Dicky grinned, touching Hector's elbow. "Punch me out. See you inna mornin'."

"Yeah sure. Only, like, don't let Sam see you. He's up 'at is desk. Better go out the side."

He walked down the stairs. The anger he felt surprised him.

"Aw, hell. It's petty. Don't think about it. A minute, two minutes, 'an Sam's gonna scream. That's all I'd need tonight. Aw, hell with it."

He walked quickly for the subway station, still angry. It was rush hour, but this was a local stop. He usually found a seat. When his train came, he did, in a corner. He slipped the paper back from his pocket and began reading. At Thirty-Fourth Street, he was reading, trying to ignore the crushing crowd, when someone touched his shoulder. He looked up.

"Hiya, Nancy! You wanna seat?"

"Oh no. I just wanted to say hello. Please don't get up."

The noise of the train was loud and screeching.

"I was only kiddin'. Come on. Take the seat. Don't try an' talk. We'll talk when we get off."

She nodded as his hand on her arm directed her to the seat. Sitting, her purse and folded paper on her lap. She smiled. "I really didn't want your seat, but thank you."

"Yeah I know. Alice would throw me out if I didn't get up. I wanted to anyway. Now, lemme read. It's the sexy part."

She laughed softly, unfolded her newspaper, and began reading.

When they got off the train, they walked slow, talking.

"Are you still working days?"

He grinned slowly. "No."

She smiled, sighing. "Yes I know. I'm stupid. It just came out."

"Yeah, I'm still workin' days, like everybody else."

"You still don't like it?"

"No. I should go back to nights. The hell with Alice."

"Aw, she just wants you with her at night."

"Yeah, I know. It was easier workin' at night, the people. I don't like the day crew."

"Ignore them. That's what I do."

He looked at her, his smile coming back slowly, his hand resting on her arm.

"You would, Nancy. I don't know why, but you would."

"You make that sound blue, as if I'm sad. Don't do that."

"Okay, sorry. You look good, Shoulders. How in hell do you keep all the men away from you?"

"Oh, you know better than that. Don't tease me."

"I wasn't. Have you heard anything from him?"

She was looking away when she answered and he wished he had not asked.

"No, I think it's better this way. I guess it is."

"Forget it. Come on up an' eat with us tonight."

"No, I'm coming up Friday. I don't want to make a pest of myself."

"Hey! Hell, you can't make a pest outta yourself. We don't feel that way. Come on. It makes Alice happy as hell to see you."

Laughing, "Besides she don't bitch at me as much when you're around."

She smiled. "No, really, but thank you. I'll be up Friday night. I turn here."

She waved as she turned the corner. He watched her walk away, denuding her in his mind, grinning. "If I was a broad built like that, I'd be a hustler. She can't an' should be."

Then, sourly, "Yeah, like I know."

When he came in the door, he smelled the deep tangent odor of frying chops. He was hungry. They smelled good. Alice was over near the stove. The table was set. She glanced at him, expressionless. He ignored the feeling in him because of the look.

"Hey, they smell great, honey. How do you feel?"

"The same way I look; just fine. If you don't like chops, it's too goddamned bad about you."

Within him, he groaned, then complained aloud. "I never said I didn't like pork chops. What in hell you jumpin' all over me for?"

"Because they're not pork chops. They happen to be veal chops."

"Oh, fer Chrissakes. Now what am I supposed to do, apologize for callin' 'em pork chops?"

"Don't bother."

The feeling in Dicky wasn't pleasant as he tried to smile, saying, "Hey, come on. Brighten up. I met Shoulders tonight on the train."

Without interest, she asked, "How was she?"

"Fine. She looks good."

"Nancy always looks good to men."

"Yeah. Whad you do today? Where were you?"

"I was here all day. Where did you think I was?"

The anger was in him. There was nothing he could do about it.

"I don't know. That's why I asked."

"I'm here every day, unless I go up to see my mother. I know you don't want a report every night on what I do, do you?"

"Alice, I'm hungry." He sat, his eyes across the room.

"Then wait, unless you want raw veal chops."

"Alice, cut it out. I don't wanna fight tonight. We've hadda fight every night this goddamned week. Cut it out."

"Yes. Well, there are two of us, ain't there?"

He inquired softly, "Alice, did you ever get knocked on your ass?"

She stood between the table and the stove gazing at him calmly.

"No, I haven't. Why?"

He shook his head, breathing deep.

"Nothin', nothin'. Feed me."

"I will when it's ready. Were eating at my mother's house Sunday."

"No, we ain't."

"Yes, we are. Kip and Freddy aren't coming up this week."

"I'm still not eatin' at your ole lady's."

She was staring at him now, her eyes were hard. He wanted to take her and choke her until the expression in them left.

"I told her we'd be up. She's expecting us."

"I'm not goin'. Feed me."

"I'm curious. Why?"

He snarled, "Because your ole lady is a self-centered, bullyin' old bitch, just like you're tryin' to be, an' your old man is a cowardly little faggot, an' it bothers me to watch him crawl. Now, you better feed me, bitch, 'cause I've had it."

She flipped the pot of string beans she had just

taken from the stove into the sink, turning to him with that blank impersonal expression that dared him and infuriated him.

He stood roaring, "You silly son of a bitch, I've had you. One a these days, I'm gonna kick your god-damned ass in. I'm gonna beat you like I'd beat a man."

Unaffected by his anger or roar, she said, "Really. I suppose you're close to it now, screaming, and you're the one questioning my father's manhood. Just re-member the consequences after you do, because I sure as hell will."

"Fuck you an' your consequences. Stick your chops up your ass."

He walked out, slamming the door behind him.

She watched as the door slammed, then sat in a chair, chin in hand, hearing the chops sizzling behind her, she stared at the door, furiously willing herself not to cry.

Dicky walked into The Uptown bar, sitting on a stool near the window. It was crowded. A new bar-tender he did not know was serving. Johnny wasn't around.

"What'll you have, Mac?"

"Beer an' a shot a seven."

The bartender poured his beer and shot quickly, making change of his dollar bill he walked away to serve.

Dicky was relieved. He was glad Johnny wasn't on. He didn't want to talk to anyone. He wanted to talk to himself.

"She's gotta have it all. Everything's gotta be her way or it's wrong. Oh hell, whadda buncha shit that is. I'm goin' back workin' nights. I mean, this broad's gone to far. I shoulda hit her in the mouth. That look a hers. Bad business hittin' a woman. Shoulda knocked her on 'er ass."

He drank the shot before him.

"Aw, hell. Think about it when it's good."

Swallowing some beer, "She can be warm, do things that ... Wonder if her ole man ever said that to himself about her mother?"

Chapter 25

Chilly Nights and Open-Toed Slippers

Kip was sitting on the windowsill in her father's bedroom. He was trying to stay awake, lying on the bed, trying to finish what had begun as a funny story, but what was now becoming a silly one, because her father had not had any sleep for two nights because he had worked a double shift, then had gone in for his regular shift last night. Kip was not surprised; concern was closer.

She knew why he didn't, and did not want him to. He wanted to save enough money to buy a house so they could move out of this neighborhood, because he felt she was being deprived of certain advantages just because of this neighborhood.

Kip wanted to tell him that she did not want to move, that she was happy. But then, all she could do was say when he showed, "All right daddy. Go to sleep. Tell me when you wake."

But he would continue as if drunk, but he wasn't, and she knew why. He continued, it seemed to her, wacky, but wonderful.

She knew that he would want her in the apartment when he woke so he could ask her all sorts of silly questions because he had no idea what kind of questions he was supposed to ask the sixteen-year-old girl that was his daughter.

He knew that he had to maintain a concern, try for a rapport, show his affection that would somehow make up for the mother she did not have. But he was almost completely lost how to go about it all.

Kip tried hard to make it easy for him because he asked the questions with an embarrassment, as if he felt he had no right to infringe upon her privacy, but that he must know she was being a good girl, not that he ever doubted she would not be a good girl.

So Kip told him almost everything she did every minute of the day, almost every minute. She never mentioned Freddy, because she was afraid her father would want to meet him and she was afraid her father would not understand him, would be disappointed in her. So she never mentioned Freddy, and as she said to Alice one day in the old man's over coffee.

"I feel so, well, so damned shitty every time I don't. I'm not ashamed of him, but it's as if I am."

But that morning, after her father gave up and

slept without telling her the end of the story, she went down to the old man's and saw Freddy for the first time in a long time and would not speak to him at first when he sat in the booth across from her. He continually swore that his father was one ill old man and had been in a hospital for the last week, but she was not the least impressed.

"Freddy, you're a liar."

"I'm not, listen."

"Well, why didn't you call, then?"

"Why? What for? You couldn't a done nothin."

"You didn't call, because you're a liar."

Then she said, because she wanted to shake him up, besides she was wondering what he would do, besides she was late, but she wasn't worried much then, "I'm pregnant."

She said it as a matter of conversation and Freddy was still trying to swear his way out of not being able to see her for a week.

"No, listen he was in this house ..."

There was a lot of doubt in his voice as he asked gruffly interrupting himself, "Who the hell toll you that?"

Looking away over his head more singing than saying, "I am."

Freddy was getting a little nervous because he was beginning to believe her. He didn't want to, but he was beginning to.

"Who told you that? You talk to a doctor?"

"Nope, I know I am."

"Awww, you ain't."

Two weeks later when Kip was finally firmly convinced she was, she was ill. She was shaky and when she got home, she curled up on the sofa, and cried because she didn't know what else to do. Then she did not even know if she wanted to marry Freddy. No, then she did not want to have anything to do with him, with anyone, least of all her father who would be waking soon.

She wondered if she should tell him. But then she thought she should wait until she spoke to Freddy first. So she marched into the old man's, all the way to the back where Tony G had a game going with Frankie, Johnny, Blood, Sully, Jimmy –who was watching Tony very carefully with a glaring warning in his eyes– and Pete. The old man was rolling. Alice was up front behind the counter speaking softly to Dicky, who was smiling at her from the other side, speaking as softly to her.

Kip bent and held Freddy's arm as he was putting money up to cover a bet. He turned, threw her a grin, then covered the bet, and was going to cover another until her fingers went to his neck and started digging. Everyone was speaking but she didn't have to because on her clean cute face there was a demand. Freddy saw it, getting up, signaling Jimmy, who nodded.

He walked to a front booth with her, asking as soon as she sat down, "What the hell's a matter with you? Are you okay?"

She nodded. At that moment, she actually detested herself because she felt weak and lonely, so she started crying becoming even more disenchanted with herself because of the tears.

He held her by her shoulders from across the table asking, a little bewildered, "Hey, take it easy. Whadda you cryin' for? You still mad at me?"

She said low, seething anger, "Yes, you bastard, I am."

Freddy grinned, faking relief, "Aw, come on."

She took a deep breath, but before she could swing, he held her, saying, "Okay, all right. Take it easy. You sure? I mean you went to a doctor?"

"Yes!" That was loud, bringing Alice's eyes to them.

He pushed her back in the seat hard because she wanted to get out about then. "Whadda you doin'? No good; listen to me, there's no sweat. So you're pregnant, I made you that way, I'm glad."

She gasped. "You're glad?"

"Yeah. I wanna marry you. Come on, honey. Nothin's that bad. It makes it easier for us."

Standing, roaring, pointing to herself, "For you. I'm the one that's pregnant."

But now Alice had one eye closed, studying the two of them. So he took her arm and they walked out. On the corner he said to her, "Listen. We can get married.

I got enough money. My old man'll be glad. Kip, hell, be happy."

She said, meaning it, "I don't want to marry you."

And he said, meaning it even more, with his chin out pugnaciously, "You gotta. That's my kid you're carryin."

"Well I'm not. I ... this kind of marriage; I hate them. It won't work. Freddy, I–"

"Oh no, yes it will. Look, I love you, the kid. Hell, that's why people get married, no? Don't tell me it won't work. You're gonna marry me, Kip."

"No, I'm not."

"Yes you are. You better believe that. Whadda you think, you can just walk away with our kid?"

Then she leaned against him because he brought her close, "But what about my father? I'm afraid of what he'll think of me."

"I'll tell him."

"No, Freddy. He doesn't know you. I'll talk to him first. He won't do anything, he'll understand."

She was scrunched up against him because the wind started then, and it was a chilly spring that year.

"Yeah, but ... Hell, no, I ... Kip, lemme do it my way. I'll go up an talk to him."

"No. I'll meet you tomorrow. I'll tell him first, then he'll want to meet you."

"Yeah, it ain't the right way."

"No, it is. I'm going up now. Freddy, the doctor said I was over three months."

"Yeah, so what? That don't matter. Kip, I should go up if he wants to punch something. At least he can punch me."

Smiling, "He won't want to punch anything. Freddy?"

"Yeah, what?"

"When you meet him, will you talk slow?"

"Yeah."

But Kip's courage faltered when her father woke. He woke happy and they spoke about a lot of things that meant nothing. She made breakfast for him while he read that morning's paper. That evening, she walked with him to the subway, because she knew he enjoyed that, and she usually did, too.

Then she went back to the apartment and wondered how she could tell him. Later she went down to the old man's and sipped coffee, but left when Jimmy came in, because he started to harass her the way he always did and Freddy was not there. She walked around a while then went back to the apartment, sitting before the television set, feeling as though she had committed an unforgivable sin, some kind of crime she would never be able to erase. And when she was about to cry she thought about it and was angry again telling herself that it was not any such thing.

So she sat in front of the television set, filing her nails, then later polishing them. She changed into a bathrobe and slippers, watching the late show and its buddy, the late late show. Her eyes were starting to burn because she was tired when her father came in.

He beamed, happy to see her awake, kissing her, hugging her, asking her to make tea for him. She did. When she came back in the living room he was sitting in his chair, the one he always sat in, reading the paper. She placed the tea and cake on a snack tray, saying, because she felt it was now or never, "Daddy, I'm not sure how to tell you this."

His good-natured face that could fall into a large smile without effort did. "Oh, you just go ahead and blurt it out, then it's over."

He was tired and she knew if he began reading the paper he would fall asleep and what he just said coincided with her way of thinking then. She wanted to tell him, let him know. "But, well, I hope you'll understand."

Without looking at her, reading the paper his finger through the cup handle, "Of course, I will."

"Daddy."

"Uh, hmm, yes, yes, I'm listening."

"I think I'm going to have a baby."

To her, it seemed as if he were still reading, as if he had not heard. So she was going to tell him about Freddy demanding to marry her, and how unsure she was because she was sure she would rather marry Jimmy if anyone. But now she couldn't, because he and Bob were going to jail soon and he still didn't know he was in love with her but she did. She was trying to explain that.

"Daddy, I think I'm going to have a baby, but ... Well, I am, because the doctor said the test said I was and–"

His head sprung up at her, his eyes rounding, his lips out, then he shouted. "You are not!"

He was sitting up in his chair now, his back not touching it. He was on the edge, and he was looking at her with anger.

She nodded her head. "Yes, I am. The doctor said so."

His finger was no longer in the cup handle. He dropped the paper on the floor, walking over to her, standing before her, bellowing her into a chair. "Do you mean to stand there an tell me you're pregnant?"

She was surprised, a little frightened at his reaction, her head bobbing numbly. That's when he slapped her, which did not surprise her, it shocked her. She was unprepared. His slap turned her head, almost spinning it around on her shoulders. Gasping, furious, holding her cheek that smarted terribly, trying to stand, "Oh, oh, you! Why'd you hit me for?"

"Yeah, I hit you. An I wanna know who the son of a bitch is. Now, who is he?"

She rubbed her cheek, finally getting to her feet. "Why did you hit me for? We didn't mean it. We couldn't help it."

Glaring at her, still bellowing, holding her upper arm, "I wanna know who he is so I can kill the son of a bitch. Don't gimme that we couldn't help ourselves."

"No, let go. He wanted to tell you. He wanted to come up, but I wanted to tell you alone. I thought you'd understand."

He yanked her, pulling her close, his face down near hers. "I do understand, you little whore. You can't tell me how many there were, can you? You don't even know who the father is. You're like your mother, no goddamned good. I thought maybe with some a my blood in you, you could be decent. You belong in an alley like the rest of her family. You think I'm gonna help you, huh? Well, you get the hell outta here. You get outta here right now and don't never come back or I'll twist your head off your shoulders, you little hallway slut."

The last he screamed pointing to the door and something broke inside Kip. She wondered if her heart was still beating because she was sure it was not. She turned and ran down the long hall and out the door.

It was late, past three o'clock in the morning. The old man's was usually closed at this time, but she went around to look anyway, because she had no place else to go and she was afraid to be alone, because she knew that as soon as she got the chance she was going to cry hard, harder than she ever had before. She hated her father, hated him for the way he had rejected her so completely, as if she were a stranger, as if she really were a slut. She thought about that and leaned against the building she was passing, a little dizzy, wondering if he were right. But why had he said those things about her mother? He had always told her how much he loved her. He had never said anything like that. Why did he say that now? What had her mother been like? But she was dead. He had no right speaking of her that way. She sneezed, took a deep breath and walked on.

Blood, Frankie, Tippy, Jimmy and the old man were in the back playing poker. Tippy was staring at Blood as if he wanted to kill him and Blood knew it, chuckling like hell. He had suckered Tippy in to bid against him for the biggest pot of the night and Tippy had gone, bidding against his full house with queens up, Tippy feeling sure he would take the pot because Blood tried bluffing with two other hands foolishly. But this hand hadn't been and Tippy was just realizing neither had the other two.

Kip saw the light in the back and rattled the door. The old man looked over to Frankie, who was sitting at the end of the booth on the other side. "G'wan an answer it."

Jimmy yawned and said, "Naw, I will; tired, wake me up a little. "

The old man rasped, "Don' let nobody in."

Jimmy ignored him, yawning again, walking for the door. When he opened it, Kip realized that she had only a house robe on. She realized that from the way Jimmy's eye brows went up and the question gleamed brightly on his face.

She swallowed close to tears because it had to be Jimmy that answered the door, she asked softly, cowered, she just couldn't take him then.

"Jimmy, is Freddy here?"

But Jimmy just held the door, frowning at her.

She nearly weeped, "Please, Jimmy. Let me come in."

"Why, what's a matter?' That was in a nasty tone but he had no intention of keeping her out, as always after watching her a while, his contrary nature asserted itself because he asked with a form of compassion.

"What's a matter? You look shook. You gots troubles or what?"

"I have to see Freddy."

"Yeah, but he ain't here."

Then suddenly before she knew she was going to, she cried, as if coughing, her hand cupped over her mouth and her head down. She turned, walking away rapidly as Jimmy said, "Hey Kip, wait a minute. Wait." Then he went after her, catching her as she turned the corner, her head bent over, still crying as if coughing in her cupped hand.

"Hey, come on. What's a matter? Come on. Stop walkin' so fast." Then he grabbed her arm. "Hey! I said stop." Looking down at her, not understanding a damned thing. "Whadda you, crazy? Walkin' aroun inna bathrobe like that there?"

But she was still crying and he couldn't understand word one because she was sobbing by then. So he said, speaking with extreme logic, "So why doncha shut up a minute?" Then softly holding her close, "Hey, come on. Ain'tcha cold? I mean, jus' try an get a hold a yourself. Come on inna hall, it's warmer in there."

They went into the hall out of the wind, standing

by a hall radiator that was just warm, a little less. He put his arms around her, holding her close, because he was cold, too. He spoke softly to her, asking her to stop crying, because he never did feel there was a damned thing tears could solve. Besides, Jimmy had a secret belief, never voiced because he did not like opening himself to possible ridicule, but he did believe that tears caused damage inside a person that would later lead to a lot of different diseases. That's why he was sure Nancy was going to die very young, and if Kip kept it up, so would she.

After about ten minutes of her shaking in his arms, he asked, "So, how come you're down here inna middle a the night with your bathrobe on only?"

"My father ... We hadda fight."

She still couldn't talk right because she was gasping, but at least he could understand her.

"Whad he do, throw you out? I mean, whatta time to."

Her head nodded. Jimmy was being extraordinarily kind, but she could not bring herself to trusting him so suddenly, and she sure wasn't going to tell him she was pregnant. That she believed would be all he needed. He would think it deliriously comical, and any compassion on his part now would have dissolved with the telling.

He smiled then, because he didn't know what else to do. "I mean, the guy can't throw you out like that, only inna bathrobe. He really did?"

"Yes."

Kip didn't want to tell him anymore and hoped he wouldn't ask. Jimmy wondered what the hell he was supposed to do now. He sure as hell wasn't going to go over to Freddy's house to get him. He had some money. He could take her to the Columbia, get rid of her, the hell with it. But for reasons, he did not want to take Kip to the Columbia. But if not, where else? He was becoming tired. He didn't want to be bothered. With some reluctance, he said, "Come on. Take you over to the hotel, getcha a room for the night."

Kip stood there, shaking her head, with a brave smile that he thought idiotic.

"No, Jim. Thanks. I don't wanna go there."

"Why not? I'll come an get you inna morning. No-body'll say nothin'."

"No."

"Yeah. Tomorra, I'll get some clothes off Alice. Don' worry. I'm not gonna try an shack with you."

That would have disturbed Kip another time, but she had enough tonight. She turned back to the radiator. He said standing beside her.

"Why, you're afraid if somebody sees you, they'll think you're shackin' with me? Aw, the hell with it. You want me to leave you here?"

Her head nodded in confirmation. She said, "I'll wait here, Freddy comes around early."

Scornfully, "Yeah, an' you'll be here frozen to death. Whadda you crazy? Don't be so stupid. Come on."

"No. Let me go, Jimmy. I'm not going there."

He pushed her ahead of him. "So I'm not takin' you there. Go on."

"No. Don't push me. Where?"

"Up Bobby's room. Go' 'head."

"What will he say? No. It's in the middle of the night. We'll wake them."

Jimmy was becoming angry now. She was stupider than he thought. But she was cute, with her curly hair tumbled all over her head. He knew he had no animosity toward her this night, more toward himself.

"So, what the hell. You think they're gonna be sittin' up waitin' jus for you? Gwan, huh?"

She walked along with him, walking close because now she was beginning to feel how really cold it was. He put his arms around her saying with a big grin, "If you wasn't so shook, I'd grab a little."

She looked at him, turning her head up. He wished he hadn't said that when she begged in a small voice that was still close to tears, "Please Jim, don't."

Gruffly, almost letting her go, "Aw, shit. I was only kiddin'. Silly bitch. You ain't got nothin' anyway."

They repassed the old man's. He said, making her move for a doorway, "Wait here. I'll be right back."

Then he ran into the old man's, running behind the counter, pouring a container of coffee, splashing milk and sugar in it, then snatching his coat and running back out. Blood, Frankie, Tippy and the old man watched, until the old man shrugged, pointing at the cards in front of Frankie, who was still looking at the door, wondering.

When he got outside, he put his coat on her, buttoning it, flipping the collar up, almost covering her head, smiling at how bedraggled she appeared. Speaking confidently almost laughing at her little-girl-lost look, "Come on, huh? Don't look so beat up. It'll be over tomarra."

She gave him a quick grin, that if he blinked he would have missed.

"You want some coffee now, uh?"

She shook her head, then took his arm, hugging it to her, saying, "Jim, thanks. I, uh, I don't know what I'd have done if you weren't here."

He flipped the container in the street. "Yeah, yeah. Shut up about it, all right? Your feet cold?"

She was wearing slippers and her toes peeped out of the front of those. "Just a little."

"Aw, they're probably numb. Why didn't you dress 'fore you went out? Man, you broads are dummies."

She grinned, then laughed softly. When he turned his head down at her, he smiled. "Yeah, sure. Shoulda waited a couple weeks till it got warm while you was at it."

Bob's arm was lying across Nancy's waist. She was sleeping on her back, he on his stomach. It was very quiet in the dark, still room. The light was out over Lefty's terrarium. He was bunched into a little puff of fur under cedar chips, sleeping soundly.

The bamming on the door woke her. She knew he was awake beside her as she felt his body jolt, then tense. He turned as she said, "Bobby, no. They can't. You said we had time."

"Mm, we do, Shoulders. Ssh, wait."

But the bamming came again.

"Bobby, they're going to–"

"No, nothin. Don't worry. Put your robe on."

He slipped into a pair of pants as the bamming continued.

She caught sight of his face for a second when he opened the door and the dim light from the hall slapped across him. His teeth were clenched, eyes shining. He was breathing hard. She stood away frightened then heard Jimmy say, "Mornin, ace. I gots some troubles for ya. Dint know whad else to do with her."

Bob answered as if he hadn't heard his voice, low, containing anger. "Whadda you doin' here?"

In Jimmy's voice, then Nancy was sure she heard a whine.

"Hey, come on. Don't get mad. I mean, what was I gonna do? Let the jerky broad run aroun' like this all night?"

He turned from the door without speaking, saying to Nancy, "Turn on the light, Shoulders."

When she did, there was that exasperating amused look in his eyes, as if he found something laughable at being awakened at past three in the morning.

Kip and Jimmy came in. When Nancy saw Kip, she

was going to chuckle. But Kip's expression asked her not to, so she went over to her, holding her arms. Kips hands were deep in Jimmy's coat pockets.

"What's the matter? Are you all right?" Smiling. "You look funny in that coat. Sit down. Are you cold?"

Bob was staring at Jimmy who was trying to grin.

"Hey, it's not my fault the broad wouldn't go to the Columbia 'cause she don't wan' people to think she's a whore. Come on uh?"

He turned to Kip, who was sitting on the bed, smiling suddenly. "You look like The Little Match Girl." Cocking his head, moving closer to her, "What's the matter kid, can we help?"

"A little, Bobby. I just wanna stay here until the morning. I'm sorry to bother you like–"

"Mm, cut it out. It's all right. Nancy, put on the coffee. Your feet cold? How come you only got slippers on?" He knelt in front of her, taking them off, rubbing her feet. "Hey, they're freezin'. Shoulders, go get that basin in the bathroom an' fill it with hot water."

She was about to leave the room to fill the coffee pot, then turned, asking, "Yes, all right. The big one, Bobby?"

"Mm-hmm."

Jimmy sat in a chair next to a table, as if unconcerned. "I tole her she shoulda got dressed 'fore she left."

Bob looked up at her, smiling, rubbing her toes, scowling playfully.

"Mm, you shoulda. What's a matter with you?"

Kip pushed her head down in the coat and in one big shiver said.

He turned his head to Jimmy. "Did Nancy put that coffee on?"

"Naw, she ain't had the chance yet. Wan' me to help her?"

"Yeah. This kid's freezin' one."

Jimmy left the room, Kip said quietly, "Bobby, I feel terrible. Let me sit in the chair. Let Nancy go back to bed. You two go back to bed. I'm all right now."

"Be quiet, Kip. Where's Freddy?"

"Home, I guess. He'll be around tomorrow."

Grinning, "I know that, honey. He's aroun' every-day. Want me to go get him?"

"No. Bobby, I'm pregnant."

"I know. Freddy told me."

A little peeved at Freddy for doing such a thing, "Why did he do that?"

"Guess he wanted somebody to talk to."

"Don't tell Jimmy, Bob."

"Okay. Your ole man threw you out, cause you told him you were knocked up?"

"Yes. Don't say knocked up. I'm not knocked up. I'm pregnant. "

He laughed as Jimmy came in the room with a basin of hot water. He took it, placing it on the floor.

"Here, put your feet in this. Ow! Hey, that's hot." He blew on his finger, winking at her as she sighed her feet into the water.

"Um-hmm, it's beautiful, thank you. Whoo, I was really cold. I didn't know how much till now."

Nancy came in, saying as she turned on the hot plate, placing the coffee pot on it. "The coffee's just going to be hot, not good. Bobby and I are the only one's that can drink it."

She sat beside Kip. "Do you want to take that coat off? I have another robe. Kip, your lips are blue."

"Yes. No I don't want to take the coat off; still cold."

Jimmy was over by the window gazing down critically at Lefty's tank. He asked Nancy who was watching him, "It got away, huh?"

Concern killed the smile as she got up going over quickly. "Why, no. Of course not."

She snapped on the light in the tank and smiled again. "Oh, you."

Jimmy was looking at her without the least comprehension, so she pointed. "There he is in the little bump. See where the chips are pushed up?"

"Uh, where? Whadda you mean, he's under there?"

"Yes, he likes to hide when he sleeps."

He looked at her a moment, his brows falling heavily over his eyes. Then he turned, glancing at Bob and shaking his head saying softly, "Holy Christ. Man, oh, man."

Bob laughed, saying, "Shoulders; make him come out."

Kip crouched slightly, watching carefully as Nancy asked. "Do we have any of those cookies left?"

He went over to the breadbox that in summer they used for an icebox. "Mm, yeah, here."

Kip asked, "You're not going to take him out of that tank are you?"

She was a little pale, Bob and Nancy grinned at one another.

Nancy answering, "No. If you're afraid, I'll let him sleep."

"I'm not as long as he's inside that tank."

Nancy put her hand in after crumbling the lemon flavored cookie in her palm. The little bump began moving when she tapped the glass side with her finger. The three of them watched her as if she were performing some kind of ritual.

Then Jimmy and Kip chuckled when a little head with deep black eyes as small as large periods peeked out from under the chips, then shook itself, turning. Seeing Nancy's hand, it crawled all the way out fitting back, rubbing its nose along its body, licking itself. Then it scooted as if suddenly making up its mind, over to Nancy's hand, where it sat sniffing and eating every once in a while, its head going up looking at her.

Kip said, "Oh he's cute! I didn't know you could train them."

Nancy's nose wrinkled as she said, "No that's nothing. Watch, wait a moment."

She let the mouse eat a while, then extracted her hand, the mouse's eyes on her. She put the cookie crumbs in her other hand, then placed her hand back in the tank, making a circle of her thumb and forefinger. The mouse wiggled through, then back, sitting beside her hand, waiting. She spread her fingers wide and he went over and under each until her thumb, then he started up her arm, she said, "Oh no. Not now."

Picking him up, placing him near his feeding dish, putting the crumbs there she put the grating back on, turning to them smiling wide, "There. See? Isn't he lovely?"

Jimmy laughed, flopping back onto the chair. Bob went over, holding her by the waist, grinning.

Kip said, "Yes, I'm almost tempted to pet him, but not really."

Nancy; "Oh, you. You're just like Alice. He can't hurt you."

"Yes, I know. But he's still a mouse."

Bob and Jimmy went down to the old man's. Nancy and Kip went to bed before the coffee perked because they were tired.

The old man was closing when they got there, he said, "Whadda you guys doin' here? What's a matter?"

"Nothin. You lock the door?"

"Yeah. Why? You goin' back in?"

"Mm, yeah. Is any of that coffee hot?"

"Yeah, yeah, it's still hot. You open up with your own keys. I'm goin' home." Then after he turned away he turned back asking, "Ey, Bob. You ain't in more trouble are you?"

He smiled his hand going to the old man's shoulder. "No, hell no. Ain't I in enough?"

"Yeah, yeah. Goddamned fools you are, both a you."

Then he turned and limped away and they watched him, both grinning Jimmy saying, "He's a funny type guy, uh?"

"Yeah, mm." Bob and Jimmy sat there in the back, playing double solitaire, drinking coffee that was cooling until after six when the papers came. They opened the store, reading the papers. Freddy came a while later, pouring himself a cup of coffee.

"It's gettin' warmer outside, Bobby."

"Mm, good. Yanks are doin' good down Florida. They'll prob'ly get off to a slow start this year." Jimmy said.

"Yeah, they usually lose down there, don't they?"

Bob smiled, winking at Jimmy, asking Freddy, "Yeah. You got troubles, Freddy?"

Freddy turned from the doorway he was standing in. "No, nothin."

Jimmy yawned, stretching saying, "Ey man, I'm goin' up, gettin some sleep. See youse later."

"Yeah."

He went out, Freddy picked up the paper he had been reading. Bob said, "She's up in my room. Leave her alone. Let her sleep awhile."

Freddy's head popped up. "Who? Kip?"

"Mm, her old man musta been pretty shook. She came up about three inna house coat."

"You sure she's all right? I mean ... Hey, I better go up there."

"No, you better not. Shoulders is up there too. Let them sleep."

"Yeah. Holy Christ, whadda'm I gonna do?"

"Don't know."

"No, I mean about her?"

Bob's eyes came over to Freddy's that were tight and jumping. "I don't know; up to you."

"What? Oh no. Hell, Bob, I wanna marry the broad."

"Go 'head."

"She's young. She's only sixteen."

"Mm, guess her ole man can make trouble you don't do somethin."

"Ahh, I'm not worried about that. Whad about her?"

"I don't know." Bob went back to the paper again.

"I gotta talk to her, Bobby."

"Wait awhile. They'll be wakin' soon. Shoulders never sleeps long."

They sold papers and cigarettes until ten, when Alice came in, just humming. She grinned, kissing them both. "Good morning, my lovely young men."

Bob's eyes went to the back as he grinned when Freddy said, "Man, somebody musta made love to her last night, she's so happy."

Alice squinted one eye and said, "You're right, love. Bobby, pour me a cup of coffee. Ya know, I just met Kip's father. He asked me where she was, if I'd seen her. Where do you have her tucked away, Freddy?"

"I ain't. He's lookin for her, hah?"

"Yep, seems a little upset. Bobby, this coffee isn't

fresh and it's cold. So, don't tell me. Talk to the ole man when he gets here. Mind the store. Let's go up, Freddy."

They left after much protesting by Alice who swore she had to go somewhere, and begged them to take her with them. But they left her and she frowned down at her lukewarm coffee because she knew she was missing something.

When they got to the room, after stopping at Marie's for ham and egg sandwiches and crullers, the two girls were sitting up in bed, giggling and laughing. Kip's smile went wider when she saw Freddy and even wider when she sniffed the food. She was hungry. They sat around the table eating and drinking Nancy's coffee, which, as promised, was only hot, nothing else, close to terrible. But they drank it because there was nothing else.

They left an hour later when Bob mentioned Kip's father was looking for her. Kip wanted to then because she wanted to finish it, end it the way she knew it was going to end. So she and Freddy left. When they were close to her apartment building, they met her father walking along the street. He came up to them, his eyes on her. She was wearing Nancy's slacks that were too long, but Nancy had folded up the cuffs inside, and a blouse and a jacket. Her father seemed tired and weary. He put his hand on her shoulder but she backed away. That seemed to add more to him and his eyes faded.

"Come on upstairs. Come on."

"No, daddy I–"

She was close to tears now that he was before her. "I just want my clothes. I'm going away. That's what you told me to do last night."

"Kip, come upstairs. We'll talk about it there, not here on the street." His eyes went over to Freddy, whose eyes were on her. He asked blankly, "Is this him?"

Her head nodded. "Yes. We want to get married."

Her father's mouth tightened and a twitch formed under his right eye. Her head went down and she started crying then. He took her in his arms patting her hair.

"No, you don't have to do that. There's doctors, they can do something, we'll–"

But she was out of his arms, then outraged. "What do you think I am? No! How can you say something like that? You really must believe I am a slut! I can't–"

Freddy grabbed her, hugging her close to him, whispering quickly, "Take it easy. Come on, stop. Let's go up with him. We can talk about it. There ain't gonna be no abortion. Don't worry about that, he just don't know what else to tell you."

Her father looked at Freddy with something close to relief. When Kip went along with him, her father followed. After an hour of arguing with no more tears, they had her father agreeing to a civil wedding set for a month later.

That day Freddy went over to his apartment and

was not chased because he met no one that was after him. He spoke to his father, who grinned and wanted to meet Kip. A week later he did, at her apartment with her father studiously trying his damnedest to be impolite.

Freddy's father enjoyed Kip, was glad she was marrying his son, did not like her father, but told Freddy that if he had a daughter and someone impregnated her at the tender age of sixteen, he would have been worse. He would have shot them.

Freddy and Kip went around searching for an apartment. They found a small one, one where they could see the river from and the drive. It was very small, but the sight sold them both. They were married six weeks later because her father wanted her to wait two more weeks, offering no reason, but she did wait. When they were married, Dicky and Alice stood up for them. They married with her father's approval, but not of Freddy, or the baby, just the marriage that he viewed as a necessary evil.

There were holes in the clouds that day where the sun peeped through when it wasn't drizzling. Freddy's father was not there, because this time he really was in a hospital in an intensive care ward. As soon as the ceremony was over Freddy took a cab there not allowing Kip to accompany him.

She did not want to go to their apartment, which was smaller than Nancy's was, alone. So she went home with her father, who kept his lips tight as if a boiling was going on inside of him, which was.

Freddy sat in the hospital to wait until a doctor would tell him his father was dead, which he did, a day later. Freddy accepted it as something that could not be helped and he knew was coming for a long time.

He gave up the fourteen-dollar-a-month apartment that his father would not leave because he would not pay any more rent than he had to, no matter the inconvenience to his son.

He had often lectured him, telling him that it was his own fault that he could not get along with colored people and that he should be ashamed of himself. Freddy never argued with his father, he just agreed with him.

His father was buried in the same grave as his mother and Freddy went home to the apartment with Kip, whose father would not attend because he said he had to work. Alice, Dicky and Hancy, Pat, Sully, Blood, the old man, Mary, Tony G and Frankie came to the funeral. Bob and Jimmy would have, but couldn't then.

In the small bedroom of their new apartment, they had a single bed with a colored television set and that's all they wanted, other than the window with the view of the river.

Chapter 26

Holy Dirt and Grass

When she came in from work that night she did not feet tired, just dull and very much in the mood for a good cup of coffee. But she knew she would be disappointed with her own if she made any, so she was making her mind up to settle for tea.

"Hi, Shoulders."

She gasped, surprised. The small lamp was glowing on the end table near Alice, who sat on the sofa. She appeared drawn and sad, as if she were very tired and her eyes were red as if she had been crying.

"Why, hi. Are you alright?"

She went over to her, placing a hand on each arm.

"Oh, Alice, you look terrible! Don't you feel well? Did you and Dicky have a fight? Alice, don't look like that. What's the matter?"

"Aw, hell, Nancy. It's all, all of it's so shitty."

Quickly as if frightened, "What? What is? Don't talk like that. You sound terrible."

"That's the way I feel."

Her face wrinkled turning sour; "Sometimes, the whole goddamned thing creeps up on you. When you least expect it, it turns out to be the way it all really is; disgusting, everything."

Softly, trying to sooth her, "Oh, stop. It's not. Don't feel that way. No matter what it is, you can get over it or used to it. Don't say that."

"Is that how you do it, get used to things?"

"Sometimes, sometimes you have to. Sometimes you can't change them."

Dismally, "Yeah, I guess so. Do you have to work tomorrow? Can you stay home?"

"Yes of course. I can call. Why?"

"Jimmy's dead."

"Who? Jimmy MacArthur? Aw, no. Don't say that. Just because he's using dope, I mean, well, he's trying to find himself, that's all. He and Peggy will go back together again and he'll be all right."

"No, Nancy, dead dead, not just because he's a junky, or was. He found himself, if he was looking, the silly fuck."

She sat on the sofa but away from Alice, not wanting to touch her now because the touching might confirm the feeling building in her and she might have to believe her. Her eyes grew darker as they opened wide.

"Alice no, not that way, not like you say. Please don't say that. Aw, aw, hell."

Alice would not turn to her. She did not want to see her. She had cried for Jimmy, and it did not help.

She would not cry anymore. If she turned to Nancy, she would, so she did not. Nancy cried, biting one hand holding the other over her eyes.

The funeral was held the next day in a non-sectarian cemetery. Because Jimmy had died in sin, his church would not bury him or allow his body to enter sanctified dirt. Most of them were there, Peggy wasn't. She did not feel her presence necessary.

The old man was there. He liked Jimmy. He had been a nice kid, kind of a funny kid. Tippy was there and he was crying. Margaret was watching uneasily. Frankie did not make it. He did not know Jimmy was dead. Had he known, he would have gone to the funeral. Jimmy had been one of his boys. But then, the broad he was with for the past three days in a motel over in Jersey was a pretty fine head, so maybe he would not have made it.

Jimmy's short fat mother was crying, had not stopped crying since hearing that Jimmy had died. His grandmother would not attend the funeral, mourning her dead at home over cold black tea.

Freddy wasn't there, but Kip was standing close to Alice and Nancy, who were holding hands, Alice dry-eyed, fingering the beads of her rosary, repeating Hail Marys silently, only her lips moving.

Everyone's heads were bowed. It was a terrible funeral. Tony G. was disgusted with it. Dicky was away from the grave, off to the side, sitting on somebody's tombstone, watching, wondering what the hell Jimmy would have thought of it all. And if Jimmy had a soul, if he did, was it laughing at all of them now? But when he thought that he felt guilty, he stood away from the tombstone and tried to concentrate on half-remembered prayers.

Nancy was thinking she should ask Alice to teach her how to say the rosary. Then she thought of Bob and what he was doing then and if she should write him? Just one more letter. Perhaps they would give it to him? It was one cold, cold day. The sun was bright but cold. She shuddered from the cold.

They started to walk away after the guy in black finished saying a non-denominational prayer, imploring some God to make room for a soul somewhere.

Dicky walked between Alice and Nancy, holding their arms, Kip holding Nancy's other. Their voices seemed flat when they spoke and they whispered. It flickered in Dicky's mind about a cemetery being about the last place anyone should whisper, but he felt he shouldn't continue with that thought too far, since it seemed a little disrespectful. He had to chuckle when he thought that, disguising it, making it sound like a cough.

Still, Alice glared at him a moment. This was not one of their good days. As a matter of fact the last few days were pretty raunchy days. They had been trying to kill one another with words. "We got new wallpaper for the bedroom, Nancy."

"Oh, yes. Are you and Dicky going to put it up yourselves?"

"Yeah. Dicky doesn't like the color; we might change it."

Dully he said, "I don't feel comfortable sleepin' with lavender-colored walls."

"Yes."

Alice had said that softly. He wondered if it was a peace offering? Then thought, the hell with it. If it was, it would still be there and if it wasn't, he just wasn't.

Dicky got behind the wheel of his new green Ford. Kip, Alice, and Nancy sat in the back. The ride out of the cemetery was bumpy. He drove slowly, listening to them.

Alice said, "The doctor gave his mother some kind of sedative. It didn't seem to take, did it?"

Kip, who was blowing her nose, shook her head. Nancy was looking out the side window. "She seems so lonely now."

Alice, brightly because Kip was making her nervous, sniffling the way she was, said, "She always was. Her mother, Jim's grandmother, was mad as hell when she found out."

Nancy turned looking out the back window as they drove through the cemetery gates, stopping, waiting for the traffic to slow, saying abstractly, "That's funny, her last name being MacArthur, too."

Dicky was watching, waiting for a break in traffic. "He never had a father, Nancy, just some guy that shacked with his ole lady, then kept goin'."

Without hearing, "Oh."

Alice caught his eye in the mirror. "I didn't know you knew that."

"Yeah, my ole lady hung around with her when they were kids. Where'd you hear it?"

"He told me; Jimmy did."

He grinned. "Yeah, you an' him. He always told you his secrets."

"Except toward the end. I guess I was teasing him too much or not listening. Bob used to listen to him all the time."

Nancy said, "Someone should write him, to let him know. Jimmy was his best friend."

"He'll find out, Nancy."

"Do you think if ..."

Dicky shook his head. "They won't give it to him. I told you that."

"Yes."

He swung the car into traffic grinning at Kip, winking. "Your nose is red."

She nodded. Alice turned to her. "Where did you say you were going to meet Freddy?"

"I don't know, he said The Uptown."

"Good. I'm beginning to feel gloomy. I wish you'd stop crying. You make me feel like I've been to a funeral."

She nodded. Nancy asked, "Dicky, would you let me out? I don't feel like going to a bar now."

He said, "No, I won't."

Alice put her hand on his arm. "Why?"

"What do you think you're going to do, go up to that apartment of yours and brood about him?"

"No, stop. I'm just not in the mood for a bar."

Kip said, "Come on Shoulders. Come with us. I'll be over my tears by then."

Embarrassed, "Oh no, Kip, that's not it. I'm sorry. I didn't mean you."

It was cold in the Uptown. There were shadows where the sun could not reach through the windows and it seemed gloomy.

The bar was empty except for Freddy end Johnny down the end. They were talking about something serious, but Freddy chuckled when they came in, smiling wide. "Hey, there they are. Set 'em up, John. This one's on Dicky."

Dicky laughed. "Ah, you little pee wee creep. Be quiet, before I sic my old lady on you."

"Christ, no. She's got too much to offer." Freddy kissed the three girls, clapping his hands hollowly, laughing at Kip.

"Well, looka you. What's the matter, mother? Whadda you want to drink?"

"Stop sounding so happy. I want a screwdriver."

He turned to Johnny to see if he had heard. Johnny nodded, waiting for Alice and Nancy to order. Alice asked her, "What are you gonna have, Shoulders?"

"I don't know. I'll have what you have."

"Gimme a scotch, John, on the rocks, with soda water out of the tap, not out of the bottle."

He bowed asking, "Make that two?"

"Oh, no," Nancy said, scowling. "I don t like scotch. Could I have a Gin Rickey?"

He shook his head, smiling. "No, I'm sorry. That's a summer drink."

Alice growled, "Who the hell said so?"

He laughed, mixing the drinks.

Dicky asked, "Howja make out, Freddy?"

"No good. I'm a half-inch too short. I'll wait'll the firemen's test comes up."

Nancy turned to him. "Were you really going to be a policeman, Freddy?"

"I was gonna try, Shoulders. I did pretty good on the mental."

Kip said, "You did very good on the mental."

He grinned, winking. "She means I passed. Hey, Maldon. Whatta you gonna do?"

Dicky shrugged. "Aw, prob'ly knock my ole lady up a couple fifteen times an' go on home relief."

"Alone."

He laughed, putting his arm around Alice's neck and she kissed it. Tippy came in with the old man and Tony G., Margaret was on his arm, still looking uneasy.

Freddy called, "Hey, come on down here. We'll sit at a table."

Alice got off her stool going over to the old man. "Hello. Are you finished saying all your prayers?"

"Aw, nah. You shouldn't talk like that. What's a matter wit you anyhow, huh?"

She laughed, holding his hand. "Are you ever happy, Frank? I don't believe I ever saw you happy once."

Low, under his breath, just loud enough for everyone to hear, "Ah, goddamn kids." Then, to Johnny loud and fiery, "Hey, you. I wanna glass fulla whisky, alla way to the top, an' no foolin' aroun' neither."

Johnny threw an inquiring glance at Dicky, who pointed to a beer glass. Johnny shrugged, pouring, handing it to him.

The old man was saying to Dicky as he took it, his voice heavy with sincerity, head nodding a few times in emphasis, "Now this here's a drink, none a them girl drinks." And he drank it, glub, glub, all the way down.

Freddy moved his tongue around in his mouth, head shaking, "I like girl drinks."

"Yer a sissy, 'at's why. Goddamn fool; like you gonna be a cop. Goddamn whole world is gonna go crazy."

"I ain't. I'm gonna be a fireman."

"Aw, Christ. 'ere goes the whole city up in smoke."

Alice chuckled. "Will you please say something nice to someone, cranky?"

"Yeah." He sat on a stool, bringing his shoulders up and head down as if hiding. Tippy walked over to the jukebox, taking Dicky by the arm bringing him with her.

"'Anybody see his ole lady?"

"Who? Peggy?"

"Uh huh."

"No. She saw him. She knows he's dead."

"What the hell happened with them? You ever find out?"

"No, Christ knows, Tip. I don't know. My ole lady says something just didn't develop in him, he couldn't understand it all. She says he did it on purpose 'cause he couldn't understand the reality around him."

Seeing the expression on Tippy's face, he grinned. "I don't know what the hell she's talkin about, either."

"Yeah, it was a shitty funeral."

"Yeah, cold."

"You think he could feel anything? I mean, under there now, how cold it is?"

"Hell no. He's dead, man. He's nothin' but a piece a meat now."

"Yeah. You wanna hear anything?"

Tippy dropped a quarter in the machine.

"No. Play something loud, anything. If you play something sad, the broads are gonna be cryin' all over the place."

"Except Alice."

"Yeah, even Alice. She' scared to."

"I better get back to my ole lady. She only met the guy twice."

"Yeah."

Alice laughed overly loud at something Freddy said. The old man turned looking down, saw Nancy and grinned. "Hey, hey, you Nancy. How are ya, huh?"

She was surprised, a little off balance. "Uh, why fine, thank you. Are you all right, Frank?"

Winking. "Yeah. They cuttin' me up, but I'm gonna be awright, okay."

Then Johnny filled his glass again because he pointed to it.

They moved two tables together in the back, playing the jukebox loud. Tony G put six dimes in the machine, Dicky forcing Nancy to play. Tony was her partner. Kip and Freddy, Alice and Dicky.

It was an electric bowling machine with a steel puck for a ball. Tony told her to shoot the puck down between the red lines. When she did, he wondered if he could bet Dicky on low score rather than high. The girls giggled and cackled when they shot, whether they made points or not.

Tony maintained a solemn poker face, Freddy a big smile, Dicky shooting while talking and making more strikes than spares. Tony and Nancy lost, Tony buying the next round for the two tables, paling slightly at the price. He would not play again unless he could have Kip for a partner, as she shot better than Freddy, since he couldn't come out and just say that he did not play anymore because he hated sore losers.

Jimmy's grandmother fixed the rag on the kitchen table just so. The big wide white kitchen echoed her voice as she spoke to the rag as if it were Jimmy, then she said, "Ah, ha ha ha!" loudly, as if she couldn't hear what it was saying anymore. So she threw it on the floor and stepped on it.

Tippy began to feel the effect of the highballs he was drinking because he was drinking three to everyone else's one. He whispered to Margaret about what a hell of a good boy Jimmy was.

She nodded to him with an empty smile, distracted, wondering where Bob was, or if she cared anymore.

John "Butch" Rigney, Jr. (1936–1967) was born in the Bronx. As a youth, Butch went in and out of a series of reform schools for stealing, and even jumping from a bridge into the Hudson River. He and his brother and sister enduring abusive parents before each leaving as teenagers. The early writings of Rigney are dated 1963, when he served in the Air Force while stationed in Alaska. After returning to New York, he continued writing what became a novel and several related short stories. Some of the chapters are dated 1966, so it can be assumed that this work was his final.

Jim Provenzano (Editor) is the author of the novels *Finding Tulsa* (Palm Drive Publishing), *Now I'm Here* (Beautiful Dreamer Press), the Lambda Literary Award-winning *Every Time I Think of You,* its sequel *Message of Love* (a Lambda Literary Award Finalist), *PINS, Monkey Suits, Cyclizen*, the stage adaptation of *PINS*, and the short story collection *Forty Wild Crushes.*

Audiobook adaptations include *PINS* (Paul Fleschner, narrator), *Every Time I Think of You*, and its sequel *Message of Love* (Michael Wetherbee, narrator). Born in New York City and raised in Ashland, Ohio, he studied theater at Kent State University, has a BFA in Dance from Ohio State University and a Master of Arts in English/Creative Writing from San Francisco State University. A journalist, editor, and photographer in LGBT media for three decades, he lives in San Francisco.

www.jimprovenzano.com

Printed in the USA
CPSIA information can be obtained
at www.ICGtesting.com
LVHW011932261024
794895LV00019B/331